# THE
# PROJECTS

## BY
## JOHN PRIBETICH

# AUTHOR'S NOTE

In January of 1986, I was fortunate enough to have my ticket punched to enter and enjoy a front row seat at the "Greatest Show on Earth". That year I began my police career in New York City, first with the Transit Police, and some years later with the N.Y.P.D. In Transit I began my career as a patrolman, riding the subways and walking the platforms of Harlem and Washington Heights. Shortly thereafter, I was accepted into plainclothes, citywide robbery unit led by the innovative, sometimes eccentric, yet always sharp-minded Lieutenant Jack Maple.

From that unit I received my detective shield, and a short time later I was promoted to Patrol Sergeant, and returned to Harlem. Following the Transit and Housing Police merger with the N.Y.P.D., I had the good fortune to be assigned as a sergeant to the 73rd Precinct Detective Squad in Brownsville, Brooklyn. After an enjoyable and exiting stay in the 7-3, I was promoted to lieutenant, returned to patrol duties, and finished my career in the Queens South Task Force.

I had completed almost twenty-seven years of service, when the fire in my belly, which had been ignited in January of 1986, finally went out. During those twenty-seven years I had witnessed, or experienced first hand, events that most civilians would find difficult to believe.

*The Project*s is a work of fiction, although most of the incidents that take place in this novel actually occurred. All of the characters and many of the locations portrayed in this novel are used fictitiously, or are products of the author's imagination. Minor liberties have been taken with the description of some of the Housing Projects, in order to fit them within the framework of the story. In most instances, I was as accurate as possible in describing both the police procedure and police jargon. I hope that my most valued critics, other cops, won't find many mistakes. If they do I'm sure I will hear about them, which is fine.

Just a quick word of thanks to the following: Detective Lieutenant (ret.) John Cornicello, who truly has blue blood coursing through his veins. Dr. Rosalie Contino, whose persistent yet gentle nudging, provided me with the impetus to complete this work. Thanks my friend in the 82nd Airborne Division, you know who you are.

Dr. Blair Kenney, my editor, you are truly a miracle worker. Thanks to my wife and two daughters, for whom my love knows no bounds.

Finally thanks, to all those men and women who step out from safety of their respective precincts, districts and public-service areas each tour, to face the unknown, to those brave men and women who begin their tours with these words that demonstrate your sense of duty and courage, "Central, show me available." Please, be careful.

# PROLOGUE

The years 2004 and 2005 were boom times for the New York City economy. The stock market was high, crime was low, tourism was up, and unemployment was down. In 2005 Mayor Mike Bloomberg had been elected to serve a second term as leader of the Big Apple. Mayor Mike was keenly aware that New York City should remain friendly to big business, and his re-election was comforting to the titans of Wall Street. People were making good money, with the exception of the men and women in blue who comprised the New York City Police Department.

Since the mid-1980's the salarys of the cops in New York City had fallen behind those of all of the other police departments in the metropolitan area. The Patrolman's Benevolent Association (P.B.A.), the largest of the five unions within the N.Y.P.D., represented all uniformed cops below the rank of Sergeant. They had become disgusted with the salary increases proposed by City Hall, so a decision was made by their Executive Board to try their luck with an arbitrator.

In one respect it turned out to be a wise decision, as the arbitrator granted the union raises of 4.5% for 2004 and 5% for 2005. Raises such as these had not been seen by N.Y.C. cops since the mid-1980s, when the Honorable Ed Koch had been most magnanimous in granting them.

The increases turned out to be a double-edged sword. City Hall agreed to the raises, but the starting salary for a rookie patrolman was then reduced. The beginning salary for a rookie cop was reduced from $32,000 to $25,100.

The police had been in great deal part responsible for the booming economy. They had brought crime down to record numbers, thus increasing tourism and giving a sense of safety to residents of the city, and now they were being asked to patrol the streets for a salary which would almost qualify a family of four to receive food stamps.

There was a reduction in the number of police officers that had not been experienced since the catastrophic police layoffs of 5,000 cops in the mid-1970s. The reduced salaries would be detrimental in attracting potential recruits, since with jobs so readily available $25,000 was considered chump change. A messenger on Wall Street could pull down at least thirty thousand, and he or she didn't have to work holidays, most weekends, and crazy hours. Most importantly, they didn't have to don bullet proof vests to go to work. The police academy classes of 1984, 1985 and 1986 had been some of the largest in the history of the Department. Now, after twenty years, those some 8,000 police officers were eligible to retire. Their final year's salary, upon which their pensions would be based, had just jumped almost 10%, thanks to the beneficence of the arbitrator.

For many of these veterans it just did not pay to stay on the job. The respect and admiration that had been displayed by a grateful citizenry right after the 9/11 tragedy had slowly vanished, and it was back to business as usual. Ever increasing "performance objective" numbers desired by the bosses, civilian complaints, and bullshit disciplinary infractions added to their desire to do their twenty years and get out.

So, when recruits were going to be needed most, the starting salaries had been reduced, and then there was the elephant in the room. The United States government had been generously giving the N.Y.P.D. federal grant money, under an Act called Safe Streets, Safe Cities. One of the main provisions of this Act was that the N.Y.P.D. had to maintain a certain number of police officers in order to receive the full dollar value of the grant. This grant money was in the millions, and now it was in jeopardy.

The money was to be used to aid the department in its crime fighting/counter-terrorism mission. Of course, many Chiefs took this to mean upgrading their take-home police vehicles, as well as re-furbishing their already lavish offices.

The recruitment problem was causing some consternation on the floors of One Police Plaza, headquarters of the N.Y.P.D.

# CHAPTER ONE

It was a September afternoon in 2005, and the summer heat was still trapped between the two apartment buildings. The wooden bench upon which Lincoln Watson sat was directly between the two eight-story buildings. The building to his right was 180 Wortman Avenue, and the one to the left was 190. They appeared to be twins, staring at one another, and it was if they were blowing hot air at one another.

The green, wooden bench was on a blacktopped walkway, on a path between the two buildings, and it overlooked a tree-lined area where grass grew in the spring and late fall, but now in the summer heat there appeared to be blades of yellow straw. The blades were bordered by sections of hanging, gray metal chain-link, strung between poles of the same color about three feet high off the ground. The chain-link roping was supposed to act as a deterrent for any young children that wished to play on the grass. The New York City Housing Authority had decided when the projects were first erected that it was unacceptable to for children to play on the grass. Apparently, they felt it would ruin the aesthetic value of a yellowed grass that even a goat wouldn't eat.

Linc was reading a paperback edition of *The Plague,* by Camus, and he hoped business would be slow enough to allow him to at least get through two chapters. The book was worn, and the pages frayed, mostly because he would stuff the paperback into his back pocket whenever a customer, or worse, one of his homeboys, approached him. He did not want to answer any questions about his reading preferences, or about why he was reading anything at all, except a video-game magazine. The reading of an actual book would make him appear soft.

Appearances were everything in East New York, Brooklyn. If one seemed to be soft or weak, the sharks would begin to circle. At first they would tell you that you were sitting on their bench, they then would want to hold some of your money. It would get progressively worse, until you had to walk around in slippers like some old skell, because all your sneakers had been stolen from you.

Linc had just started his third year at Long Island University's Brooklyn campus, and *The Plague* was required reading for a philosophy course he had decided to take as an elective. Although he would never admit it to any of his boys, Linc enjoyed reading, and that enjoyment was one of the reasons he was able to maintain a 3.2 average at the school- - The Deans List, if his friends only knew. He was hoping to get his degree in Speech Pathology, in order that he might, one day, be able to help his brother.

Linc got up off the bench, stuffed Camus into his back pocket and began to stretch his solidly built, six-foot frame. He pulled off his dark blue Yankees cap, tag still attached, and ran his free hand along the top of his fade. He looked down at his brand new white Nikes, untied, of course, and was satisfied that they were still scuff free. Out of the corner of his eye he spotted someone moving toward him. Hoping it was a customer, he quickly discovered it was Tarface.

"Tarface, man, whats you doin out of that lobby, dawg? Silky sees you, he gonna beat your ass."

"Pfft, I ain't fraid of that muthafucka b, you know that. Besides, you supposed to be steerin muthafuckas into my lobby. I ain't seen no one, cept that skell bitch, Latrice, you sent in bout half hour ago. And she only bought three rocks, man. You been sending them into ShortFinger's lobby?"

"Nah, son," Linc said. "I wouldn't play you like that. Just been real slow, is all. Scary slow, like these bitches know something. Listen, man, I'm gonna be getting Harris off the bus little while. You cover fo me? "

"Yeah, yeah, man, I got ur back," Tarface said, hitching up his sagging denims, as he slowly strolled back towards the lobby of 180 Wortman. Linc spotted Shortfinger coming out of the lobby of

190 Wortman. He yelled, "You better get back in that lobby you nosy muthafucka. You didn't miss nothing."

"Ah, fuck you, man," yelled Shortfinger. "You think you the boss or some shit?" He rolled his shoulders, and slowly turned around, and headed back towards his lobby.

Linc laughed, as he watched his friend walk back into the lobby. He laughed at their bravado, knowing that if Silky, who ran the crack trade in the Linden Houses, saw Tarface and Shortfinger out of their respective lobbies, he would sooner put a bullet in their ass then listen to their excuses. All three friends: Linc, Shortfinger, and Tarface were twenty-years-old and had known each other since they had gone to Public School 306, located right across the street from 180 Wortman, on Vermont Street.

Linc had never wanted to become involved in the drug trade, but had been forced to join out of financial necessity. Following his father's untimely death, when Linc was almost twelve, it had become difficult for his mother to provide for two growing boys. When Linc was a senior in high school, he realized that asking his mother to pay for college was out of the question.

He had noticed his two friends had never wanted for money. Both were walking around sporting Iverson's on their feet, and wearing nothing but Rocawear and ENYCE. Linc wasn't stupid. He knew how they suddenly came into new found riches, but he would never ask. That was another unwritten rule of the projects. When it came to money, you kept out of other people's *bizness*. He also knew that his friends would rather Linc stay out of the trade, since they both felt that with his brains he could actually go somewhere, hopefully out of the projects.

Linc had been desperate though, so he asked Silky if he could make some *change*. Silky, who for some reason, had a soft spot for Linc, agreed to let Linc *steer*, a much less dangerous job than handling the product itself. That would be left up to guys like Shortfinger and Tarface. A *steerer* evaluated a prospective customer. If he felt comfortable that the customer wasn't *5-0*, or, worse, intent on ripping off a stash, he steered the customer to a particular lobby. Tarface and Shortfinger were not too thrilled with Linc's business decision, but he explained it would be only temporary, until he finished paying for college. Tarface and Shortfinger, on the other hand, knew that they would be in the game for the rest of their lives, however short those might be.

Although he had known Tarface and Shortfinger all his life, Linc sometimes had trouble remembering what his friends' real or *government* names were. In their neighborhood you were known by your street name. It made it all the more difficult for the cops to determine someone's real identity. A street name was generally derived from some kind of perceived or actual deformity one possessed, or, in the case of Tarface, from an incident that had become part of street lore.

Shortfinger's name had come, of course, from a deformity, not congenital, but rather complements of the New York City Housing Authority. Shortfinger and his family lived in the same apartment building as Linc, 220 Wortman Avenue. One glorious summer afternoon in 1994, a nine-year-old Shortfinger, whose real name was Devon Timmons, hurried to finish his lunch, so he could join his friends for some basketball on the courts at Stanley Avenue. He finished his sandwich and headed for the front door of his apartment.

The Housing Project's front doors were all steel fire doors, installed as a precaution. In the event of a fire in an apartment, if that massive door stayed shut, the fire would be contained to the one apartment. The problem, however, was that if the door to the outdoor terrace on a particular floor was open, the wind came through the terrace door, causing a vacuum, and any open apartment door on that floor would quickly slam shut. The noise from that slamming door was slightly louder than cannon fire.

As Devon opened the door to step out of the apartment, he heard his mother call him back inside. Devon took one step back inside the apartment, neglecting to remove his left hand from the door jamb. At that moment, LaQuan, a twelve-year-old boy from apartment 6C, exited the terrace, having just finished smoking the

4

Newport he had lifted out of his mother's bag. LaQuan's opening of the terrace door created the vacuum needed to cause a two-hundred-pound steel fire door to slam against the left hand of Devon Timmons.

The result was a pinky severed just above the knuckle at the first joint. Amazingly, Devon did not feel a thing for about ten seconds, and then his pain receptors kicked in. He looked at the ground and saw the top half of his pinky lying on the tiled hallway floor. Devon observed blood spurting out of the severed member, and he began to scream.

He screamed so loud he actually woke up his uncle Bernard, who had taken up residence on the family couch. Bernard, his mom's brother, had asked to stay for a weekend about four months before the incident, swearing he was "this close" to getting a job. The mother had doubted it. It was now 1994, and Bernard hadn't worked since Reagan was President, but she had a soft spot for her only brother.

Bernard jumped off the couch, a bit groggy due to the many gin-and-cokes he had consumed the evening before, and realized he had an emergency situation on his hands. Devon's mother screamed that she was calling 911, but Bernard had watched enough television to know that if he got Devon to the hospital quickly enough, the doctors might be able to reattach the severed part of the pinky. For a moment, he stopped to wonder what type of glue they used to accomplish that feat. Anyway, if he got Devon to the hospital in time, he might be a hero in his sister's eyes, even though he hadn't given her a nickel since he began his *temporary* stay at the apartment.

Knowing he had not a moment to lose, Bernard looked for something sterile. He grabbed a once used napkin off the kitchen table, ran over and picked Devon's pinky part off the floor. He wrapped it in the napkin, picked up the screaming Devon, and raced down the stairs to the street. He ran right to the bus stop on the corner of Wortman and Vermont, knowing livery cabs were always at the stop waiting to take riders who were frustrated with the consistently slow bus service.

Bernard, with Devon in tow, jumped into the first livery cab they saw. Bernard directed the driver to get to Brookdale Hospital, on the double. The driver, who himself had a taste or two that morning, drove west on Linden Boulevard, driving right past Brookdale Hospital. When Bernard asked where the fuck they were going, the driver explained that Kings County Hospital would be better equipped to deal with Devon's severed pinky. The driver further explained that he had been an ambulance driver in the army during the Vietnam War, so he knew what he was talking about.

Bernard yelled that he didn't care if the driver was that big eared, fuckin' Dr.Spock, he wanted his nephew to be taken to Brookdale. The driver then began yelling at Bernard that he should be grateful he was getting free medical advice. If he didn't like it, maybe him and that short-fingered boy should just get the fuck out of his cab.

Bernard, his head throbbing from the overload of gin and cokes and the tremendous pressure he was now under, decided to punch the driver in the back of the head in order to get him to shut the fuck up. He did so, and the driver slammed on the brakes, causing both Bernard and a screaming Devon to slam into the back of the passenger seat. Bernard grabbed Devon's good hand and dragged him out of the car, all the while threatening to one day kill the driver.

Fortunately, a 6-9 Precinct car had just turned onto Linden Boulevard. Bernard flagged it down, explained what had happened, and asked if they would be kind enough to take them to Brookdale. The police got them to the hospital within minutes, but the surgeons there were not equipped to conduct a reattachment. The doctor explained that the only hospital in the area equipped to perform the reattachment was Kings County.

Bernard promised himself that he would pick up a real good bottle of vodka, maybe even Georgi, for that cab driver, and when the driver received, and hopefully shared the gift, perhaps the

6

driver could tell him a thing or two about the bursitis Bernard seemed to be developing. As for Devon, from that day on he was forever known as *Shortfinger*.

Tarface's street name had been arrived at in much less painful, yet more humiliating circumstances. It had happened when he and Shortfinger were twelve years old and both had begun dabbling in criminal activity. Like many other youngsters who had an inclination towards criminal activity, both Shortfinger and Tarface began with strong arm robberies.

These types of robberies were seen as a natural progression for the disadvantaged youths of the projects. Trapped inside their apartments, they were bombarded with television commercials of games, clothes, and sports equipment. Of course, they would ask moms or pops to buy these items and as much as the parents would have loved to, it was difficult enough for them to make sure everyone had enough to eat and clothes to wear.

Once these commercial-watching young men reached the ages of twelve and thirteen, they were seen as old enough to be trusted to go out into the street and play on their own. Besides, moms and pops, especially mom, were becoming more and more heartbroken, having to tell their sons each day that they could not afford to buy him the expensive video games or high-end sneakers they desired.

Once out on the street, however, these young men began to see some of those advertised items that they longed for, actually possessed by young men more fortunate than themselves. Perhaps their moms and pops didn't have as many mouths to feed and were able to pay for the goods. It was just a matter of time before the criminally-inclined figured out the easiest way to possess these valuables -- just take them.

Stealth was sometimes used, but more often than not a beat-down was administered in order to purloin the desired objects. It was a sort of twisted Darwinism. In the housing projects, the strong took from the weak. You also quickly learned that if there was a chance you were going to get an ass-beating in your attempt to appropriate a desired object, it was best to enlist two or three of your homeys in order to accomplish your desired conquest.

It was a hot, July summer day in 1997 when Thomas Williams (soon to be known as Tarface) spotted one of his most desired objects -- a purple, ten-speed mountain bike. The bike was currently in the possession of Lamar, a skinny twelve-year-old from the Boulevard Projects. Lamar was sitting on the white banana seat of the bike, on the corner of Flatlands and Van Sicklen Avenues, enjoying a bag of Salt and Vinegar chips. Thomas spotted Lamar, eyeing him as a lion would an antelope that had strayed too far from the pack. Thomas sized up the situation, knowing that Lamar had made a number of tactical errors. First, he was in foreign territory, almost four long blocks from his home projects. Secondly, he was alone, and third, he was much too engrossed in enjoying his Salt and Vinegar chips.

Lamar, savoring the taste of his chips, had four of his five fingers in his mouth attempting to lick off every last granule of salt. Thomas slowly crept up behind him. Thomas moved as quietly as possible, but Lamar's street radar kicked in and he spotted Thomas just as Thomas rushed up on him. Lamar, who almost became known as Shortfinger himself, fell to the pavement, sliding his fingers out of his mouth just before his head hit the concrete, and his mouth snapped shut. Thomas jumped on the fallen ten-speed bike and began pedaling east on Flatlands Avenue, and he made a sudden left turn onto Schenck Avenue, unaware of the street paving project that had begun that morning.

*

The Linden Houses Summer Block Party had been scheduled for the very next day, and an urgent call from Councilwomen Woods to the Deputy Commissioner of Transportation had initiated the last minute work. The councilwoman had explained to the Deputy Commissioner that she had been mortified and embarrassed at last year's fete, when Monsignor Ryan, from St. Laurence Church, had almost broken his ankle.

The Monsignor had explained to the disconcerted councilwoman that the uneven pavement had been the cause of his fall. What the Monsignor failed to mention, however, was that before his arrival at the Linden Houses Block Party, he had attended two other block parties. Desiring to be a gracious guest at the last affair, the good Monsignor had sampled the punch that had kindly been provided by the elderly women from the local Baptist Church. In an effort to smooth over any denominational gaps between the two faiths, the Monsignor helped himself to a number of glasses.

The punch, of course, had been delivered and set up by the spouses of the elderly women, and these gentlemen had been keenly aware that the day's festivities would be much more entertaining if a fifth of Ronrico Rum was secretly added to the punch. The Monsignor, who was all too familiar with the taste of the grape, never strayed far from the punchbowl until it was time to bid all adieu. By the time he had arrived at the Linden Houses affair, he was walking as if he were on a small skiff in the Bering Sea.

He headed straight for the punch bowl, and he was about four feet from the table on which it sat, when the ninety-five-degree heat and his previous liquid consumption finally got the better of him. He went down as if he had been shot, with the ligaments in his left ankle stretched to their breaking point. Thankfully, he was able to grab onto one of the six-foot speakers that had been set up for the musical entertainment. The speaker broke his fall, saving his foot from a cast.

Not wishing to see any further indignities inflicted upon his boss, the Monsignor's aide, a gentle, non-drinking soul named Torres, managed to lift him up and hobble him away. A call by Torres, under the direction of the Monsignor, was made to Councilwoman Woods the very next day. The Monsignor hoped, Torres stated, that by the time next year's affair rolled around, the pavement problem would be rectified. That phone call not only ensured that the street would be repaved, but also that Thomas Williams would finally inherit a street name.

*

Thomas, who was generally aware of any new developments in his neighborhood, had apparently not been apprised of Councilwoman Woods' concern for the wellbeing of the local Monsignor. He had also underestimated Lamar's swiftness afoot, similar to that of an antelope, as well as overestimating his knowledge of ten-speed mountain bikes.

Lamar had leaped over the three foot high chain link roping that separated the sidewalk from the grass, and, cutting across the grass, he picked up a small piece of broom handle that had been left by one of the pavement project workers. Thomas began to slow the bike down when he saw the newly finished paving project, which gave Lamar the time to reach the back wheel of the bike and throw the broom handle into the spokes. The handle didn't actually go into the spokes, but the noise of the broom handle hitting the back wheel was enough to terrify Thomas, the novice mountain bicyclist.

Thomas squeezed the left handlebar brake, assuming that, as on all other bikes he had *borrowed*, this would cause both wheels to stop. However, only the front wheel came to a stop, an abrupt one at that. Thomas flew over the front handlebar, over the yellow tape that indicated fresh tar had been applied to the street. The left side of Thomas's face skidded along Schenck Avenue, absorbing tar along the way.

Some witnesses, Shortfinger and Linc among them, claimed the skid was at least twenty-feet long, and many of the observers felt that if you went that far on the street, you should be required to have a license plate attached to your ass. The skid was in actuality only five-feet long, but a new street name was born, and Lamar vowed never to leave the Boulevard Houses again, no matter how good those Utz Salt and Vinegar chips that he had stolen from Stanley Avenue bodega were.

Linc arrived at his street name in a less dramatic fashion. Linc wasn't even technically a street name. It was short for his real first name, Lincoln. Many people in the housing project, especially the elders, admired Linc's real first name, thinking he was named after The Great Emancipator himself, but Linc knew better. Both Lincoln and his brother Harris had been given their names as a favor to their grandmother.

It really could not even be considered a favor, because his mother, a gentle, non-confrontational woman, did not want to argue with her mother. The grandmother while growing up had loved watching cop shows. Her two favorites were *The Mod Squad*, a cop show that ran from the late 1960's into the early 70s and *Barney Miller*, a popular cop show in the early 70's.

When her daughter, Elizabeth, had had her first son, the grandmother had pleaded with her and the boy's father, Delbert, to name the boy Lincoln. At first both parents thought it admirable that the grandmother felt that much respect for Abraham Lincoln, especially since she had never had an inclination to study history.

The grandmother had said, "No, you fools! The name is from Lincoln, on *The Mod Squad*. He was one handsome, low-talking, kick-ass, black man. Matter of fact, I think he might have been named for Abraham Lincoln, so we'll killing two birds with one gun."

Both Delbert and Elizabeth knew better than to argue.

They also agreed to name their second son Harris, after "the funniest and most handsome detective I've ever seen!" Detective Ron Harris was a black, squad-room detective in the comedy show *Barney Miller*. However, Captain Barney Miller always addressed him as Harris, and the name Ron was rarely mentioned, so "Harris" stuck in the mind of the grandmother. Whenever his brother, Harris, complained about his name, Linc would be quick to remind him that thankfully his brother had not been named Barney, after the Captain from the show.

\*

Linc gave Tarface a sign that he was going to walk over to the bus stop at Wortman and Vermont, to make sure Harris, came off the bus. Business was still slow, and Silky knew that Linc insisted on making sure his fifteen-year-old brother got off the bus safely each day. Linc had arranged his school schedule in order that he could make money and also tend to his brother every afternoon. It was unusual, since Silky had no sympathy for anyone who worked for him, except, for some reason, Linc.

The M.T.A. bus was just pulling up when Linc reached the bus stop. The bus's air brakes let out their familiar hissing sound, and the smell of the diesel fumes felt comforting to Linc. The front door of the bus opened like an accordion, and Harris bounded down the steps.

"How was school, little man?"

"Im-m-mm not l-little, Li-Li-Linc! Cu-cu-cut that sh-sh-shit out!" his brother said, stuttering.

"You watch your mouth, little man, or I'll be putting a speed knot on top a your head. You got a lot of homework?"

"Ye-ye-yeah. A lot of ma-ma-math."

"All right. Get up to the house and get busy. I made you a bologna and cucumber sandwich. It's in the frigerator. Moms should be home in a little while. I'll be up sometime after dinner."

Linc waited for the bus to pull out of the bus stop before telling his little brother it was okay to cross Wortman Avenue. He continued to watch Harris until he entered the lobby of their building. He knew that once his brother was in the building he would be safe, as the tenants looked out for one another, most having lived there all their lives.

The apartments were handed down generation to generation, and rarely was someone lucky enough to escape the cycle. Most of the kids never left their housing project grounds, except to take a subway ride into Manhattan every-so-often. Most would never even cross the Verrazano Bridge, only a few miles west on the Belt Parkway, to explore a world only seen by them on television.

Linc turned around and began walking back towards his bench, when he heard the gunshots. He began running towards the front of 180 Wortman when he saw two males, wearing hoodies, leap the chain link and sprint across the grass towards Cozine Avenue. Out of the corner of his eye, he observed Shortfinger pull out his 9 millimeter Llama and begin firing at the two males. It was chaos, as women who had been gossiping with one another on benches, jumped off them in order to tackle their young ones, who were now frozen still, staring-wide eyed at the violent commotion unfolding before their innocent eyes.

"Stop, Shorty, the kids!" screamed Linc. "Tarface!" Linc and Shortfinger ran into the lobby of 180 Wortman and saw their friend lying on the blood-stained tile floor. One of the mailboxes had been opened, and inside lay a 9 millimeter Beretta. Tarface had evidently seen his foes approach and pulled open the mailbox to retrieve his gun, but he was too late. He had been shot in the stomach and the neck, and the neck wound would soon prove fatal. He was gasping for air as Linc knelt next to him and cradled his friend's head in his arms. Blood began to saturate Linc's pants.

As warm teardrops began rolling down his cheeks, Linc pleaded with his friend, "Don't you be leavin me, cuz! You got to hang in. The ambulance is comin!" A gurgling sound, along with blood, came out of Tarface's mouth.

"Linc, you gotta bounce man," screamed Shortfinger. "You all full of blood. The po-po will be taking you in. I'll answer up their questions. Just take my gat and get back to your crib, get to Harris man."

The approaching sirens were piercing the afternoon air as Linc stood up, stuck Shortfinger's gun in his pocket, reached into the open mailbox and pulled out the Beretta. He tried to place the gun in his rear pocket, but Camus was stuffed in there, so he placed the weapon in his waistband, as he ran out the front door of the lobby. Running across Wortman Avenue, his eyes still full of tears, he finally remembered. Thomas, yes, Thomas Williams was Tarface's real name.

# CHAPTER 2

In all of the New York City Police Department, which was comprised of approximately 35,000 sworn members, there were only seven three-star chiefs, and only three positions that technically outranked those chiefs-- the Chief of the Department, the First Deputy Commissioner and of course, the Commissioner himself.

Chief of Personnel Vito Arena was one of those three star chiefs, and one would think that he would have been happy to attain such an exalted rank, but he wasn't. He had been informed that the Personnel slot was just a "temporary" one, until the Chief of Detectives job opened up. To Arena, that was his dream job. He had been in the Detective Bureau for most of his thirty-five-year career, and no boss knew the intricacies of the Detective Bureau better than he.

So when the former Chief of Detectives finally retired, Vito began polishing the pinky ring he had purchased when he first became a third-grade detective thirty-one years ago, and when, two weeks ago, he had received the notification to report to Room 1400 in One Police Plaza, the Commissioner's office, he called his wife and told her something good was about to happen.

He had gone to the Commissioner's office and waited in the anteroom. Vito was nervous. He had spent enough time on the job to know that no matter what one is told, or even promised, it's not official until the papers are signed. He had worn his best Armani suit, the gray one with a light-blue shirt and a gray tie with dark-blue stripping. Running his fingers through his thick, dark hair, only recently invaded with gray streaks, Vito began to silently say a Hail Mary.

"The Commissioner is ready to see you now, Chief," said the Commissioner's secretary, who held the rank of Captain.

"Thanks, Brian," said Vito, as he stood up, pulled down the cuffs of his sleeves, and walked into the Commissioner's office.

The office was, of course, lavishly furnished, but what caught one's eye was the desk. It was an imposing piece of furniture, made of a heavy mahogany, but its history was even more impressive. The desk had been built for then Commissioner of the New York City Police Department, Theodore Roosevelt, in 1894. It had remained in the office of the Commissioner for over one-hundred-years now, a reminder to the men who sat at that desk that they had big shoes to fill.

The present Commissioner, John "Jack" McKean, had done a fine job, continuing the policies of the former Commissioner, which had led to double-digit crime decreases. The former Commissioner had left to make his fortune in the world of corporate security. McKeon, who had risen through the ranks to become Chief of Department, was the logical choice for the P.C. slot, and the Mayor was a logical man. Everything had been running smoothly, until the decision was made to lower the starting salary of the rookie cops.

"Sit down, Vito, how bout a cup of coffee?" said McKean.

"No thanks, boss. As much as I'd love to use your private bathroom, I think it wise to forego the coffee."

"Okay, Vito, we have to go over a couple of things, so I'll get right to the point. I know I had mentioned to you that I would consider you for Chief of Detectives, but we are entering a crisis period which directly affects the Personnel Bureau. I'm sure you have heard about the lowered salaries for rookies, and, with the shitload of retirements coming in, I'm anticipating a dire shortage of recruits."

Vito did not like where the conversation was headed.

"I'm going to have to institute some discreet policy changes, and you're one of the few men I can trust. So, until further notice, you are to remain as Chief of Personnel, at least until this crisis has passed."

Vito thought to himself, *what a fuckin jerk job*! He had to say something. "Commissioner, with all due respect, can I be honest with you?"

McKean gazed at Vito with his piercing blue eyes and slowly said, "Sure, Vito. Go right ahead."

Vito could feel his guinea temper rising, but he knew he had to maintain his composure. "First of all, you told me I had the Chief of Detectives job, not that I would be "considered" for it. Second, a fuckin monkey could run the Personnel Bureau, and I appreciate your "trust," but I know there are quite a few bosses in your inner circle that you probably trust more than me." Vito took a deep breath and asked the question that had been consuming him since he was told about losing the Chief of Detectives job. "By the way, who got the Chief of Detectives slot?"

"I gave it to Danny Coyle."

*Of course he gave it to Coyle, part of the Irish Mafia.* Rumor had it that when McKean was a rookie cop, Coyle's dad had been McKean's training sergeant. The only time Coyle might have stepped into a detective squad room was to get a free cup of coffee. Vito had the urge to tell McKean that Coyle couldn't find his ass with both hands, but he kept his mouth shut.

"Okay, boss, I understand," he said instead. "So what are these discreet policy changes' that you spoke about?"

"Well, to start with, Vito, I need you to know that these changes need to be instituted, because, as you well may know, if we drop below a certain number of cops our Safe Streets federal grant money will be in jeopardy-- money that we desperately need in order to continue to fulfill our mission. That is, to keep this city one of the safest in America."

*Please stop dispensing the bullshit,* thought Vito, *and get to the point.*

"So, in order to fill the upcoming academy classes we may have to loosen up some of our standards. Now, of course, I know certain requirements are written in stone. For instance, the required number of college credits and the consequences of failing the entrance drug test are just two that I can think of offhand. But if the extensive background checks are stretched out, or if we are a

16

little more lenient in our residency requirements, those sorts of things will surely help fill the classes."

*Yeah sure*, thought Vito. *So we will have recruits with possible criminal records living in New Jersey patrolling the streets.* "Are you going to give me written guidelines Commissioner?" asked Vito, already knowing the answer.

"No, Vito. I am going to leave the guidelines up to your discretion. I just want you to know that I expect that the academy classes of January and July of 06' will be full. I don't want us losing one cent of that federal money, understood?"

"Sure, boss. I understand what I'm to do," said Vito, in a slightly sarcastic tone.

"Fine," replied McKean, looking at his watch, "Well, you better get busy. And please give my regards to your wife, Mary."

"You got it, boss," said Vito.

*

Vito returned to his office, knowing what McKean wanted from him. He wanted Vito to fall on the sword. He had been around long enough to understand the Machiavellian ways of working in One Police Plaza. Whenever it was discovered, and it would be discovered, that the N.Y.P.D. had not completed full background checks before admitting individuals into the police academy, the media would have a field day. They were actually going to swear these people in as probationary police officers. The more Vito thought about it, the more he kept coming to the same conclusion - McKean had not forgotten about Fort Surrender. That could be the only reason why McKean was setting him up to take the fall on this.

*

It had occurred when Vito was an Inspector, the Executive Officer of Brooklyn South Detectives, and McKean had just become Chief of the Department. One evening in the 66th Precinct, which covered Brooklyn's Borough Park neighborhood, a cop had locked up a high ranking Hasidic, for leaving the scene of an accident in which there had been serious physical injuries. In addition, it was discovered that the Hasidic driver had a suspended license.

The cop had brought the prisoner back to the precinct for arrest processing, when a large group of Hasidics had come into the precinct, demanding that the Hasidic prisoner be released with a summons. The Desk Officer refused, informing the head Hasidic that the prisoner had committed a felony, according to the Penal Law. This failed to satisfy the Hasidics, and they continued to demand the release of the member of their sect.

The Desk Officer ordered the crowd to leave the precinct, and at that point all hell broke loose. The Hasidics stormed into the cell area in an attempt to free their compatriot. The cops that attempted to stop them were assaulted, one officer sustaining a broken-eye socket as a result of the melee. Only reinforcements from the Brooklyn South Task Force had saved the precinct from being completely overrun. Once the precinct had been cleared, within an hour, the desk officer received a phone call from the Chief of Department's office directing the Desk Officer to release the prisoner with a Desk Appearance Ticket. The Desk Appearance Ticket (D.A.T.) mandated that the prisoner appear in court in a month to answer the charges. The only problem was that it was against department policy to issue a D.A.T. for a felony crime. The Desk Officer pointed this out to the Captain from the Chief of Department's office.

At that point, the Captain asked the Desk Officer where he lived, and the Desk Officer, who held the rank of Lieutenant, replied that he lived in Staten Island. The Captain then informed the Desk Officer that he hoped the Desk Officer had an E/Z Pass, because he was going to need it to drive to his new command in the Bronx. This was known in N.Y.P.D. parlance as "highway therapy." The Desk Officer got the message, and to much outrage from the cops in the 66th Precinct, the Hasidic prisoner was released with a D.A.T. From then on all the officers within the precinct began to call their own stationhouse, "Fort Surrender".

Inspector Vito Arena had been outraged when he had arrived at work the next day to find that cops had been assaulted within their own precinct. He had his detectives interview the officer with the broken-eye socket, in order to determine whether the officer would be able to identify the individual that had assaulted him. The officer felt he could provide a positive identification. When the officer had recovered from his injury, Inspector Arena had his detectives escort the injured cop on a canvas of the Hasidic neighborhood.

After two days of canvassing, the cop spotted the assailant coming off the subway at New Utrecht Avenue and 50th Street. The assailant was quickly arrested, and Arena directed the detectives to process the prisoner in the 67th Precinct, which was located in East Flatbush, and was almost a one-hundred-percent black community, occupied predominantly by people from various nations of the West Indies. To say the least, it was quite different from the Borough Park neighborhood, where the Hasidics resided.

*Let them try and storm this precinct,* Arena thought. He knew he had to act quickly, as the phone calls from One Police Plaza would be coming in shortly. The Hasidic community was very insular, and someone had to have seen the prisoner being arrested on the street in broad daylight. Phone calls to the Hasidic leaders, no doubt, had quickly followed after the arrest, and the political clout of that particular community gave them the freedom to call the high command at One Police Plaza, demanding the release of the cop's assailant.

Arena placed a phone call to a well respected, much-read, police beat reporter from the Daily News, Mike Dealy. Arena explained the situation to Dealy, asking if Dealy could do him a favor and make inquiries of the N.Y.P.D's Deputy Commissioner of Public Information (D.C.P.I.). Arena delineated what he would like Dealy to ask, and impressed upon him the urgency of the situation. Arena had fed Dealy information on other cases before the information had become public, giving Dealy a jump on the competition, so Dealy owed him one.

Dealy quickly made the call to D.C.P.I., wanting confirmation that Brooklyn South detectives had made an arrest in the case of the badly beaten police officer from the 66th Precinct. He further stated that he had discovered that the prisoner was being processed at the 67th Precinct, and said he was immediately going to write an article for the morning edition extolling the perseverance of the detectives involved in the case, especially considering the heinous crime. The D.C.P.I. rep informed Dealy he would get back to him.

At that moment, one of the head Rabbis of the sect called the Chief of Departments office (a number which he had on speed dial) expressing outrage that a member of his congregation had been arrested for no known reason. The Rabbi went on to say that whatever crime the man had supposedly committed, the Rabbi could produce fifty witnesses who would testify that the man wasn't there. A flustered Chief McKean informed the Rabbi that he would get back to him. To add to his developing migraine, Chief McKean then received a call from D.C.P.I., asking about a supposedly great collar made by Brooklyn South detectives, a collar that seemingly was going to generate press for the department in one of the city's major newspapers. McKean wondered what the fuck was going on.

The next call McKean's office received was from Inspector Vito Arena, who just wanted to inform the Chief that his men had made an arrest on the assault of the uniformed officer in the 66th Precinct. The officer had made a positive identification, and was one-hundred-and-ten percent sure that the man arrested was the miscreant that had broken his eye-socket. He further stated that he had spoken to the Brooklyn District Attorney's office and it was agreed that the assailant should be charged with Felony Assault, due to the seriousness of the injury, and was therefore ineligible to be released with a Desk Appearance Ticket.

When McKean's lieutenant informed him of Arena's call, McKean knew he was boxed in. If he ordered the prisoner to be released with a D.A.T., or if he had the charges lowered to Assault

Third Degree, a misdemeanor, the papers would have a field day. The minority communities would read the articles, and once again accuse the N.Y.P.D of giving favored treatment to the Hasidic community. McKean had to admit that Arena had pulled a slick move, and a man like that should be kept close by. McKean was of the notion that revenge was a dish best served cold.

*

Well, if they needed a fall guy, Arena figured he would give them what they want, but he was not going to stick around for the fallout. He had decided he was going to pull the pin. He had thirty-five years on the job and was fifty-six years old. He still had enough time to do policing, but it was going to be somewhere else. He had heard the Commissioners jobs in both Nassau and Suffolk Counties were going to be opening up and with his qualifications he knew he could make a good run at either job. Knowing he might be blamed for the "lowered standards" fiasco, he hoped he would be firmly ensconced in another department by that time.

A week after his meeting with McKean, Arena summoned to his office the Commanding Officer of the Applicant Processing Division, Inspector Bill Moss. Moss was everything Arena hated about working in One Police Plaza, a conniving weasel who should never call himself a cop. When Arena came into Personnel as Chief, he had done a background check on all the bosses that would be working for him. It wasn't a complete check. All he did was to run their arrest history, because that would tell him all he needed to know.

Moss, he discovered, had made only five arrests in his three years on patrol. To Arena that meant two things: Moss had spent quite a bit of time working inside the station house, and when he was on patrol he was wearing blinders. Once Moss got on the promotion track, he did the minimum time required in a command before he got himself re-assigned to cushy jobs such as teaching in the Police Academy, or he got lost somewhere in Headquarters. Each time he summoned Moss to his office, which was not very often, the first thing Arena did after Moss left was wash his hands.

But, there was no avoiding this meeting. Arena called out to his aide to send Moss in.

*

Moss knew of the meeting between Arena and the Commissioner, and he had reached out to all his contacts from his extensive time at Police Plaza to find out what had been discussed at the meeting. All he had gleaned from the Commissioner's aides was that the meeting had something to do with the upcoming academy classes. Moss was frustrated, because he always wanted to stay one step ahead, and when he was notified of his upcoming meeting with Chief Arena, he was uneasy. He had been able to stay inside the big building long enough to know he had to cover himself. So, as he did with most meetings in which he did not know every topic to be discussed beforehand, he set his cell phone on audio record.

*

After being summoned by the Chief's aide, Moss walked into the big office and took a seat in front of the Chief's desk. *The balls on this pasty faced, skinny son of a bitch*, thought Arena. *He sits down without my asking him to take a seat. Now he can sing for a cup of coffee, the arrogant little fuck..*

"Good Morning Chief. You needed to see me?" said Moss. Arena continued to stare at Moss, and all of a sudden he began to laugh. He didn't understand why, but while staring at Moss, the Chief pictured his guest wearing a brown bowler, in a suit much too tight, with pants much too short. Arena had conjured up that image, while imagining Moss selling bottles of that cure–all elixir out of the back of a covered wagon in the Old West. *Oh shit,* thought Arena. *I need a vacation.*

"Something funny, boss?"

"No, no, just thinking of a joke I recently heard. Anyway I'll get right to the point. The department is in jeopardy of losing federal funding in regards to the Safe Streets, Safe Cities grant if we do not fill the two upcoming academy classes for 2006. So, in order to ensure that we fill those classes, I've outlined some

22

changes in regards to our recruitment and retention of those individuals interested in becoming police officers. First off, I need you to contact the Department of Civil Service and have the fifty-dollar police entrance examination fee suspended, until further notice.

"Then, reach out to the Department of Education, and ask if we could utilize various junior high and high schools throughout the city to conduct walk-in entrance exams, each and every Saturday, starting A.S.A.P. Make sure most of these schools are in minority neighborhoods, in order to give us a leg up on minority recruitment.

"Now, as far as residency requirements, let these potential recruits know that they will be accepted into the academy, even if they do not live in the five boroughs or the contiguous counties. However, they will have to sign an affidavit stating that they will move into our required residence areas within one year after being sworn in. Are you following me so far, Moss?"

"Absolutely, Chief," replied Moss.

"Well, I don't see you writing anything down, but then again, you're probably recording this whole conversation."

An anxious Moss looked away from Arena and stated, "Chief, I'm actually kind of insulted that you would even think I would do such a thing."

"Yeah, yeah, whatever. Okay. Let's get this over with. Finally, in regard to background checks of potential recruits, I want you to let the applicant investigators know that the extensive background checks we normally conduct are to be delayed. Of course, I want warrant checks to be conducted, but if it is a bullshit warrant, like turnstile jumping, disorderly conduct, shit like that, give the potential recruit the opportunity to clear it up. The decision as to what is, and is not, an acceptable warrant should be decided by the investigator's Lieutenant.

"Stress to those Lieutenants however, the importance of filling these classes, which is going to be difficult enough, considering the starting salaries they are offering these recruits. I want these investigators also to know that the usual interviews of the recruit's friends, neighbors, past employers, etc., are to be delayed until these recruits graduate from the academy and assigned to commands. In that way they can be counted towards our federal grant money. Capisce, Moss?"

"No thank you, Chief. It gives me heartburn."

The Chief shook his head at Moss's ignorance of, as far as Arena was concerned, the greatest of the romantic languages.

"About the background investigations, Chief. I don't think a delay will be any problem, since the Applicant Investigations Unit just got hit with a slew of retirements. Now that the contract has been settled, a lot of cops from the 1985 and 1986 classes have put in for retirement. I was going to ask you for approval to bring in additional investigators to replace the ones we are losing."

"How many have put in their papers?"

"As of right now, an even dozen."

"All right, replace half. This could be a benefit, since their case loads will double," Arena said. "Okay, Moss, that's it. You have quite a bit of work to do, so I think you should get going on this."

"Sure thing Chief. Just one final question. Will these policy changes you have just spoken about be sent to me in a memo, or some type of Operations Order?" asked Moss, knowing what the answer would be.

"Do I look like some kind of fucking idiot to you, Moss?" the Chief answered, as his voice began to reflect his anger at the question posed. "Do you actually think I would put any of what we discussed in writing?" Arena stared at Moss, whose deodorant was not working as advertised at the moment.

Moss slowly stood up and backed out of the Chief's office, trying to keep an eye on Arena. He had heard the stories about Arena's temper. A Captain had remarked that he had witnessed Arena actually punch a suspect who had been arrested for shooting at a cop. Who knew what a madman like that would be capable of?

Moss ran back to his office and immediately pressed the playback button on his phone. The whole conversation was crystal clear. Moss was elated. Now, at least, he couldn't be held responsible for policy changes that would inevitably create a shit-storm.

Less stringent background checks on potential recruits were not without precedent in the N.Y.P.D. In the late 1960's, the Vietnam War had been in full swing, and civil unrest was erupting throughout the city. Protests, sometimes violent, were almost a daily occurrence, as America's youth raged against the war, social injustice, and deteriorating race relations. Cops were desperately needed, and hiring began at a frenzied pace. Background checks were cursory, and while thousands of those officers turned out to become great cops, quite a few of them turned out to be problems later on for the N.Y.P.D.

For example, two graduates from 1969 were Louis Eppolito and Steven Carracappa. Eppolito was able to get on the N.Y.P.D., although some of his immediate family members were members of the Gambino crime family. Carracappa had been arrested and found guilty of possession of stolen property, but that was seemingly ignored, as a police department desperate for warm bodies overlooked past misdeeds that would have automatically disqualified a candidate in earlier years. In 2006, both men were found guilty of eight counts of murder and conspiracy to commit murder. The department was failing to heed the words of George Santanyana, "Those who fail to learn from the mistakes of their predecessors are destined to repeat them."

# CHAPTER 3

It was a Saturday afternoon in late September, and Linc was sitting at the kitchen table in the two-bedroom apartment he shared with his brother and mother. It had a cookie-cutter layout, like all the apartments in the Linden Houses. You walked through the front door and you stepped into a hallway to the right. A short walk down the hallway brought you to the kitchen on the left, which was attached to a living room. Continuing down the hallway, you came to one small bathroom on the right, directly across from the living room entrance. Past the bathroom the hallway led directly into the master bedroom, with the second bedroom on the left.

The Watson's apartment was sparsely furnished, with a hand-me-down couch and love seat in the living room, both pieces sitting atop a ten-year-old mocha colored rug. The apartment was painted in the standard Housing Authority Yellow, and the heat from the radiators was generated through old cast iron pipes that clanged and groaned, notifying the tenants that they would be sweating shortly.

Linc was studying for his first test in Phonetics, which was to be given on Monday. His mother, Dolores, was standing right behind him in the cramped kitchen, packing her dinner, as she got ready to go to work. Dolores worked for the Transit Authority as a subway clerk. Thankfully, she did not have to travel far, as her steady assignment was the Junius Street stop on the #3 subway line, in Brownsville. Linc constantly worried about his mother's safety, as he knew there were some rough-ass gangs in the numerous Brownsville projects. And she worked the night shift, from 3 p.m. until 11 p.m.

Dolores was non-confrontational but tough, and she possessed that street smart sixth-sense, which could be partially attributed to the fact that she had been born and raised in the projects. She had met her late husband, Delbert, in one of the Transit Authority safety training classes, when they had both gotten jobs with the Transit Authority. Delbert, before he had been murdered, had worked as a subway car inspector in the New Lots yards at the end of the #3 line. A senseless act of violence, all too common in the projects, had ended the life of the man she loved.

*

Delbert Watson, had been a kind, gentle man, who arose every morning at 4 a.m. in order to make sure he wasn't late for his 5 a.m. to 1 p.m. shift at the New Lots yards. He worked hard, volunteering for any available overtime, and saving as much money as possible, in order to one day get his family out of the projects. When Delbert came home from work, he always made sure to kiss his wife and convey his love for her, as she walked out the door to work her shift at Junius Street.

It had been a beautiful Brooklyn summer afternoon, in July of 1996, when Delbert Watson, at the age of young age of thirty-three, had lost his life on the streets he had desperately wanted to escape.

It was a Thursday, and Delbert had taken the day off from work to watch his son, eleven-year old Lincoln, play a baseball playoff game at the field next to George Gershwin Junior High School. Delbert had brought Harris along so he could watch his older brother, a brother he idolized. At the time Harris was seven years old, a normal, healthy boy who saw only sunshine every morning he woke up.

They watched Lincoln play shortstop on the all-dirt, sun-baked infield. The outfield grass was an emerald green, a sharp contrast to the clear, azure blue sky. The sky was so beautifully blue that it demanded you constantly look up towards it and realize that even the greatest of painters could never duplicate that magnificent color on a canvas.

The game was getting out of hand, as Lincoln's team was up by seven runs and it was only the top of the third inning. Lincoln was doing well, having two hits and driving in four runs.

Delbert suggested to Harris that they take a short walk to the bodega on Stanley Avenue so Harris could grab a cold soda, and

27

also bring one back for his brother. Harris, concerned that his brother would miss them, yelled to Lincoln, who had been standing in the on deck circle, that they would be right back. Lincoln acknowledged his father and brother with a wave.

Harris began to drag his father by the hand, and Delbert laughed, picked up his skinny son, and threw him onto his shoulder.

As they walked down Stanley Avenue, his legs kicking in the air, his stomach resting on his father's big right shoulder, Harris began playfully punching his father's heavily muscled back. "Cmon, Dad, let me down before any of my friends see me!"

"Listen up, little man. You're never too old to have fun with your pops," said Delbert, gently lowering him to the ground. As they approached the front entrance to the bodega, Harris ran ahead and yanked open the front door. He waited at the door until his father could see him go inside, then he ran into the store and up one of the food aisles to the rear of the market, where the soda and beer were cooling in the refrigerator.

*

The two fifteen-year-old project kids needed money, and they knew that the Arab running the bodega made a money drop on Friday morning, so Thursday afternoon was the opportune time to stick up the place. The smaller one had a thirty-two-caliber revolver in his pocket to show the Arab that he wasn't fucking around, if it came to that. The bigger one felt he didn't need a gun. If anyone stood in their way, he would just administer a severe beat-down. They both had ski masks sitting on top of their heads, ready to pull down at the right moment, and thin racing gloves. The smaller one went to the back of the store, grabbed a grape Nehi, opened it, and began drinking from the bottle as he walked up to the counter, where the Arab owner stood. The bigger one was already standing nearby, reading a magazine. Suddenly, Harris burst into the store and ran to the back. The one with the gun recognized the kid, and he also knew his brother.

The smaller kid nodded to the bigger, and they both pulled down the ski-masks.

"Give it up, A-rab man," said the smaller one, now displaying the small black revolver he had been carrying.

Delbert, as was his habit, glanced through the glass door before entering the bodega. He saw the two boys pull down their masks, and now the smaller one had a gun pointed at the bodega owner. He knew both boys from the projects. They were both only a few years older than Lincoln. These were just kids, he thought. He didn't see Harris, who was probably in the back of the store, examining every bottle of soda in the case. Delbert stepped inside.

"Hey, young blood, put down the gun and get back to your building before someone gets hurt," said Delbert.

The smaller one, stunned, recognized the man blocking their escape. It was the skinny kid's pops. "Nah, man. You gots to get the fuck out of here, or you be the one getting hurt."

"Don't be the fool, son. Nobody hurtin nobody. You and your homeboy just get on out of here, this shit's done."

The smaller one began to panic, as he heard the skinny kid yell for his father to come to the back, to help him pick out a soda for his brother. The smaller one had a bad feeling that the big man blocking the door recognized him. He could tell by the way the big man was staring at him. *Fuck this*, he thought. *This ain't no Spofford juvenile bullshit deed.*

Knowing he and his partner had to get away, he raised the gun and pointed it at the big man's chest. He pulled the trigger, and the gun, although small, almost jumped out of his hand. The big man fell backwards, crashing into a Goya bean display.

"Oh, shit," yelled the bigger kid. "Let's jet, muthafucka!" Both boys leaped over the outstretched, twitching legs of Delbert Watson, burst through the front door, and ran south on Van Siclen Avenue.

Delbert was lying amidst the cans of Goya beans, and the store owner, an immigrant from Yemen, was staring at him. His chest was heaving, as the small caliber bullet had pierced his aorta, causing blood to spurt from the inside of that vital artery into his chest cavity. Delbert was drowning in his own blood. He could see the face of his younger son, crying, the warm tears dropping onto Delbert's own face. Strangely enough, he could not hear anything, and perhaps that was good, since no father wishes to hear his son cry. Harris's handsome face began to fade, and Delbert Watson drew his last breath on a dirty floor in a bodega in Brooklyn.

*

It was right after that traumatic event that Harris began stuttering, and, as Linc grew older, he realized that the public schools were ill-equipped to deal with his brother's speech impediment. Harris had been left back one year in school, as he could not express himself well enough in some of his classes to move up to the next grade.

Linc was determined to help his brother and others like him, so he decided to become a speech-pathology therapist. His college courses were difficult, but Linc was driven to succeed, knowing that his father would have wanted him to. He desperately wanted to get a good job in the therapy field, and quit drug steering for Silky, but Silky's money was needed to pay for college and to help out his mom. When his mother had asked him how he was paying for college, he said that he had taken out student loans. She would be devastated if she knew how he was really paying for his tuition.

*

Linc had just finished reviewing his Phonetics class notes, when his cell phone rang, it was Bam-Bam, Silky's muscle. Silky wanted to see Linc right away.

Linc put away his book, and told Harris he would be right back. He exited his building, crossed Wortman Avenue, and entered the lobby of 180 Wortman. He rode the elevator up to the eighth floor and turned left. Silky's apartment was 8B, the last one on the left.

Linc knocked on the door of Silky's base of operations. Bam-Bam opened the door, and nodded to Linc, who stepped inside the apartment. After hearing the door close, Linc placed his hands against the wall. Silky trusted no one but Bam-Bam, and all who entered his apartment were subject to a frisk. Bam-Bam's large hands ran along Linc's arms, to the front of his chest, and across his back. The hands then ran along his waistband, into his crotch area and down his legs. Bam-Bam grunted his approval and pointed Linc towards the living room.

Silky was sitting on a plush, black leather couch, watching a mixed martial arts bout on his 54-inch Sony television, with surround sound, of course. Lying on an adjacent couch was a light-skinned beauty, wearing nothing but a shear, black negligee and was perusing through "Jet" magazine. Silky threw a rolled-up twenty-dollar bill at her. "That's for you baby. Now you get that fine ass of yours down to Micky D's and get youself a couple a them high protein fish sanwichs. That way you can get your strength back up. You come back a little later and Silky'll burn that protein off you."

She smiled and slowly arose from the couch, bent over and kissed Silky on his cheek. Never acknowledging Linc, she brushed by him on her way into the bathroom.

"Well, well, if it ain't my college edumacated home slice. How you been, boy? Have a seat," said Silky, pointing at the couch, where the beauty had just lain. Silky stood up, stretching his lanky, 6'3" inch frame. He was three years older than Linc, and, like Linc, he had been born and raised in the Linden Houses. His street name had come from his silky, smooth ways, especially with the ladies. It also didn't hurt his reputation with the opposite sex that he oversaw all the drug action in the Linden Houses and had just opened up a small operation in East Flatbush.

"Yo, my heart's out to you for Tarface, man." Silky said. "I know how tight you n the brother was. I know it was those punk muthfuckas from the Boulevard Houses and payback gonna be real. I gots a plan in motion right now, and you gonna be the main character, cuz."

Linc wasn't sure where Silky was going with this so he asked, "How you mean, Silk?"

31

Silky walked over to the kitchen table, picked up a white sheet of paper and handed Linc the paper.

Linc had seen the same paper hanging in the lobbies and elevators of the apartment buildings throughout the Linden Houses. It was basically a recruitment poster for the N.Y.P.D.

"What the fuck I want this paper for?" asked Linc.

Silky smiled and said, "You gonna be the po-lice my brother. I know a friend of a friend that be five-o, and he tell me that those muthafuckas be desperate for cops. Says they ain't gonna be checkin shit on brothers. Not that you got to worry. You ain't never been locked up anyways."

"Nah Silk. Member I got that summons for loitering in the lobby of 190. They won't take me," said Linc, hoping to convince Silky that it could never happen.

"Pfft, that ain't shit B. You took care of it, and it wasn't nothin but a summons anyway."

"Yo, man. I had to go to downtown Brooklyn Criminal Court for that summons. It weren't like it was a traffic ticket or sometin. I had to show up in person!" Linc was desperate to get Silky off the subject. He remembered he had been smart enough to give the cop issuing the summons Silky's address of 180 Wortman, Apartment 8b. Even though he had no identification, the cop had believed him, seemingly happy just to be able to write a summons.

"It weren't nothin, man, I'm telling you, word to God," said Silky. "They ain't gonna deny you for that petty bullshit. Yo, Bam-Bam, make youself useful and fire up some tree, man."

Bam-Bam dutifully removed a zip-lock bag from his pants pocket, and quickly rolled a joint. Lighting it, he took a deep inhale and passed it to Silky. Silky took a quick toke and passed it on to Linc.

Linc realized he had an escape route from all the foolish talk and also took a toke. "Now there you go, Silk. You know I taste the herb every now and again, so I ain't never gonna be able to pass no piss test."

"Chill, cuz. My boy tol me they gonna be telling brothers way head o'time when they gotta piss. Gonna give you plenty a time to clean out, they ain't gonna be doin no random shit. Now listen up son. This shit is a done deal," said Silky, hard-looking Linc. "You gonna get your skinny ass down to Gershwin next Saturday, and you gonna take that test. I'm gonna still bankroll you as if you still be steerin for me, and you get to collect government money from u job as a po-po.

"You ain't been right since your boy got lit up in the lobby, so you get some time to chill. Once you get out of that police school you gonna volunteer to work this precinct. Ain't no muthafuckas wanna work this hood, so I know they gonna put your ass in the precinct on Sutter."

Silky took the joint back, took a long draw, and put his head back. After making sure his lungs were full of the smoke, he began to exhale slowly, enjoying the high he was beginning to feel. "You got the college they want, and I'm setting you up with an address at my aunt's crib in Ozone Park because my boy tol me that they don't want no brothers workin in the precinct they be livin at. See, I got this shit covered. Once you in the precinct you can be feedin us all kinds of nefarious shit, man. Undercover car plate numbers, narco raids, but, most def, any shit on those Boulevard punk assses. Then we get payback for your boy. We decimate those muthafuckas. You feelin me, cuz?"

Linc began thinking about it and he knew he had no choice. The more he thought about it, it really wasn't such a bad deal. Silky would still be paying him, plus he could collect money from the cops. He would explain to his mother that it was only temporary, until he received his degree and started teaching. Besides, Harris was becoming old enough to take care of himself. In addition, he wouldn't have to move out of his apartment, so he could still help out Harris if need be.

As far as school was concerned, he knew a few of his classmates were cops and firemen, so they were able to work out both school and their jobs. More importantly, however, was the death of his good friend. This might give him the opportunity to discover who was responsible for Tarface's death. Linc knew that if he had not gone to the bus stop to meet Harris, it could have easily have been him lying dead in that lobby. "A'ight Silk, I'll be there next Saturday."

# CHAPTER 4

No one knew exactly where Shawn had come from, nor did they know how old he was. Shawn had the mind of a twelve-year-old, but, he was most likely somewhere in his mid-twenties. They knew Shawn lived in the projects, but which one was anyone's guess. He appeared in the 75th Detective Squad office every day around noon, and stayed until he became bored or hungry.

Boredom was generally not a problem, since the 75th Precinct Detective Squad was the busiest in the city, and Shawn either raided the refrigerator in the squad kitchen, sometimes eating dishes lovingly prepared for a detective by his wife, or waited for someone to buy him a couple of slices of pizza.

Shawn wore an old army fatigue jacket whether it was January or July, a black woolen hat, faded blue jeans, and an old pair of Chuck Taylor, black, Converse sneakers. He carried no identification, except a toy plastic five-star sheriff's shield. The shield had been presented to him by Detective Kevin Monahan at a *swearing in* ceremony held in the detective's meal room. Shawn enjoyed the shield almost as much as the six Devil Dogs he had eaten on that glorious occasion.

Shawn mentioned his mother once in a while, on the few occasions he did speak, and she tried her best to administer to Shawn's hygiene. However, on certain hot days during July and August, the detectives would not allow Shawn into the squad office, as he smelled like an "unwashed ass." He would be directed to go home and tell his mother to give him a bath, or else the detectives wouldn't play with him. The next day Shawn would show up, smelling as fresh as a flower, wearing a big smile on his face, and he would park himself in any detective's chair that was available.

Whenever a new detective, or a supervisor, was assigned to the 75th Squad, Shawn would just stick his thumb in his mouth, as would an infant, and stare at the newcomer. Feeling uneasy, most

35

would attempt to strike up a conversation with Shawn, but they were met with a continual stare. A veteran detective would inform the newly assigned individual that Shawn helped out by taking out the trash, even though each precinct had its own cleaning crew. Sometimes, Shawn would actually take out the trash, along with anything else lying on or near a detective's desk.

Shawn's penchant for picking up any bags lying near a detective's desk was now causing Detective Matty Boyd's migraine to become almost unbearable. As an eight-year veteran of the 7-5 Precinct Squad, Boyd should have known better than to leave a paper bag full of evidence lying near his desk. When Boyd stepped into the interview room to speak to his homicide suspect, Shawn had spotted the bag, and ever on the hunt for food, preferably something sweet, he quickly opened the brown paper bag.

Eyeing only an old blue sweatshirt with some red stains on it, Shawn decided the best place for the paper bag would be in the black contractor's bag in which he had dumped refuse from the various garbage pails around the office. He then dutifully dragged the contractor's bag down the steps to the first floor of the precinct, took it out the back into the parking lot, and tossed it into the dumpster.

Everything had gone smoothly for Boyd, up until the point of the missing evidence. It was his last case in the 7-5 Squad, and it had been what detectives called a "ground ball." He had just gotten a written statement from his suspect, Stanley Devins, in which he fully admitted to stabbing to death his longtime friend, Tooky Remis. Boyd loved to label his cases. He had decided to call this case the, "NO, NOT THE SNICKERS!" homicide.

*

Stanley, just three weeks before his arrest by Boyd, had been released from the Green Haven Correctional Facilty. Once back in the world Stanley rekindled his friendship with Tooky, a friend of his since childhood. Having served sixteen years for a homicide, Stanley had been paroled, but was finding it difficult to survive in the outside world. He had become *institutionalized*, having spent more than half of his thirty-five years in various prisons.

Once released, Stanley was no longer being fed three times a day, working out, watching television, and socializing with those of his own ilk. Now he had to find work, constantly report to his parole officer, perform random piss tests, and deal with civilians, most of whom he considered assholes.

Furthermore, he had discovered that Tooky had become one of those assholes. Sure, it had been *stand up* for Tooky to let him use his crib, but he never let Stanley forget it. Every day, at least once a day, Tooky reminded Stanley that it was Tooky's house, even though it was no more than a small, shit-smellin apartment.

On the day of his arrest, Stanley had had enough. Being a gracious guest, he had bought a six pack of assorted candy bars, which he placed inside the refrigerator, since he liked his candy cold. Displaying great generosity, he even informed Tooky that he could help himself to <u>one</u> of his candy bars, but to make sure it wasn't the Snickers. Stanley went out on another fruitless search for gainful employment, and returned to the apartment looking forward to biting into the perfectly chilled Snickers Bar. When he went into the shit-smellin apartment, he observed Tooky lying on the couch, watching an episode of Jerry Springer. Tooky was also picking at his teeth with a toothpick, as if he was trying to dislodge a nut from within. Stanley went directly to the refrigerator, and upon opening it, discovered that the Snickers Bar was missing from his assortment pack of six.

"Why, you no-count muthafucka," said Stanley.

"Yo, dawg. This my crib, that my refrigerator, anything in it be mine," Tooky said, while staring at the television, intently watching a mother and daughter punch each other, after the daughter had  discovered the mother was pregnant by the daughter's boyfriend.

"Yea, yea cuz, you be right," Stanley replied calmly, as he walked behind Tooky, who was now sitting up, thoroughly enthralled with the drama unfolding on the television screen. He had become so entranced with the show that he never felt the cold, sharp edge of the razor, sliding across his neck, severing his jugular vein. Blood began pouring out of the blood vessels from his completely severed neck onto his blue sweatshirt.

He tried to stand up, but Stanley grabbed the top of his forehead, and snapped his neck back. "Hope you enjoyed my Snickers, muthafucka!" Stanley then walked over to the phone, dialed 911 and told the operator that he wanted to report a homicide. Three weeks of civilian life, with nothing but assholes, was enough for him.

*

"Okay, which one of you assholes hid my evidence bag?" asked Boyd. "Cmon, no fuckin around. I want to get this done so I can meet Monahan later. My last day here, and you guys still won't give me a fuckin break." All the detectives were either pecking away at their keyboards or on the phone.

Suddenly, Boyd heard a growl from one of the desks, "I seen Shawn over by your desk a little while ago." The information came from Benny Archer, a large, black, well-muscled detective who said very little, but when he spoke, people listened. "Yeah. See if you get that kinda help from those Applicant Investigation bitches you gonna be workin with," said Archer.

Shawn had just walked into the squad room, smiling proudly at the task he had just accomplished. All the waste paper baskets were empty, so he was suprised he heard Detective Boyd scream out his name. "Shawn, did you just pick up a paper bag that was lying next to my desk?"

"Yeah. Just some old shirt. Threw it out."

"Threw it out where?"

"Where else, stupid? In the dumpster." Shawn began to get somewhat nervous as he saw Boyd's light blue eyes begin to blaze. Shawn never liked Boyd because he was always playing tricks on people, including Shawn. He was glad Boyd was leaving, just as long as Boyd's partner, Monahan, never left. Shawn was unaware, however, that the brown paper bag containing a delicious turkey and swiss hero, with hot sauce and onions, left every Friday in the refrigerator, was left for him by the short, blond haired detective Boyd, who was always playing tricks on people. Included in the bag was, of course, two Devil Dogs.

"Well, you better get your skinny black ass down to that dumpster and get me that bag, or I'm going to stick one of these cowboy boots up that ass," said Boyd.

*That is another thing,* thought Shawn. *What kind of a detective would wear stupid looking shoes like that.* Shawn was beginning to feel a little uneasy, so he ran into the meal room, sat down, stuck his thumb in his mouth and began watching television.

The ever-present Fox News Channel was on, the only show ever on the television, unless the Yankees were playing. Any Met fans in the squad office had given up asking to put the Mets on, since the response was usually, "We don't get minor league baseball on this set."

Shawn sat in the seat, stuck his thumb in his mouth and stared at the television set, refusing to look at Boyd, who was standing in the doorway.

"I swear to God," said Boyd, "if they have someone like you in that Applicant Unit, the first day I meet him I'm gonna poison him to death. I shoulda did it to one of your Devil Dogs a long time ago." Boyd was resigned to the fact that he was going to be dumpster-diving shortly, looking for his evidence bag.

*

After eight years in the 7-5 Precinct squad, Boyd had been stuck at third-grade detective. He became unbearable when the Personnel Orders were published, and promotions to second-grade detective consisted of detectives from inside units, such as the Mayor's Security Detail, Internal Affairs, and the Intelligence Division. Very rarely did a detective from a precinct squad get second-grade. Not only was there prestige with receiving promotion to second-grade, but a substantial increase in pay. A second-grade detective made just a little under sergeant's pay. A first-grade detective ranking, the pinnacle of a detective's career, gave him a little less pay than a lieutenant.

After the last round of promotions had been published, Boyd became fed up, and called a captain he knew in the Applicant Investigation Unit. The captain explained that they were shorthanded and were looking to pick up experienced detectives. There would be plenty of overtime, but no chance for promotion to second grade. Boyd did not care, as he was becoming burned out at the 7-5. He was handling twice as many cases as a detective in any other precinct. Besides, he would be getting a take-home car, and what could be easier than conducting background checks on twenty-something-year-old recruits?

As Boyd lifted his five-foot, six- inch body into the dumpster, he began to think that he would never get a grade promotion out of the 7-5 because he was his own worst enemy. Boyd loved arguing with people almost as much as he liked bustin balls. He had graduated from the police academy in December of 1982, been assigned to the 7-5 Precinct, and his problems had begun within four months.

He was able to get a seat in a patrol car by volunteering for the midnight platoon, and he hooked up with a five-year veteran named Donnie Floyd.

The Floyd and Boyd team moniker produced an unending flow of jokes around the muster room at roll calls. One night the Floyd/Boyd team, out on patrol, turned onto Essex Street off New Lots Avenue, and they saw the second floor of a two-story house fully engulfed in flames. They pulled their patrol car onto the sidewalk in front of the residence, jumped out, and ran inside the home. They were able to awaken all the residents, and, after three trips into the smoke-filled house, they managed to get everyone out to the safety of the street.

Unbeknownst to the partners, during their rescue effort the lads from Engine Company 290 and Ladder 103 had arrived on the scene and decided that the police car in front of the fire location was a bit too close to a fire hydrant. Not ones to pass up causing some problems for the boys in blue, the fireman decided to bust out the rear windows of the patrol car and run the hose from the fire hydrant through said rear windows.

When their patrol sergeant showed up, both Floyd and Boyd were receiving oxygen from the local E.M.S. crew. Both officers were oxygen deprived, they reeked of smoke, and Floyd's back was in great pain from his having had to almost carry a 250 pound woman down the stairs.

"What happened to the side windows of your R.M.P.?" the sergeant asked.

"No. We're fine, Sarge. Thanks for asking. What are you talking about with the windows?" asked Boyd. The Sergeant pointed to their patrol car, and they saw the huge hose, leaking plenty of water, running through the two back windows.

"Why those motherfuckers!" screamed Boyd, suddenly feeling an onrush of oxygen fill his lungs.

"Forget it, Boyd, don't start anything. You guys are in enough trouble for failing to safeguard your vehicle."

After receiving a Command Discipline penalty of two vacation days, Boyd plotted his revenge. The way Boyd's mind worked, it didn't take him long to compose a flyer which declared that free government cheese would be available, first come, first serve, on Sunday morning starting at 5 a.m. at 480 Sheffield Avenue. This just happened to be the firehouse location of Engine 290/ Ladder 103. The partners then plastered the flyers around the neighborhood of the firehouse.

On that morning, hungry residents were lined up, almost forty strong, in front of the firehouse door. Floyd and Boyd were strategically parked down the block, ready to observe the ensuing uproar. Sure enough, at 5: 15 a.m., impatient residents began banging on the front door of the firehouse. When a sleepy fireman answered the door, he was met with demands for free cheese. Of course, the fireman didn't know what the fuck the people were talking about, so he shut the door hoping to grab a few more hours sleep. This only enraged the hungry crowd, and they began screaming, while still banging on the door. The expected call over the police radio, of an unruly crowd in front of 480 Sheffield Avenue was soon transmitted.

Boyd/Floyd answered, informing Central that they would respond forthwith. First, however, they decided to eat their breakfast and drink their coffee. After all, who would want to eat cold eggs or drink cold coffee? While dining, they continued to observe the irate group screaming at the firemen, all of whom were standing in front of their firehouse, hoping the crowd did not decide to storm the place.

Satisfied that their efforts had caused the firemen a great deal of angst, the partners decided to break up the crowd. They pulled up to the scene, and were immediately confronted by the leader of the group, who quickly showed Floyd the flyer.

"This looks pretty official to me," said Floyd.

"Well, then, you tell those muthafuckers to start handing out the cheese!"

"I'm sorry, sir, but the cheese was distributed, as it says on the flyer, by the Federal Government, so it's a federal matter. Best thing to do is go home and contact your councilman and inform him of this injustice. Either that or call the F.B.I." said Boyd.

"Ain't this some shit. Why would they do that? They supposed to be helping people."

"Well, you know firemen. They take anything that's not nailed down. Why do you think they wear those big boots when they go in to those house fires? If you notice they even wear those boots when there's not water on the ground!" observed Boyd.

The crowd broke up, and the partners informed the firemen that they hoped they would be able to get back to sleep. They then resumed patrol.

Following that incident, especially since it involved firemen, everyone wanted to work with Matty Boyd. Whenever his partner, Floyd, took a day off, cops were clamoring to work with the Merry Prankster. Cops would offer to buy him his dinner, plus beers after work, if only Matty would ask the Sergeant if they could be his partner for the night. Matty was also a good cop. He always met his summons quota, and would bring in at least four quality collars every month.

From patrol, he went to the precinct anti-crime unit, where he first partnered up with Kevin Monahan. They were a great team, leading the precinct every year in gun collars, and before long both were assigned to the precinct robbery, or R.I.P. unit. From there, they made the natural progression to the precinct detective squad, where they both received the coveted gold detective shield.

*

Even in the detective squad, Boyd could not stop with his pranks. They could become especially vicious if he disliked a person, and there was perhaps no person whom Boyd disliked more than their precinct squad lieutenant, Ed Fisher.

Fisher had become the squad lieutenant almost three years ago. He had spent all of his time as a lieutenant, prior to his arrival at the 7-5, in the Chief of Detectives Office at One Police Plaza. His downfall came when he took a shit where he ate.

Fisher had Fridays and Saturdays off, while assigned to the Chief of D's Office. On Sundays, he would work from noon to eight, a tour in which he knew things would be quiet, and nobody would ask him to do any work. Every Sunday dinner, he would treat himself to Chinese food from the Woo Hop restaurant, which was only a short walk from One Police Plaza. It was the only time he could eat Chinese food, since his wife, Mary Beth, was a born-again Christian, and she refused to let any food made by godless people enter their home.

On this particular Sunday, Fisher was sitting at his desk, reading a memo from the Chief, which had actually been addressed to another lieutenant. He had pilfered the memo from the top drawer of that lieutenant's desk and was reading it in hopes that he could get some dirt on his co-worker. Fisher began to feel the rumblings from some of the Moo-Shu Pork that he had consumed for dinner, and decided he had to utilize the men's room, quickly.

Unsure whether he would be able to make it all the way down the hall, Fisher made a career-changing decision. He knew the Chief of Detective's office had been left open for the cleaning crew, and he had always desired to see what the inside of a Chief's bathroom looked like, so Fisher grabbed a set of Personnel Orders to read and made his way into the Chief's office.

The bathroom was more opulent than Fisher ever imagined. It even had a shower. While standing, he unbuckled his pants and slid the pancake holster containing his five-shot Smith and Wesson off-duty revolver off the belt. He did not want to chance the gun sliding off when he took a seat. He sat down and placed the holster on the floor, just in time, as the Moo-Shu pork had completed its journey into his bowels.

Fisher was only able to read two pages of the Personnel Orders when he thought he heard voices outside the Chief's office. In a panic, he stood up, performed the proper hygiene maneuvers, buckled his pants, and quietly slipped out of the bathroom. He did not flush the bowl, as the whooshing sound of the water might alert the voices he had heard coming from outside the office.He would come back and flush after he had completed his investigation.

When he stepped out of the Chief's office, he was relieved to discover that the voices were of two cleaners arguing in his office about who had better French fries, McDonalds or Burger King. He quickly dismissed the two cleaners, and was about to go back into the Chief's bathroom to finish tidying up, when his phone rang. It was his wife, Mary Beth, demanding that he come home immediately.

She explained that their fifteen-year-old son had gone to a party, and Mary Beth had discovered from a church-going friend that girls might be at the party as well. No one was answering the phone at the party house, and Mary Beth was afraid that one of those "hussies" might try to take advantage of their poor son. Fisher tried to explain to his wife that he had very important police work to do, but Mary Beth would have none of it, and insisted that he better get home right away.

Flustered, Fisher looked at his watch, and noticed that he only had a half an hour to the end of his tour, so he figured *what the heck, why not beat the job for thirty minutes*. He packed up quick and left. On his way home he remembered the unflushed bowl, but he figured he could blame it on one of the Mexican cleaners, since everyone knew they would just shit anywhere.

Unfortunately for Lieutenant Fisher, the Chief of Detectives decided to respond from his home to a police-involved shooting within the confines of the 1st Precinct that Sunday evening. After everything was wrapped up at the shooting scene, the Chief figured he would go to his office to await the reports on the shooting, and perhaps order something to eat, since he had not had dinner. The 1st Precinct bordered One Police Plaza, so returning to his office was not out of his way.

As the Chief entered his office, a sour stench invaded his nostrils, almost knocking him off his feet. Curiously, there was a faint odor of Chinese food intermingling with the horrid smell, dissipating whatever appetite the Chief had developed. He held his breath and entered his bathroom, fearing that a dead body had been dumped therein. Upon entering the room, the Chief began retching as he viewed the unflushed bowl. Holding his nose, he used his left foot to depress the lever, flushing the noxious material into the New York City sewer system.

Out of the corner of his eye, he spotted what appeared to be a small caliber revolver inside a brown pancake holster. The holster was tucked up against the wall, in back of the toilet bowl. Using his foot, the Chief slid the holster away from the wall and kicked it to the bathroom door. He then went back to his desk, opened his briefcase and pulled out a pair of rubber gloves he often utilized when visiting crime scenes.

In reality, what had happened in that bathroom was a crime, since the toxic odor had almost killed the Chief. Picking up the holster, he removed the revolver and located the serial number on the weapon. He then placed a call to the Internal Affairs Action

Desk and asked the sergeant there to run the serial number of the weapon.

Since it was the Chief of Detectives, the sergeant put his crossword puzzle to the side and immediately ran the numbers in his computer. "The gun comes back to a Lieutenant Edward Fisher, Chief. And it seems he is assigned to your office."

"I know where the fuck he is assigned Sergeant," said the Chief.

"Is there anything we should know, Chief? Do you want us to open a case on this?"

"If I wanted a case open I'd tell you Sergeant. I'm going to handle this myself," said the Chief, wanting to make the conversation as short as possible, since he knew all calls to the Action Desk were recorded. "Thanks for you're help, Sarge."

The I.A.B. Sergeant heard the click of the phone as the Chief hung up, and was extremely disappointed, figuring he had missed the opportunity to open up a case on a lieutenant, a case which looked like it would have been a ground ball. *It isn't every day that you get the chance to harpoon a lieutenant* thought the sergeant. Disconcerted, he returned to his crossword puzzle.

One of the liabilities of working inside during your entire career, as Lieutenant Fisher was doing, was that your weapon becomes an afterthought. The only time you remove your weapon from your holster is when you had to qualify at the range, which is only twice a year. Cops who worked the streets would have known they were missing their weapons within minutes after leaving that bathroom, since they are constantly placing their hands or forearms against their guns, ensuring that the mechanized pieces of metal that might save their lives were still there.

The next morning, at 7 a.m., Lieutenant Fisher received a phone call from his immediate boss, Captain Ken Brown. Immediately, Fisher remembered the unflushed bowl! That could be the only reason why his Captain would be calling him this early in the morning.

"Morning Lieutenant. Did you leave anything at work last night?"

*How very odd,* thought Fisher, *that the Captain would put the unflushed bowl into those terms. If one thought about it, I guess I did leave something.*

"Uh, morning to you too, Cap. No, I can't recall leaving anything at work, but I did see a couple of Mexican cleaners go into the Chief's office right before I left, and I think they planned on using the Chief's bathroom."

"Oh, yeah? Well, did those Mexican cleaners also rob you of your gun?" asked the Captain.

*Holy shit,* thought Fisher, *my gun! How could I have forgotten my gun, I had been in such a rush to get out of there that I left my gun on the floor!*

"Um, I'm not really sure I know what you're talking about, Cap," mumbled Fisher.

"Listen, Fisher," the Captain said. "Don't make this any worse than it already is. Just be thankful you are not here right now. The Chief was so pissed he couldn't even speak. He thought he might have to get a hazardous materials exposure number, after smelling what came out of your ass. And then you didn't even flush the bowl. What are you, some kind of animal?

"After what you did, the Chief felt it only appropriate that you be sent to a shithole, so effective immediately, you're transferred to the 75th Precinct Squad. I'd keep my mouth shut and maybe after four or five years, I would request a transfer, if you last that long there. Make necessary arrangements. Your first tour is today, a 1600 hour start. Have fun Fisher!"

*

From the moment Fisher first arrived at the 7-5, Matty Boyd disliked his new supervisor. Gossip travels at lightening speed with the N.Y.P.D., and the detectives in the squad knew about the incident in the Chief's bathroom before Fisher even had a chance to unpack. Boyd gave the new lieutenant two days before he asked the lieutenant if he was sure he had his gun, as Fisher was walking out the door to go home. From then on they became enemies.

Boyd especially loathed the facts that Fisher never left his office, that he was afraid of the streets, that he disliked minorities, and that he was an just an all-around douchebag. The detectives in the 7-5 also discovered that Fisher, while he had been assigned to the Chief's office in One Police Plaza, had made sure that he attended the COMSTAT sessions on the 8th Floor at every opportunity. He would grab a cup of coffee, and become positively joyous as he watched Precinct Commanding Officers, Squad Lieutenants, and Sergeants and Narcotics Supervisors get grilled and lambasted at these inquisitions.

Now, however, he was one of those Squad Lieutenants, and he was deathly afraid of having to appear at the podium, and attempt to explain why his squad had so many open cases. Fisher always attempted to schedule some kind of training or re-qualification class on COMSTAT days, just so he would not have to appear at the podium. He would send poor Sergeant Dover in his place.

Every detective in the squad had respect for Dover, as they knew he always had their backs and he knew as much about each of their cases as they did. Dover's competence was a double-edged sword however, since Fisher also felt comfortable feeding him to the lions at COMSTAT, knowing Dover would be able to handle any questions posed to him. This, in turn, would make the 75 squad look good, and make Fisher seem as though he was an excellent squad commander.

About six months after Fisher had arrived, things came to a boil when Fisher did not respond to a cop-shot incident that had occurred on Fulton Street and Shepard Avenue. When a cop is shot, the precinct empties out, but Fisher begged off, telling all who would listen that he was in the midst of a big report that was due to the Chief of D's office forthwith.

That was the final straw for Boyd. About a week after the cop-shot incident, Fisher and his wife Mary Beth began receiving phone calls concerning the sale of their home, located in a lily-white suburb of Nassau County. It seems an ad had been placed in the "Amsterdam News", which was published in Harlem and was read predominantly by members of the Afro-American and Caribbean communities.

The house was listed at quite a bit less than market value price, because, as the ad explained, the Fishers needed to sell right away. After almost a week of the Fishers telling potential buyers that they had no intention of selling their house, the phone calls ceased. Of course more than one caller screamed at Fisher, "Why aren't you selling? Because I'm black?" Mary Beth had become so upset that she felt the need to take an additional Xanex during the day.

Her Xanex intake increased again two weeks later, when the mailman began to deliver various magazines to the Fisher home, magazines with such titles as *OUT, The Advocate,* and *Hot Male Models.* They were all addressed to her husband, Edward. As a God-fearing Christian, Mary Beth was appalled at the contents of the periodicals, yet she perused each and every page of the magazines. After a thorough examination of the contents of the magazines, she phoned her husband and asked for an explanation. A befuddled Fisher professed his love for his wife and explained to her that he would never think about looking at a man that way. Fisher, who was thinking about paying a visit to the Psychological Services Unit, explained to his wife that it was all a big mistake, one that he would rectify shortly. Fisher knew that Boyd was behind the mental torture escapades, but he could not even look at Boyd by that time, so he called Monahan, Boyd's level-headed partner.

"Kevin, you better explain to your undersized partner with the Opie Howard haircut that enough is enough. Doesn't he realize that he is sinking himself? A Palestinian will become a member of the Knesset before I put him in for second-grade. Let him know the shit stops now!"

Monahan was a bit perplexed, unaware of what the lieutenant was referring to, but than again, if it involved Boyd and his pranks, Monahan was better off not knowing. "You got it, boss. I'll talk to him right away."

Monahan relayed the message to Boyd, who gave a wry smile and said, "I'll bet she's lying in bed with those magazines right now. 10-4, Kev, I'll cease and desist."

*

Boyd's career in the 75 was essentially finished at that point, but he could not bring himself to leave. More to the point, he did not want to leave his long time-partner, Monahan. When he finally had enough, and over some beers at P.J. McKeefery's, he told Monahan about his intention to leave, the ever laconic Monahan told Boyd he understood, and that Boyd had to do what was right for him and his family. Boyd knew however, that Monahan had taken it hard, and that was the reason he wasn't present for Boyd's last tour. Monahan would not have been able to stand watching Matty sign out in the Command Log for the last time.

Accompanied by Sgt. Dover, Boyd loaded the Snickers murderer, Stanley, into the back of the unmarked Crown Victoria for the ride to Central Booking.

As he was about to slide into the passenger's seat, he heard, "Hey, Boyd, that's it. No goodbyes, kiss my ass, see you when I see you?" It was one of the 75 Precinct Training Sergeants, John Kolitoski.

"Yeah, John. You know me, I owe too many people money in this place, so I figure better to just slip away in the dead of night. How's it going, pal?"

"Same ol, same ol, my brother. I'm doing the Operation Impact shit with the rookies that graduated from the academy about four months ago. They call this the "welfare group" because of the shit money they're making. I was told to keep my eyes wide open with this group, since most of them never had complete background checks done. Heard they locked up one of these rookies at Rodman Neck range while he was qualifying. He had an outstanding murder warrant from Virginia that popped."

"Yeah, that's smart," said Boyd. "Lock up a murder suspect while he's got a gun in his hands. Well, I'm the man to clean up the mess, my brother. Starting Monday I'm headed over to Applicant Investigation, and I think I'm going to be doing some of their investigations. Thirty hours a month of boo-coo overtime, man, just for doing backgrounds. No more dealing with knuckleheads like my friend Stanley in the back seat here."

"Okay, Matty. Listen, you be safe and stay in touch. Hey, you do have your gun on you, don't you?"

Boyd laughed, as he heard the Sergeant yell, "Hey Linc, gas up the RMP, and make sure you check the back seats. Give the car a good toss."

# CHAPTER 5

Linc had breezed thru the Police Academy, but unfortunately had to put his college studies on hold for the six months when he had attended the training. Now, however, he had settled into a steady shift, 8 p.m. by 4 a.m., and he was able to take his required courses during the day. He and his fellow rookies were part of Operation Impact, a crime fighting strategy developed in One Police Plaza, in which a high crime area was saturated with academy graduates.

For his first four months he was stationed on various foot posts in the northern section of the precinct. The foot posts were predominantly on Jamaica Avenue, Fulton Street, and Atlantic Avenue. He very rarely saw any of the project gang members, as the projects were in the southernmost sectors of the precinct. In any case, the projects were patrolled by Housing Bureau cops from Public Service Area 2, located on Sutter Avenue in Brownsville.

The areas that Linc now patrolled were inhabited mainly by Dominicans, Puerto Ricans, and, to a lesser extent, Cubans. That portion of the precinct had suffered a rash of shootings, some resulting in homicide, and most came courtesy of the ruling drug gang in the area, La Compania. The gang was ruthless. Even Silky and the other project gang leaders would never consider infringing on their turf.

Linc had made some good collars, mostly drug offenses, and he had even made three gun arrests. It was like second nature to Linc, as he observed things in the streets that only a seasoned narcotics cop could understand. He knew who was steering, and he knew who was holding product. He knew to check a dude's sneakers or inside a brother's crotch area, when a search of clothes revealed nothing. It was the same way with guns. Crooks are like cops. They always feel for their gun. If one arm is swinging while the dude is walking and the other is hanging down close to the body, there is a good chance the boy is packing. If a brother is walking stiff, and keeps adjusting the front of his pants, more than likely he's carrying a gun in his front waistband.

He had also been able to help out Silky. Since the Housing cops from P.S.A. 2 were on the same frequency as the 7-5 and the 7-3 Precincts, he was always able to give Silky a heads-up on any narcotics runs in the Linden Projects. He utilized a *burner* cell phone that had been provided to him by Silky, and the phone was generally changed once a week. Of course, he had his own cell phone, in case his family or his sergeant needed to get hold of him. Linc also provided Silky with descriptions and plate numbers of all the unmarked cars in the 7-5 Precinct. He had even volunteered to deliver paperwork to P.S.A. 2, and while there he recorded the descriptions and plate numbers of all their unmarked vehicles, which he relayed to Silky.

Each precinct maintained a Street Narcotics Enforcement Unit (S.N.E.U.), and the members of that unit were responsible for identifying known drug locations within their precinct, and ultimately locking up buyers and sellers at those locations. The officers assigned to the unit were responsible for drug dealing only within their precinct. They concentrated mostly on hand-to-hand sales observation arrests. They did no undercover buys, and very rarely would they get to arrest a major dealer.

Narcotics units, on the other hand, were assigned to the Organized Crime Control Bureau. They had the freedom to move from precinct to precinct, and they utilized their own undercover officers to conduct drug buys. The one, or sometimes two, undercover officers were assigned to a particular Narcotics *module*. They would make a number of buys at a known drug location, each buy recorded, and all the drugs vouchered. Depending upon the size of the drug operation, the undercovers could make buys at a location over a number of weeks. Satisfied that they had identified all the *players* in a particular gang, the module would conduct an early morning raid on the location, locking up all individuals they had recorded selling to the undercover.

The chief advantage of operations run by Narcotics was that the dealers never knew who the undercover cop was, since they sold to such a large number of people during a day. The dealers were charged with narcotics sale for each time they sold to an undercover. This gave Narcotics, unlike the Precinct S.N.E.U, the luxury of developing major cases.

Linc was also able to provide intelligence to Silky whenever he had the opportunity to visit the S.N.E.U. office, which was quite often. Each time Linc made an observation drug arrest, the S.N.E.U. cops would de-brief Linc's prisoner. The debriefing was in an attempt to find out who the prisoner worked for, if he knew anyone carrying or selling guns, the location of "chop shops" for stolen cars, etc. More often than not the prisoner replied, "No speakie Ingles."

The only time prisoners would provide information was if they knew they were in big trouble with that collar, and that providing information might ultimately help them in obtaining a reduced sentence. Most of the time however, they knew that a small quantity, hand-to-hand observation arrest, would be pled down to either a disorderly conduct or loitering charge. They figured that rather than snitch and wind up in the weeds off the Belt Parkway with a bullet to the back of the head, they would just take the pinch, and more than likely be sentenced to time served, or some bullshit community service.

Growing up, Linc's feelings towards the police had been that their presence in the projects was just a fact of life. Both his mother and father had emphasized the need to respect the job that they performed, and yet conveyed to him that as a young male black in the projects he needed to be cautious in his dealings with cops. Many cops, they told him, had never encountered an environment like the projects. Quite a few had never had dealings with blacks, and had preconceived notions that all young black men were trouble. It was these cops that Linc had to be wary of, they told him. If the officer told him to stop, he should stop. If they told him to raise his hands, he should follow that command.

Since both his parents had worked for the Transit Authority, they also made him aware of the heroic actions they had witnessed done by the Transit Police. His father would always tell him the story of how he had seen a Transit cop crawl under a train, while the third rail was still electrified, to rescue a man who had fallen off a platform between two subway cars.

His mother would become upset when recounting the story of a Transit cop being stabbed on the Junius Street station platform by a crazed individual who had jumped the turnstile. Although stabbed twice in the shoulder, the cop bravely fought back, subduing the individual and finally arresting him.

Linc's only negative encounter with the police had been the summons he had received for loitering in the project building. He knew he had deserved the summons, and it actually could have been much worse, considering what he was really doing in the lobby.

*

His most vivid memory of dealing with the police, of course, was of the day his father had been murdered. He remembered standing in the on-deck circle, with his heavy aluminum bat, which had the name Tony Gwynn labeled on the meat end. His dad had bought the bat for Linc when he had turned ten years old and had begun to play Little League baseball.

There were teammates on first and third, when he heard a sharp *whoop*, the universal signal indicating the arrival of a police car. All eyes turned to look at the gold Chevrolet Caprice that had pulled up in front of the entrance gate on Stanley Avenue. The umpire behind the plate raised up both arms, called "time out", and stepped back from the plate. Linc looked at the car and caught a glimpse of a young male in the back seat. It was his brother. His brother Harris was staring at him through the back window, and he was crying. Where was his father? A terrible, tight knot began to form in the pit of Linc's stomach. Where was his father? He had seen him and Harris not fifteen minutes ago, Harris across the top

55

of his father's shoulder, kicking and laughing, pounding his little fist against the middle of their father's back.

A large, black detective, looking sharp in a light-gray suit, a black shirt, and a light-gray and maroon-striped tie, slid out of the passenger seat and walked slowly towards the entrance gate onto the field. There was a pained expression on the detective's face as he approached Linc's coach. The detective whispered into the coach's ear and the coach pointed at Linc. At that moment Linc wanted to drop the bat his father had bought him and begin running, running as fast as he could, across Linden Boulevard, away from the projects. But then he looked at his brother sitting in that back seat, alone and afraid, and he began running towards the police car.

He reached the cop's car and began pounding on the glass window, frightening Harris even more, Linc screaming, "No, no, no!" The black detective, holding Linc's bat in his large hands, pulled Linc away from the vehicle and softly said, " I'm gonna need your help here, little man. You can't be going weak on me now. Your momma and that little man inside the car gonna be looking to you for strength. Don't you go soft on em'."

Linc thought he noticed the big man's eyes begin to water, and he just nodded. He slid into the back seat, and his brother wrapped his shaking, skinny arms around his neck. Linc just stared straight ahead, as the detectives drove him and his brother back to their apartment. When they reached the apartment, two detectives were already there, consoling his weeping mother. They stepped inside the apartment, and their mother arose from her chair and ran to the boys, dropping to her knees. She grabbed both her sons around the waist, and began to wail. Linc looked at the big, black detective, who just nodded, as Linc rubbed the back of his mother's head, gently repeating, "Everything is gonna be all right, momma. I'm gonna keep us safe."

Two detectives remained with the Watson family until friends and relatives had filled the small apartment, people who would comfort and care for the threesome during their time of desperate need. His father was waked at L.J. Funeral Home on Liberty Avenue, and on the first day of the two day service, the black detective and his partner, an older white guy, stopped in to offer their condolences.

Following his father's burial, the black detective would call every few weeks to give his mother an update on the investigation of the case. The detective was honest. He informed Dolores Watson that, unless someone on the street provided information, the case had reached a dead end. The detective said, however, that since it was a homicide, the case would never be closed. No matter how many years passed, someone would always work the case.

It was a shame, thought Linc, that he could not remember the black detective's name, especially now that he was assigned to the 7-5. He was sure the detective had retired, as ten years had passed since that horrible day. He knew that he could never inquire about that detective's whereabouts up in the squad room, since too many questions would be asked, and it might be discovered that he was actually from the Linden projects. Linc had to remain quiet concerning his relationship to the projects. Never in his wildest dreams had Linc ever thought he would be wearing the blue uniform of the N.Y.P.D., but his innate desire to care for his family had forced him into the situation, and that was all that mattered.

During the debriefings of his prisoners in the S.N.E.U office, Linc would study the pin maps the S.N.E.U. cops had hanging on the walls. The pins were of various colors, green indicating pot sales, blue for cocaine and crack, and red for heroin. The pins were placed on the map indicating various locations of the precinct where those particular drugs were sold. The placement of the pins were based on the cop's observations, but many were the result of "kites." "Kites," Linc had learned, were complaints called in by the public, to either 911 or the precinct itself. The callers, almost all anonymous, would call and complain about drug dealing at a particular location. Those locations were then placed on the pin maps, and each kite was supposed to be investigated. Linc advised Silky to have his boys call in, either to the precinct or 911, and complain about drug sales at various locations within the Boulevard Houses. In this way, the S.N.E.U. cops would concentrate their enforcement efforts in that area, leaving Linden Projects alone.

One of the S.N.E.U. cops had taken a liking to Linc. Teddy Jolich was one of the Patrolmen's Benevolent Association delegates for the 7-5 Precinct, and he was always complimenting Linc on the collars he brought in. Jolich was a big guy, his head and neck were the same diameter, and other cops often said that you could tell how old Teddy was by counting the rings around his neck. His constant red face was a source of puzzle to many cops, as they didn't know if the cause was Teddy's fondness for the drink, or his high blood pressure as a result of his being fifty pounds overweight. His heart matched the size of his head, though, and there was nothing Teddy would not do for the cops he represented.

Whenever Linc brought in an arrest, Jolich made sure Linc shared in any food purchased by the S.N.E.U. cops. The P.B.A. delegates for a precinct generally had a great deal of pull within the command, and Linc became the victim of his own successes. Jolich had approached Linc's boss, Sergeant John Kolitoski, and recommended that Linc become the sergeant's steady driver.

"This kid is wasting his time on a footpost, Sarge. He has great street-smarts, and he could learn so much more being in a car with you. Besides, your driver just got promoted, and you can't drive around by yourself. And listen, he doesn't know I'm even asking you this."

Kolitoski had been a sergeant in the 7-5 for fourteen years, racking up more commendations and medals than anyone else in the precinct. He had begun to become burnt out on patrol, so recognizing his special skills, the commanding officer had given him the Training Sergeant slot. "Yeah I know Teddy," said the Sarge. "I've been watching him. He does have that sixth sense, especially when it comes to spotting guns. I don't know, though.

58

He is awfully quiet, I don't know if I could ride around for eight hours with a mute."

"C'mon, Sarge, give him a shot. If it don't work out, you could always bounce him back to a footpost."

"Yeah, guess you're right. I'll give him the notification to start next week."

Linc had brought another drug collar into the S.N.E.U. office, and he was greeted by a gushing Teddy Jolich when he entered the room. Jolich conveyed the news to Linc about driving the sergeant, and he was somewhat taken aback by Linc's somber reaction. Linc enjoyed the freedom of working by himself, and it gave him the opportunity to phone Silky whenever he needed with any intelligence the drug boss could use.

"You're fuckin kiddin me, right, Linc? Guys would give one of their nuts to be the sergeant's steady driver, and especially a great cop like Kolitoski! Hey, if you don't like it you can always go back to your shitty foot posts."

Linc knew that Teddy was right. The sergeant's driver slot was a most desired position, and turning it down would set off alarms. Linc had come to realize that cops noticed every little thing, and if he refused the job, Linc would be under a microscope. Hell, he thought, he wasn't staying on this job forever. He was hoping three, four years, tops. "Yeah, you're right, Teddy. Thanks for stepping up. You really didn't have to do that."

"No bro, you deserve it." Jolich said. "Hey, stick around. We got Detective Monahan coming down as the Federal Tag Police!"

As Jolich explained it, he and his partner had locked up the two Simmons brothers, Mal and Al, once again. The brothers operated a small weed business, on the Brownsville border, and both had been caught doing a hand-to-hand sale. This was the fourth time the 7-5 S.N.E.U. cops locked up the obnoxious brothers, both of whom knew that they would be out on the street the next day, plying their wares.

The brothers, while under arrest, would never shut up, constantly making disparaging remarks about their arresting officer's perceived, or actual, physical shortcomings. They went over the edge however, when they unanimously decided that Officer Teddy Jolich looked like "that ugly muthfucka Shrek, only with a red face instead of green." At that point Julich called up to the 7-5 Squad office and asked if Detective Monahan would not mind playing the role of Federal Tag Police.

He only made that request for the most obstinate shit-heads that he collared, and he would generally use Detective Boyd, who had originated the prank. But Jolich knew Boyd had taken the day off, so he hoped Monahan could perform the prank just as well, and somehow he knew Monahan could pull it off.

As he was explaining the ruse to Linc, he heard Mal Simmons yell, "Hey, pumpkin head, when we going down to the bookins? I gots shit to do tomorrow." Jolich's red face suddenly became a tinge redder, and one might have thought that the top of his head would explode when he replied, "Easy, home skillet. You and your ugly brother might have a problem. Seems a federal agent wants to talk at you. We got a warrant for that dump you live in, and we made an interesting discovery."

The brothers looked at one another, and Al said, "Federal? What the fuck you talking bout, slim. We just handlin' a little weed. Ain't nothing federal bout that!"

At that moment the office door opened and in walked Detective Kevin Monahan. Monahan gave a slight nod to Jolich and Linc. He stood about 6'1, his blue pinstripe suit hanging perfectly over his broad shoulders and 190 pound frame. His light-brown hair was thinning a bit at the top, and he sported a traditional cop moustache, but of all his physical characteristics the one most striking was his eyes. Linc had never seen a lighter green set of eyes.

Linc had often heard the veteran cops in the locker room speak of the detective partners, Monahan and Boyd. When discussing Boyd, they would laugh hysterically, recalling the various pranks and scams he had pulled on people, but when speaking of Monahan they took a more reverent tone and referred to his toughness and courage.

Linc, who felt he could read people fairly well, could understand the toughness. Monahan exuded a sense of strength that Linc had encountered perhaps once or twice, from street-hardened gangstas. His whole aura said, "You do not want to fuck with me."

"Yo, yo. Who the fuck invited the Marlboro Man?" squealed Mal, who then became suddenly silent, as Monahan stared at him and his brother with his piercing eyes.

"Listen up fellas," Monahan said. "I don't have much time. I'm Federal Special Agent Bauer from the Federal Tag Division. As you well know, Officer Jolich contacted me to conduct an investigation when he discovered all the pillows in your apartment were without the required federal tags stating, "Do not remove under penalty of Federal Law." I examined your pillows and discovered that someone had ripped the tags right off. So now, since it is only the two of you in that hovel you reside in, both of you are going to be charged with a federal crime, unless one of you admits to the act."

Both brothers sat stunned, staring at Monahan. Mal suddenly smacked his brother, Al, on the back of the head, "You stupid shit! I tol you don't be fuckin with those tags. Pillow ain't barely made it out of the bag and you be rippin the shit off."

"Yeah. Well," said Al. "That tag keep getting in behind my ear, botherin the shit out of me."

"Then just put the tag into the closed end of the pillowcase, you stupid muthafucka!"

"Okay, okay, boys," said Monahan. "So you're saying Mal, that Al was the one that perpetrated the crime?" At that point, Linc actually had to step out of the room, as he was laughing so hard.

"Na, man, we bof did it. I can't let my brother do any federal time by hisself."

"Okay, this is what's going to happen. After you get arraigned on your marijuana charge in Brooklyn Criminal Court, Federal Marshals will be waiting to escort you by plane to Fort

Leavenworth, Kansas. You will be remanded there, since that is the facility we house Federal Tag violators, until your federal trial."

"Kansas? Ain't that where that girl and her dog got fucked up by that hurricane and they wound up where all the little people live?" inquired Al.

"Yeah, something like that," said Monahan "Only hurricane season isn't for a couple of months. Hopefully you won't still be there."

The once-talkative Simmons brothers were silent as they were transported to Brooklyn Central Booking, all the while contemplating hurricanes, flying dogs, and little people wearing ugly fuckin shoes.

# CHAPTER 6

Boyd had been right. Monahan did not wish to be present on his partner's last day in the squad. He and Boyd had been partners for close to fifteen years, between anti-crime, the R.I.P. Unit and finally the Detective Squad. Civilians would never understand the bond that develops between partners within the police world. Although Monahan did not have a family, outside of his brother, he realized that even if married, he would never be as close to his wife as he was to Boyd.

Boyd who was married, for a second time, had three children, but he had spent more time with Monahan during the last fourteen years than with his wives and kids. His first wife could not accept the fact that Boyd wanted to work a case, to bring justice to a grieving family, rather than spend time with her. It was just one of the myriad reasons why cops had one of the highest divorce rates out of all professions.

Together, the partners had seen things that human beings should never have to see. They had truly witnessed man's inhumanity to his fellow man. Boyd knew that he could never express his feelings of sorrow and frustration to his family, or to other cops for that matter, only to Monahan, for Monahan was bearing the same burden, and the indelible bond that develops between partners was strengthened all the more by the knowledge that his life was, at times, in the other's hand. Each time they went out together to canvas for witnesses, to chase down leads, to sit on a stakeout, they knew shit could go real bad in an instant, and at times like those they had no one but each other.

Monahan pulled over into the 7-11 parking lot on Beach Channel Drive, intent on easing another burden he carried, one even Boyd knew nothing about. As a matter of fact, only one other person knew of Monahan's burden, and that was his brother, Timothy. Timothy was a Catholic priest, serving the poor parish of

St. Jerome's in East Flatbush, and Monahan had opened up to him, not only as a brother, but as a priest.

Monahan went inside the store and purchased the $500.00 money order, slid it into an envelope, and addressed it to the Mikens family of Beaufort, South Carolina. There was no return address on the envelope that Monahan would slide into an anonymous post office box that stood on one of the corners of Beach 116 Street. Monahan had just turned fifty-five in October of 2005, and he had been sending the money orders stuffed envelopes to the Mikens family since January of 1978.

*

Monahan had always wanted to be a cop, just as his father had been, except that when Monahan became old enough to take the police exam, the city had laid off thousands of cops due to the budget crisis. Times were bad. He remembered his father running to the bank to cash his New York City payroll check, unsure if it would bounce. His father knew of his son's aspirations, but somberly told Kevin that perhaps he should think about another field of endeavor.

Kevin figured that after he had a three-year stint in the Marines the economy would have rebounded. He enlisted and was sent to Parris Island for six months of boot camp, in July of 1975. While there, he became friends with a southerner, Dwayne Clinton, who lived in a small town outside of Hinesville, Georgia, a place about one hour southwest of Parris Island. Generally northerners and southerners remained apart, even through the crucible of boot camp, but the young men had been talking one day, and Dwayne learned that the Irish kid from New York knew quite a bit about college football, which was a religion in the south.

Of course, the Irish kid loved Notre Dame, while Dwayne lived and died by the Georgia Bulldogs. They told each other of their conquests of beautiful women, both fabricating most of their stories, and spoke of their aspirations once out of the Marines. Their desires were similar, in that Dwayne hoped to make a career in the Corp, just as his father had, while Kevin wanted to follow in his father's footsteps in the N.Y.P.D. The only concern Kevin had about their relationship was that Dwayne would go on an occasional racist rant, but Kevin chalked it up to Dwayne's upbringing in the Deep South.

Kevin had grown up in the Edgemere Projects, which were located between Beach 58th Street and Beach 51st Street and Beach Channel Drive in Rockaway. His family and his cousins, the McKeeferys, had begun renting their apartments in 1960. The project buildings, at the time, were primarily inhabited by cops, firemen, and Transit Authority workers. The population was close to ninety-percent Irish, and remained so until the mid-sixties, when more and more black families began to fill the apartments vacated by whites, who had decided that Long Island would be the optimal place to raise a family.

Through sports, Kevin had begun to socialize with many of the black males his own age, especially through basketball and Little League baseball at O'Donohue Park. Eventually, the Monahans and McKeeferys left the Edgemere Projects, but only to move west some fifty blocks, into the area known as Rockaway Park, but Kevin returned to the projects often, to see many of the black friends who had been his teammates in basketball and baseball.

He knew that some of the best hoops games he could find were still at the Edgemere Projects, which in a few short years had become almost one-hundred-percent black. Kevin's feelings towards a person of a different nationality or race, was that the person should be judged as an individual. No matter the color of their skin, or the birthplace of their ancestors. He knew just as many white assholes, as he did black or Hispanic ones. An asshole was an asshole, no matter the color of their skin. He felt uncomfortable when Dwayne would occasionally speak disparagingly of blacks.

After graduation, many of the Marine graduates in Monahan's class, Monahan included, were forced to wait at Parris Island until their orders came down, orders that would send them to Marine bases around the globe. One night, set to enjoy a forty-eight- hour pass, Dewayne and Kevin were picked up by Dewayne's older brother, Bobby Lee. The two newly-minted Marines jumped into the pickup and headed into Beaufort, South Carolina. They hit some of the local bars in the City of Beaufort, and, as young Marines do, they began to get hammered. Each Pabst Blue Ribbon was accompanied by a shot of Jack Daniels, and it wasn't very long before they all began slurring their words.

Bobby Lee suggested a couple of honky-tonks outside of town, where they were sure to get more bang for their buck, and they wound up in a small, smoky joint called the Overlook Inn. Peanut shells littered the floor, and country western singers George Jones and Conway Twitty were in the air, as Kevin heard about, "cheatin spouses, drunken nights and rooms to rent for jus fifty cent."

Kevin felt he had listened to, "she's actin single, so I'm drinking doubles" far too many times, so he suggested that their steel bunk beds back at the base wouldn't be so bad at that moment. The Clinton brothers had had their fill also, so the boys stumbled outside and loaded themselves into the pickup truck. It was just before midnight, and Bobby Lee was having difficulty navigating the rural back roads. As they came around a bend, Bobby Lee spotted a young black male walking along the side of the road. He mumbled to his brother, "Hey, Dwayne, how bout me and you show Irish how we feel about integration in the south?"

Dwayne smiled and nodded, as he reached behind to the back seat to grab a 35 ounce wooden baseball bat.

"Hey Irish, wake up. We're gonna show you some Southern hospitality," said Bobby Lee.

Kevin felt the truck come to an abrupt halt, and when he opened his eyes he saw the two brothers alight from the pickup and begin to run towards the rear of the vehicle. They were chasing what appeared to be a young black male, wearing a gray sweatshirt and blue jeans. Dwayne caught up to the young man, leaped onto his back and knocked him to the ground. Kevin wasn't sure if the black male had done something to the brothers when they had passed him on the road, but he was getting a bad feeling.

He made his way out of the truck just in time to see Bobby Lee slam the wooden bat onto the back of the prone male. Kevin heard an ear-piercing scream, as Bobby Lee hit the male again on the legs. Dwayne then grabbed the bat from his brother and brought the weapon down onto the male's upstretched arm, breaking his forearm. Kevin got to Dwayne, but too late, as the bat was brought down onto the young man's skull. Kevin laid out Dwayne with one punch to the jaw, and as Dwayne fell, Kevin recovered the bat in time to hit an onrushing Bobby Lee in his shoulder. Bobby Lee backed up and stared at Kevin.

"What the fuck is wrong with you guys? This guy could be dead!" cried Monahan. "We have to get him an ambulance."

"We ain't getting him shit, Irish. This here's the way we do things down here," said Bobby Lee. "And you ain't saying shit bout what happened, cause both me and my brother seen you beat this boy mercilessly. It's your finger prints gonna be all over that there bat, boy."

Kevin's head was spinning, as he knew Bobby Lee was right. It would be his word against the two of theirs, unless the black kid woke up, but that didn't seem likely. Kevin knelt down and felt a very slight pulse in the male's carotid artery, but his eyes were listless, blood was coming out of his ears, and unless he got to a hospital within minutes, Kevin knew he was not going to make it.

"You guys are fuckin animals!" yelled Kevin. "We have at least get to a payphone to let someone know he is here!"

"Yeah, we can do that," answered Bobby Lee.

Kevin noticed that Dwayne had not said a word, and he wouldn't even look at Kevin. "Dwayne, listen, man, we have to report this," said Kevin.

Dwayne said, "Report it? Get court- martialed and spend the rest of our lives in a fuckin Federal prison? You're gonna be just as guilty to them, Kevin, you know that. Military code says you should have stopped it. Then what happens to your police career, or my career in the Marines? We would be fucked, man!"

As they climbed into the pickup truck, Kevin almost became sick to his stomach as he looked at the dying young man one more time. At the first phone booth, Kevin jumped out and dialed 911. He reported to the operator that he had spotted a black male lying on the side of Route 21, by Beaufort National Cemetery, and that the male needed immediate medical aid. He hung up. Not a word was spoken in the pickup during the entire ride back to the base.

Kevin never uttered another word to Dwayne during their remaining short stay at Parris Island. He checked the local newspaper, *The Beaufort Gazette*, the next few days after the incident and discovered that Walter Mickens, a male, black, twenty-three-years old, had been discovered beaten to death on the side of Route 21. Mickens, the story read, was one of three sons of Ida and Thomas Mickens of 76 Burnside St., Beaufort, South Carolina. Kevin wrote down the address and placed it in his wallet.

The orders for the remaining Marine graduates came down within a few days. Kevin was shipped overseas to a base in Japan, where he proceeded almost to drink himself to death in order to erase the memory of Walter Mickens. He dreamed of the bat, swung by Dwayne, crashing down onto Micken's skull, and when the nightmares were extremely bad, Kevin would dream of Mickens, who would prop himself up onto an elbow, look at Kevin and ask, "Why ain't you helping me man?"

Kevin knew that if he continued drinking, he would wind up in either a detox ward or in a coffin, so he put in his application to join the Marine Force Recons. The Recons were an elite, special forces type unit within the Marine Corp. It was said that the Marines were the toughest of all the armed forces, and the Recon Marines were the toughest of the Marines.

Kevin did well on the aptitude exam, and was shipped back to Camp Pendleton, California for six months of some of the toughest training a man could endure. Kevin viewed the tortuous training as penance for his actions. He would push himself past exhaustion during strength and obstacle training, to the point where he would actually pass out, or he would wait until the very last second to pull his parachute cord on low level jump training. It seemed to him that he had a death wish.

His instructors thought of Kevin as the perfect Marine, a lean, mean killing machine, but none knew what drove him. Kevin graduated at the top of his class, and his Recon group became part of the 2nd Marine Division. He had been awarded the Expert Badge when it came to rifle and pistol skills. An Expert in marksmanship really meant something, as he was competing against some of the best shooters in the armed forces. Those skills earned him a slot in the Scout/Sniper platoon.

He and his unit were shipped out to Saudi Arabia, as there had been rumblings of problems developing in Iran. Kevin was actually grateful for the deployment to Saudi Arabia, for their strict Moslem laws prohibited alcohol, and Kevin knew that alcohol opened doors of his mind that he would much rather keep closed. He also viewed the extensive training exercises in the hot, barren desert as having a cathartic effect on his psyche.

When he returned to the States, he was packing a rock-solid 195 pounds onto his 6'1 frame, but more important, he had never felt so mentally alert. During that January of his return to Camp Pendleton, he started out sending two-hundred dollar money orders to the Mikens family every month. After six months as a firearms instructor at Pendleton, Kevin mustered out of the Marines in July of 1978.

When Kevin returned to Rockaway, he took a job as a lifeguard at Rockaway Beach, and during the winter he picked up jobs doing house painting, all the while waiting for the Department of Civil Service to give the go-ahead for an N.Y.P.D. entrance exam. Finally, in 1979, the first entrance exam in almost a decade was administered. Kevin did well, so now it was just a matter of waiting and staying out of trouble. In 1980 Kevin's dad, John, was finally promoted to Captain, after the freeze on promotions had been finally lifted, but the brief joy was overshadowed by the sudden death of Kevin's mother from cancer that winter. She never got to see her son finally achieve his dream. Kevin was sworn in a little over a month after Joan Monahan had passed away.

Kevin entered the academy in January of 1981, and upon graduation in July he was assigned, much to his chagrin, to the 107 Precinct in Fresh Meadow, Queens. His father, grief-stricken after the passing of his wife, called in some favors, and had his son assigned to one of the quietest precincts in Queens. Kevin knew how hard his dad had taken his mother's death, and rather than fight his father to get assigned to a busier command, Kevin let it be.

While at work, one hot summer July day in 1981, Kevin received devastating news. His sergeant called him in from patrol to inform him that his dad apparently had had a heart attack during one of his daily swims in the ocean off Rockaway. The lifeguards had pulled his body out of the water, and, despite their best efforts, they had been unable to revive him. Kevin knew that no matter what the coroner's report would say, his dad had died of a broken heart, and now Kevin had lost both his parents within a matter of two years. He was suddenly alone in the house on Beach 114 Street, and although his brother, Timmy, stayed with Kevin for about a month after their dad's death, he had just entered the seminary and needed to return in order to complete his studies to become a priest.

His dad had been given a full inspector's funeral, and many of the cops that had come on the department with his dad were now Chiefs. They all informed Kevin that if he ever needed anything, all he would have to do is ask. Kevin immediately asked to be transferred from the 107th Precinct to the much busier 75th Precinct. By the time Kevin returned to the 107 Precinct after his Death in Family leave, the orders transferring him to the 75th Precinct were cut. Once Kevin arrived at the 7-5, he knew he had found a home.

*

After Kevin had dropped off the Mikens envelope, he drove to the house on Beach 114 Street. Parking in the small driveway aside the house, he entered the home and checked his machine for any messages. The one message was from Boyd, informing Kevin that since no riding Homicide A.D.A.s had been available to come to the 7-5, Boyd had to draw up the Snickers homicide at the D.A's office, and it could be a while before he was done. He told Kevin that he hoped to meet him at P.J. McKeeferys, but if not he would speak to him the next day.

Kevin quickly changed his clothes within the silent house, and after making sure to leave the kitchen light on, he stepped outside. The slapping of the ocean waves onto the hard Rockaway beach sand made Kevin relax, as he walked south towards the Ocean Promenade. He took deep, salt-air-filled breaths, as he gazed upward at the kind of a clear, starlit sky that only seemed to be found over oceans or deserts. Kevin turned right on the Promenade, and knew he could never think of living anywhere else. The Rockaway peninsula was surrounded by water, and contained some of the most beautiful beaches one could find anywhere. Yet it was only some ten miles from Manhattan.

Kevin continued along the Promenade, until to 116 Street, Rockaway's main thoroughfare, where he made a right and began walking north until he came to P.J. McKeeferys. He felt comfortable making McKeeferys his watering hole for a number of reasons. The first was that the bar was across the street from both a firehouse and Transit Police District #23. The chances were therefore good that the joint wouldn't be held up, and a fire wouldn't consume the place. The second, and more important reason, was that it was owned by Kevin's cousins.

*

The place had been purchased by his now deceased Uncle Pat in the late 1980s. Ann and Pat McKeefery had eight sons, of which only three remained in Rockaway. Johnny, Dennis and Tom were left to care for the bar their father had put his soul into. Actually, just Dennis and Tom managed the bar, although one would think that the oldest, Johnny, would have been the father's choice to take over the establishment.

Before passing, the father, Pat, had sat down and solemnly discussed the future of the pub, his pride and joy, with Dennis. "You know I love your older brother, but I want you and Tom to take over the place when I'm gone. Johnny has a sickness."

Dennis's face turned pale, as he could not believe his older brother was suffering from some undisclosed illness. "Oh shit, Pop. What's wrong with him?" Dennis asked.

"He's a fuckin kleptomaniac, is what's wrong with him!"

The family knew that if given the chance, Johnny would steal a hot stove, and had been aware of this for some time, especially after Johnny almost received a dishonorable discharge from the Air Force during the Vietnam War.

Johnny, who never missed a meal, had joined the Air Force specifically because he had heard they had the best chow. Assigned to McConnell Air Force Base in Witchita, Kansas, following boot camp, Johnny escaped being sent to Vietnam by becoming a chef. Upon first arriving at the base, he claimed to have graduated from the prestigious Culinary Institute of America. Although he couldn't cook an egg, Johnny was blessed with one of the greatest of Irish traits, bullshitting. It was said that Johnny, if given the opportunity, could convince the Pope to give up his miter in favor of a Yankee hat.

Wrangling his way into the base kitchen, Johnny found the best chef, and was able to convince him that he was the chef's new assistant, there only to carry the food to the officer's quarters. Once in the officer's quarters, he would convincingly assure the brass that he had cooked the meal they were about to enjoy, and that only they should be the recipients of his special talents. The brass were immediately impressed with the portly New Yorker's culinary ability, and decided he would best serve his country by remaining stateside.

It was not long however, before Johnny managed to get himself into trouble. Deciding that the Air Force was not paying him what he was worth, Johnny began removing what he considered extra food supplies from the kitchen. He would load the food into the back of a truck, and at the checkpoints he would inform the guards that he was headed into town for a special wine desired by the Colonel, and ask them how dare they question the Colonel's private chef. He would then proceed to make stops at various restaurants in Witchita, unloading his wares at a very good price.

After a few months of this business venture, Johnny made a delivery to a restaurant the manager of which had just returned from two tours in Vietnam. Concluding that the Johnny was depriving hard-working airmen of food, the manager placed a call to the Provost Marshal at the base. Caught red handed in a sting operation, Johnny escaped punishment only because the base commander did not wish to have the obvious lack of security at the camp publicized.

The fat one-time chef was confined to the base for the remaining two months of enlistment. He returned to Rockaway, joined the American Legion Post on Cross Bay Boulevard, where beers were only $1.50 a glass, and spoke about his exploits as a test pilot to all those who did not know him.

His brother Dennis, on the other hand, was a bona-fide Vietnam War hero. A standout basketball player at Bishop Loughlin High School in Brooklyn, Dennis had had the world waiting for him when he graduated from the prestigious high school. A number of colleges, particularly St. John's University, wished to utilize Dennis's basketball skills, and he was offered a full scholarship. In addition to the scholarship offer, he was also contacted by his Uncle Sam, informing him that his draft number was up, and that they wished to develop his skills as an infantryman.

Dennis could have escaped the draft by going to college, but as his father had done in World War II, he decided to serve his country. He assumed he would do a quick year in Nam, come back and continue his basketball career in college. Little did he know that it only took a short time in that beautiful, small Asian country to drain the life out of a nineteen-year-old boy.

He landed in Saigon in early January of 1968, assigned to the 3rd Brigade, 1st Air Calvary Division of the 7th Calvary. Ironically, Dennis McKeefery was assigned to the "Garry Owen" Brigade. Without realizing it, he was part of a brigade whose name was derived from an old Irish drinking tune, a tune he had probably heard many times in the Irish pubs in Rockaway, where he had searched on sunny, summer Sundays for a father looking for relief from working two jobs and a house full of eight sons. Legend had it that the Garry Owen tune had been the last song played for General Custer before he and his men from the 7th Calvary traveled to their deaths at Little Big Horn.

The Tet Offensive had just occurred, and the North Vietnamese Army, along with the Viet Cong, pushed to capture the ancient city of Hue. The Marines were engaged in fierce fighting inside the city, and the Garry Owen Brigade had landed just north of the city in early February. Their assignment was to relieve the personnel in the Military Assistance Command, located just outside of the city. Once that was accomplished, they were to push into Hue from the north, cutting off any escape route of the North Vietnamese Army.

The relief of M.A.C.V. was completed, and the Garry Owen Brigade marched into Hue. One of the first villages they approached had been deserted, and they soon discovered why. In a shallow creek bed just outside the village, dozens and dozens of villagers were lying in the dry bed, their skulls crushed by the rifle butts of the AK-47 rifles carried by the N.V.A.

Nineteen-year-old Dennis McKeefery witnessed a scene so brutal that his hands began to shake, and his knees began to buckle. One of the men in his company jumped into the creek bed, to help what appeared to be a lone survivor of the massacre. When the soldier lifted the body, there was a sudden explosion and the soldier's face was shredded with shrapnel. He turned and looked at Dennis with the one eye still left in his head, outstretched his arms and began grunting through a hole that had been the soldier's mouth. The soldier took two steps towards Dennis and dropped, succumbing to his wounds.

The Brigade continued their southward march towards Hue, engaging in sporadic firefights with N.V.A. troops along the way. After a week of fighting, they reached the northern outskirts of the beautiful, ancient city. There was an eerie silence as the men began to search buildings, the quiet occasionally disrupted by gunfire in the distance. Dennis had had trouble along the march, as he was unfamiliar with Elephant Grass and rice paddies. The only grass he had known were the small square plots between the project buildings in Edgemere.

Many of the southerners, as well as the Midwestern farm boys, had never been inside a city, and so were unfamiliar with conducting building searches within an urban setting, but Dennis felt right at home. The years of playing Ringolevio and Kick the Can in the Edgemere Projects, street games endemic to those raised in New York City, became invaluable when a soldier was hit by sniper fire as he was crossing from one building to another. Dennis studied the urban terrain and, utilizing burnt-out cars, garbage bins, and building corners, he was able to pull the soldier to safety, all the while under fire from the unseen sniper. He saved the soldier"s life, and was eventually awarded a Bronze Star for his actions.

After a three-week stay in the recaptured city, the Garry Owen Brigade was sent to various hotspots throughout South Vietnam. Dennis, like many other soldiers, quickly became disillusioned with the strategy of rescuing a country for people who never wanted American troops there in the first place. To get through the days and erase the horrific images that were floating through his mind, Dennis began smoking pot and drinking heavily. It also eased the pain in his legs, which were beset by rashes that screamed to be raked by sharp fingernails, and were constantly swollen. The symptoms were later associated with exposure to

"Agent Orange," an insidious poison that was dropped from planes to destroy the bucolic Vietnamese countryside.

Dennis finally returned home in time for Christmas in 1968. When he had left for Nam, the top songs were "Daydream Believer" by The Monkees and "Happy Together" by the Turtles. Now the Fifth Dimension was singing about the Moon being in the seventh house, and Jupiter aligning with Mars, but Dennis found himself constantly listening to a song by a Motown artist named Edwin Starr, and the opening line was "War, what is it good for? Absolutely nothing!"

College was a distant dream, and a sixteen-ounce beer had become his orange- juice substitute for breakfast. He bounced from job to job, eventually winding up doing rail repairs in the subways for the Transit Authority.

When his father had passed away and left the bar to Dennis and Tom, Dennis knew he had to stop drinking. After eight hour days of inhaling steel dust, followed by eight to ten sixteen-ounce "oil cans" of Fosters beer, Dennis knew he was killing himself. The Viet Cong and N.V.A. had tried to kill him, he thought, and now he was doing to himself what they couldn't do. He also knew that a drunk running a bar would be like a pyromaniac working in a match factory, so he stopped cold turkey, and each day seemed better than the one before.

*

The bar itself had a smoked, glass-block front, which prevented any nosy pedestrians from taking account of who might be taking a drink in the middle of the afternoon. As Kevin stepped inside he heard the warm, raucous laughter endemic to most of the Irish pubs that populated the Rockaways. The dark, laminated oak floor was dotted with burn marks from the countless cigarettes that had been crushed underfoot in bygone days, pre-Mayor Bloomberg. The bar was dimly lit, and, with the glass-block front inhibiting any sunlight, it was difficult to know if it was night or day, especially depending upon the number of pints one had imbibed. Behind the bar were signs, denoting various counties in

Ireland, as well as the usual humorous signs, such as the one informing patrons that their bar stools could be cleaned for only ten cents.

Kevin, as was his habit, strolled to the end of the bar, a cop custom that allowed him to observe all who entered the establishment. Dennis had drawn a pint of Guinness for his cousin, and met Kevin as he pulled up a stool.

"When you get a chance, cuz, back that up with a wee bit of Tullamore Dew," requested Kevin.

"Tough day, pal?" asked Dennis. "What time is your now ex-partner showing up? I just love getting my balls broke."

"Last I heard from him he was still down at the Brooklyn D.A's office drawing up a homicide collar he made. Honestly, Den, I don't think he's gonna show."

"Homicide collar, on his last fuckin day? You two should have opened this place up and been drinking ever since, talking about all the time you two knuckleheads spent together."

"Talking about the past sometimes makes today and tomorrow seem even shittier. A clean break is probably healthier in the mental sense, for both of us. What time did Tom get out of here?"

Thomas McKeefery was the same age as his cousin Kevin, both born only a few months apart in 1955. Tom was considered the most stable of the eight boys. After graduating from high school, he had picked up a job pumping gas at a local gas station, and within a year he was managing the place, all the while attending night school at Queens College. He received a degree in accounting, and was hired by a small firm in midtown Manhattan. At the firm he rose to a managerial position and remained there until his father passed away. Now he took care of all the administrative duties involved in the bar, while also working behind the stick during the day.

"He left about six, said he would call you tomorrow," said Dennis as he sipped a club soda.

The bar began getting crowded, and Dennis eased away to tend to the other customers, coming back occasionally to fill Kevin's beer and shot glass. As Kevin continued drinking he became maudlin, sliding dollar bills into the jukebox in order to hear "Danny Boy," again and again. He knew it was selfish to feel that Boyd was abandoning him, and he came to realize that it was the fear of the unknown that worried him most.

Every day for so many years he had the same partner. As he became older, the sense of familiarity and order had become more important to him, and he couldn't help but think that now Boyd was fucking that all up. Continuing to drain his beer and Tullamore, the image of a darkened road in South Carolina flashed through his mind, as he feared it would.

The only solace to Monahan was that the two red-neck killers of Mickens were no longer polluting the earth. DeWayne was killed in an I.E.D. explosion in Iraq, while his brother Bobby-Lee was killed in a car crash just outside his hometown of Hinesville.

Dennis, looking down at the end of the bar, saw his cousin place his hands over his face and begin to shudder.

"Hey, don't take it so hard, pal," said Dennis, as he walked over to his cousin. "Listen, I know what you're going through. You rely on another guy with your life, and then the relationship ends. I lived with guys in the Nam for 24/7, we fought together, some died together, then it was all over. But I'll always remember each and every one of them. Think about it. It wasn't going to last forever anyway, Kevin. It had to end sometime. You'll still have memories."

"You of all people should know that memories are fucked up!" yelled Kevin, as he stood up and staggered out of the bar, hoping to fall asleep before he received a visit from Walter Mickens.

# CHAPTER 7

As the days and weeks passed, Lincoln actually began to look forward to going to work. He found patrolling the 7-5 with Sgt.Kolitoski similar to riding the Cyclone rollercoaster at Coney Island. The ride would begin nice and slow, and everything would be calm, but in the back of your mind you knew something exhilarating was going to happen at any second. Then the drop came. Your ass tightened up, there was a knot in your stomach, and your palms were sweating. But you felt so alive!

You could feel the adrenaline surging through your body, as the lights and sirens of the police car were switched on, as you stomped down on the gas pedal, racing to another cop's voice over the radio-- a voice screaming for help, or perhaps a call of shots fired. As a matter of fact, he had never felt the adrenaline rushes that he had recently experienced since riding the Cyclone.

Riding with Sgt. Kolitoski had been the right move, as Linc got to see more of the precinct and was able to develop better intelligence to give Silky, but as time passed, Linc realized he was not sending Silky the amount of information he had provided in the past. He was actually becoming caught up in the excitement of police work. He was becoming addicted to the adrenaline highs. Linc figured he would enjoy the highs while they lasted, at least until he received his degree and was able to start teaching.

He knew he could never make a career as a cop, as he saw on the veteran officers the physical and mental toll police work took on a human body. Many of the veterans were divorced, and Linc heard the locker room whispers of the alarming number of cops who had committed suicide. The cops would say "he ate his gun." On the late shift tours, many of the cops had a deathly pallor, they ate like shit, and Linc observed that a few of them had blank, far-away stares. The emotional ups and downs during a tour had to have a debilitating effect on a person's body. *No thanks*, thought Linc, *not for me.*

Linc thought he would never meet a white boy with a better sense of the streets, or its people, than Kolitoski. The blond haired, blue eyed, white boy from East Bumfuck, Long Island had it going on. He could read the streets, knew when a brother was playing him, and knew when things might turn to shit. That knowledge had probably saved Linc's life once.

They had been conducting a bullshit seatbelt checkpoint by the Pink Housing Projects, on the corner of Loring Avenue and Crescent Street. One of the things that Linc hated about patrol was issuing summons. So he tried to get away without having to give out any tags, but Kolitoski would have none of it. He explained to Linc that he was doing him a favor by having him write tags, otherwise the other cops who were forced to write summonses would bust Linc's balls, because he was the Sergeant's driver, and it would appear as if Linc were receiving special treatment. "You never want to give another cop any ammo against you," Kolitoski would say.

On that particular afternoon a small, white Toyota had pulled up to the checkpoint. Inside the vehicle was a Hispanic family, and Linc knew there would be trouble when he saw a small baby on the lap of the mother, seated in the front passenger seat. The father was driving, and three younger children were in the back, none belted in. The only person wearing a belt in the entire car was the father, and he had probably put it on when he spotted the checkpoint. Linc looked at Kolitoski and watched as the Sergeant's face began to turn beet red, his jaw muscles tightening. Linc had seen this before, whenever Kolitoski encountered unbuckled kids in a car.

"Get the old man's license and regy, Linc, while I have a chat with the mother," Kolitoski said slowly, as he strolled over to the passenger side window. Kolitoski motioned for the woman to roll down the window, but the roll-down mechanism was broken, so the woman just opened the door. Kolitoski silently reached inside the car and pulled the seatbelt strap back and forth, making sure it was operable. He then screamed into the mother's face, "What are you doing, using your baby as a fuckin airbag?"

The woman stared at Kolitoski for a few seconds, and then she began to wail. This caused the baby to start crying, and all three children in the back joined in. At that point, Linc thought the father was going to begin to start crying.

Kolitoski realized what he had done, and he attempted to calm everyone down, but to no avail. "Where do they live, Linc?"

"Right here in the Pinks, Sarge."

Kolitoski then pointed at the father and said, "Okay, listen. I want you to pull into the parking lot right here, and I want to let you know that I am going to come back looking for your car. If I find you did not get a car seat tomorrow, or if I see you driving around with those kids in the back unbelted, you are going to be in a world of shit, mi amigo, comprende?"

"Si,si, lo siento," said the father, who could not start his car fast enough so that he might get away from the crazy gringo that caused his whole family to cry, and would now force the father to open and drink half the bottle of Padron Tequila, usually reserved only for special occasions.

As the hysterical Hispanics pulled away, a call came over the radio of a possible D.O.A. at a nearby apartment in the Pink Houses. Technically, the Pink Houses were a housing project covered by the Housing Bureau cops assigned to P.S.A. # 2, but the unit covering the Pink Houses informed Central that they were currently on a prisoner transport, and would arrive at the D.O.A., with a delay. Kolitoski radioed Central that he was close to the location and he would respond to handle the job until the assigned Police Housing unit showed up.

Linc drove up to the location at 1260 Loring Ave, and he and Kolitoski exited the vehicle. Linc locked the patrol car and noticed a young black teen sitting on the bench in front of the apartment building. *The kid is a steerer,* thought Linc, *just as I sat on the same type of bench in front of my project almost two years ago.* Linc knew the seller would be in the lobby, just as Tarface and Shortfinger would have been in the Linden Houses. He had missed the lookout, the one responsible for alerting the steerer and all others involved in the operation, that 5-0 was on the premises. When Linc had been steerin, he had told Silky he never wanted a lookout. He never trusted them. For the most part, they were crackheads who received compensation for looking out in the form of crack. Linc had wanted to look out for himself.

Sure enough, as Linc and Kolitoski entered the lobby of 1260, two young men were leaning against the wall as if they were waiting for the elevator. One would be the gunman, or enforcer, there to ensure that the stash, money, or both, were not ripped off by a rival gang. Linc knew, and he was sure Kolitoski knew as well, that the gunman's weapon would be hidden, likely in one of the sixty-odd mailboxes along the wall. If the gunman had had the piece on him, he would have jetted up one of the stairwells as soon as he had seen the two cops approach the lobby.

If Silky had employed an enforcer, Tarface might still be alive, but Silky was too fuckin cheap to pay a gunman. Gunmen made good money, but they also took the greatest risk. If there was a gun battle, the enforcer was going to be right in the middle of the melee. Silky was also so cocky and confident that he never thought Boulevard would have the balls to attempt to rip off his stash.

Both young men were wearing Jordans with untied laces, baggy blue jeans, and Roc a Wear sweatshirts. Each one had a blue Yankee hat atop his head, worn backwards, of course. Kolitoski approached the young men. "So what are you guys, part of the Neighborhood Watch team?" he asked sarcastically.

His question was met by the requisite teeth-sucking, as the two teens stared at the Sergeant.

"Don't be sucking your fuckin teeth at me, home slice. What are you two doin in this building?"

"We be vistin my God cousin," said the shorter of the two.

"How does that work, being a God cousin? Can you describe the familial relationship between you and your God cousin?"

The two looked at each other as if Kolitoski was the stupidest person they had ever met.

"Familiar relationship? Man, that is fucked up! You think I would be havin sex with my God cousin?" the shorter one asked.

Linc had to turn away or risk laughing out loud in front of the two project thugs.

Kolitoski said, "Okay. Listen, Masters and Johnson, we have a job in this building. When we come down, you two brain surgeons better not be in this lobby. Got me? Oh yeah, one more thing. I've been looking in all the stores for hats like that, where the brim is in the back, but I can't seem to find any place that sells them like that. All the hats I see have the brim in the front. Where can I buy the ones that you got?"

The two teens looked at each other and began shaking their heads, thinking that nobody could possibly be this dumb. As they began to stroll out of the lobby, the taller one turned and enlightened Kolitoski. "Listen up, po-po. You just buy a regular hat and then turn it around, just like this." Thinking that Kolitoski could be mentally disabled, the tall kid demonstrated how the hat thing worked.

*

*Thankfully,* thought Linc, *the apartment that contains the D.O.A. is on the third floor.*

Kolitoski refused to take the apartment building elevators, for a number of reasons. They often broke down, and it was sometimes up to a one-half-hour wait before either the Fire Department of the Police Emergency Service Unit showed up to free the trapped passengers.

Also, Kolitoski had explained, a cop could learn a lot from the stairwells. If someone was hanging out in a stairwell, you made sure you identified them, and filled out a Stop, Question and Frisk form. Kolitoski had said that since a many of the rapes in the project buildings happened either on the stairwells or the roof. If a rape pattern developed in a particular Housing project, the detectives could search through the UF-250's, the N.Y.P.D. form number for the Stop, Question and Frisk, and hopefully the shithead you had identified in the stairwell would lead to a collar.

The graffiti on the stairwell walls were also a wealth of information to a cop. A cop could tell which particular gang ran a project building from the graffiti, or if someone's street name was tagged over, a cop knew a beef could be developing. Linc had never known that the cops would read the shit tagged on the walls, and he had passed the information on to Silky, who then made sure the Linden Houses had the cleanest stairwells of all the projects.

The partners reached the third floor and found apartment 3D. Kolitoski had taught Linc never to knock on a door without first putting his ear to it. One never knew what they might hear before entering an apartment, especially on calls of domestic disputes. Another defensive tactic Linc had learned was that after knocking or ringing a doorbell he should always step to the side.

Kolitoski had told Linc of how he and his partner had once responded to a domestic dispute, and when they had knocked on the door, luckily they stepped to the side. A drunken wife thought her cheating husband had returned to the apartment to apologize, and, the women decided a pot of boiling water in his face would be her reply to his asking for forgiveness. Kolitoski and his partner had only caught the splash off the back wall, but both cops had suffered minor burns on the backs of their necks from the incident.

Linc always knew when he was about to be given an informational tidbit, as Kolitoski would always preface his statements with the same line. "Listen carefully Linc, because I'm about to tell you something that might save your life one day."

As Linc and Kolitoski pressed their ears against the cold, steel door of Apartment 3D, they heard what sounded like a video game blasting, along with yelling and laughing. Kolitoski nodded to Linc as he rang the bell, and they both stepped away from the door. Kolitoski then began rapping on the door with his nightstick. After a minute of banging on the door, the noise in the apartment subsided, and someone inside yelled, "Who?"

"Police. Open up the door, please," yelled Linc. The sound of the television was lowered. Footsteps approached the door. On the other side of the door a number of deadbolts were unlocked, and the door opened slightly. A dark skinned male, about twenty-five-years-old, peered out the small opening. The male then closed the door, and unlocked the thick chain that had kept the door from opening completely. The door opened and the male said, "Bout fuckin time!"

He turned his back to the cops, and began walking towards the living room. The apartment was hot, and a mélange of odors permeated the apartment air. The twenty-five-year-old was shirtless and was wearing a pair of black Under Armour shorts. He was heavily muscled from the waist up, but his calves and thighs were of normal size. From the "Book of Kolitoski," Linc knew that the male had probably done time in prison. Kolitoski had explained that in prison, the crooks would generally work out their upper bodies with bench presses, pushups, dips, and curls, but they neglected working out their legs. Linc noticed the amateurish prison tattoos splayed across the male's back and arms, indicating that, indeed, he had probably been upstate.

The male walked into the living room to join two other males who were sitting on a couch, facing a large-screen television. The other two males were perhaps a little younger and smaller than the one who had answered the door. All had their shirts off in the hot apartment. The video game, Grand Theft Auto was on pause on the television screen. At least five quart bottles of Old English beer, or O.E., as it was commonly called in the projects, were sitting on a glass table in front of the males.

"Someone call in a possible D.O.A. in this apartment?" asked Kolitoski.

"Ain't nothin' possible about it. She dead!" said the male who had opened the door.

"What's your name, champ, and what's your relationship to the deceased?" asked Kolitoski.

"My name be Truth, and I'm her grandson."

"I need your government name, Truth."

"Tyrell Simpson," replied the male, who seemed to be greatly inconvenienced by the whole matter. He was just itching to start up his video game once more.

"Do you live in the apartment with the deceased, and what happened to her?"

"Yeah, I be livin here, and I don't know. I ain't no doctor."

Linc heard a noise from the kitchen area, and, he saw there a small brown-and-white pit bull tearing apart a quart carton of Chinese food. A number of spare rib bones were lying on the floor, but the pit bull seemed intent on lapping up the remainder of the Chicken Chow Mein in the box. The pit momentarily stopped his quest to look at Linc, and then attacked the spare rib bones, apparently afraid that Linc might decide to help himself to some ribs and Mein.

The kitchen was a disgusting mess, with dishes piled over the top of the sink while cockroaches darted back and forth over the greasy kitchen counter.

Linc became aware that Kolitoski was alone in the living room with the three men, so he walked over to stand behind his Sergeant.

Kolitoski said, "So, last name is Simpson heh? Like the cartoon? Surprised your friends don't call you "Homer" instead of "Truth."

Truth's two friends, who had been sitting on the couch, one hand continually grabbing at their respective crotches, put their free hand to their mouth and began laughing.

"They could call me that, but then they would suffer a beatdown," said Truth, now staring at his two, suddenly silent buddies. "You here to tell jokes, funny man, or you here to see about my Grandmoms?"

"Yeah, I'm gonna see your Grandmoms, but before we do go into the bedroom, I need to have your homeboys' bounce. This could be a potential crime scene, and we don't need anyone else disturbing it."

"Crime scene? Yo, the old lady died cause she old. Ain't no crime in that!"

"Fine. You want them to stay, Tyrell? Then I'm gonna have to get good government I.D. from both of them."

The older of the two males suddenly stood up, not enthralled with having to provide identification to the police. "Yo, Truth, it's a'ight, we got's shit to take care of anyway. You be strong, cuz, you know we sorry bout your Grandmoms." Both males then went through an intricate system of handslaps with Truth, and the long good-bye ended in hugs. Linc thought Kolitoski was pushing it too far. After all, Tyrell did live in the apartment, and if he wanted his boys to stay, they should stay.

Once Kolitoski was satisfied that both males were out of the apartment, he nodded to Linc to follow him into the bedroom. They heard Grand Theft Auto restart on the television, Truth apparently deciding to play by himself.

As they walked down the hallway to the bedroom, Kolitoski said, "Never fails, Linc. Ask them for I.D. and they can't get out fast enough. We didn't need those other two knuckleheads in the apartment, especially when we couldn't see them. They had all been drinking, and who knows what Truth's relationship with them is like. They could have started arguing about the video game, and the next thing you know we're breaking up a fight. Always best to have the odds on your side. People think that we're just doing shit like that to bust balls, but my concern is making sure both you and me sign out in one piece at the end of our tour."

They opened the bedroom door and were hit by the pungent, unmistakable odor of death. Linc went over to open a window, and then he heard Kolitoski's voice, "Linc, no, not until were sure what happened. Here, use this for now." The Sergeant pulled out a small tube of Vicks vapor rub, dabbed a glob onto his finger, and he put some of the rub under each nostril. He then handed the tube to Linc, "Invest in a tube, pal. It could save you from a bad case of the nauseous. Also keep in mind that if you have to sit on a D.O.A. from natural causes, and the smell is real bad, think *coffee*."

"Coffee? You know I don't drink coffee, Sarge."

"No, knucklehead, not to drink. You check out the kitchen, hopefully you find some ground coffee from a bag, or a can, you cook it on a low burn on the stove, and the coffee smell overcomes the death stench. If it's not an obvious natural D.O.A., and there is any possibility there was foul play involved, all bets are off. You touch nothing and you suffer in silence, my man, like cops have been doing for a hundred years."

Kolitoski then stepped out of the room and into the hall, "Hey, Tyrell, what time you find your Grandmoms like this?"

The television was lowered, and Tyrell yelled back, "When I got up. About one o'clock."

"I guess they must have cancelled his early morning Mensa meeting," said Kolitoski.

Lying on the bed was a light-skinned black woman. She appeared to be lighter than her normal color, as lividity had begun to set in. The blood had started to leave the upper portion of her body, and pool in her lower extremities. The woman had a tranquil look on her face, as if she was happy that she was finally at peace. She must have foreseen her passing, as on her nightstand, she had placed all the vital information needed for those responsible for her final trip. A birth certificate and Social Security Card identified her as Adele Minton, born in Mobile, Alabama on October 13th, 1936. She had turned seventy just over a week ago.

Mrs. Simpson, nee' Minton, had also written down, in a beautiful, flowing script, her doctor's name and all the medications she had been taking. Kolitoski spotted a vial of Nitroglycerin pills on the nightstand, so it was apparent the woman had heart complications. There were no signs of violence or struggle, but final determination as to the cause of death would be made by the Medical Examiner.

"You're a long way from Mobile, Alabama, Ms. Simpson," said Linc, "I pray you rest in peace." With that, both cops made the sign of the cross.

*

Adele Pitt had been sent north from Mobile when she was twenty years old, her mother and father not wishing to subject their oldest daughter to the indignities and injustices suffered by blacks in Alabama at that time. She rode a bus up to New York City, settled in with an aunt on Gates Avenue in the Bedford-Stuyvesant section of Brooklyn, and found a job with the Piels Brewing Company on New Jersey Avenue in East New York.

The 1950's and 60's were heyday years for breweries in Brooklyn, with famous-name beers like Rheingold and Schaefer, setting up shop in the Borough of Churches. Brooklynites would claim they had the best beer in the "woild", and it was all because of their "wawda."

Adele, a beautiful, gentle woman, soon met Darnell Simpson, another employee of Piels, and they quickly fell in love, got married and moved into an apartment in the Pink Houses, only fifteen minutes from their work.

Adele and Darnell were only able to have one daughter, Dell, a name derived from a combination of Adele and Darnell. Dell married too young, and was not as lucky as her mother in her choice of husbands, as the young man liked to drink and could not hold down a steady job. He soon abandoned Dell, leaving her with two sons, Thomas and Tyrell. Dell took back her surname, and also completed the required paperwork to have her sons retain the proud Simpson name. An all too familiar cycle, distinct to the projects, began, as Dell and her two young sons moved back into the apartment she had grown up in.

The Piels Brewing Company, along with Schaefer and Rheingold, had closed its doors in the early seventies, as many breweries had found it more profitable to set up shop in Pennsylvania. Darnell found a job in a printing shop in lower Manhattan, while Dell, landed a job as a bus cleaner with the Transit Authority. Adele stayed home to take care of her two grandsons.

Then tragedy struck. On one rainy night in July of 1992, a car skidded through a red light on Linden Boulevard, striking and killing the only daughter of Adele and Darnell Simpson. Not long after, on a cold February morning, as he stepped outside their apartment building, Darnell Simpson had a massive heart attack and was dead at the young age of fifty-nine. Adele knew his heart had been weakened when his angel and princess, Dell, had been taken from him much too soon, and now Adele, at the age of fifty-seven, had had to raise and care for her eleven-and nine-year-old grandsons.

She did the best she could, and the older boy, Thomas, at twenty, had joined the Army, as did many other young New Yorkers right after 9/11. Thomas had been enraged that foreigners had attacked his home city, murdering thousands of innocent people in the process. He had become a paratrooper with the 82$^{nd}$ Airborne Division and had been deployed to Afganistan in January of 2003 as part of Task Force Devil. His current rank was Sergeant, E-5, and on the day his grandmother passed away, he was still in Afganistan.

Tyrell was a different story. Adele had always felt Tyrell had inherited the worst of his father's bad genes, and he was first arrested at fifteen for a strong-armed robbery. By the time Adele died, Tyrell had been in and out of prison so many times she had lost count. She would take never-ending bus rides, upstate to places with names like Coxsackie and Elmira. Those bus rides, and talking to her youngest grandson on a phone through a plexiglass window, surely hastened Adele's demise.

Linc noticed a small, black purse on the nightstand. The purse was empty, except for one quarter and two pennies. *The son of a bitch,* thought Linc. *He probably bought the Chinese food and beer with his grandmom's remaining money.*

All of the sudden there was loud banging at the front door.

"Who the fuck?" yelled Tyrell.

"Open up, asshole, before we kick it in!"

Kolitoski recognized the booming, yet comforting, voice of Shock, whose real name was Police Officer Steve Hannigan, a Housing Bureau cop from P.S.A. #2. Kolitoski knew that right beside Hannigan was his partner, Police Officer John Fulfree, whose nickname in the projects was Awe. Kolitoski walked out of the bedroom into the hallway, and watched as Tyrell, while uttering a few "muthafuckas" under his breath, opened the front door, and the two huge housing cops walked into the apartment.

"Ty-rell, my man. Don't tell me you were stupid enough to kill someone in your own apartment and then stick around!" shouted Fulfree. Fulfree was a large, black, bald headed cop, whose eyes were as black as his skin. His biceps were as big as most people's necks, his shirt so tight on his bicep that it would have been difficult to slide a quarter between it and his skin. The only difference between him and his partner, Hannigan, was their skin color. The two had been partners so long that it was said they could finish each other's sentences.

They had been partners working the East New York/ Brownsville Housing projects going on twenty years, and they were now locking up third generation crooks. Shock and Awe knew all the players in the projects, and Linc hoped they did not recognize him from his steering days at the Linden Houses. Everyone in the projects knew Shock and Awe, along with the many stories associated with the two gigantic cops. Like most urban legends, the stories began to take on lives of their own, but one story Linc knew to be true.

*

A fifteen-year-old girl named LaShonda had dropped some acid at one of Silky's impromptu parties. She left the party and made her way to her own building, where, instead of getting off the elevator at the seventh floor on which she lived, she continued up to the top floor, fourteen. Acid, the vilest of hallucinogens, had taken over the young girl's mind, convincing her that the only way to escape the projects was by flying away. LaShonda made her way to the roof, intent on soaring towards the wispy cirrus clouds above her, clouds that seemed so close that she might well be able to grab one, and just float away-- to a place where gunshots would never be heard, children did not go hungry, and young girls could live out a childhood that LaShonda had only seen in Disney movies.

As luck would have it, Officers Hannigan and Fulfree had been conducting a vertical patrol in the very same building, and, as the cops were about to enter the stairwell on the fourteenth floor, one of the tenants notified them that she had observed a girl go through the door that led to the roof. The cops, figuring the girl was up there to fire up some weed or liaison with her boyfriend, cautiously entered onto the graveled top roof. They had only taken a few steps on the roof when they observed LaShonda standing on the roof ledge, her arms outstretched. The cops walked quickly towards the girl, and as she heard their approach, she bent her knees, ready to take flight.

Fulfree was closest, and he dove towards her as she began to push off the building. The huge, black cop was able to grab her ankles as she jumped off the ledge, in her mind, towards the clouds. Her momentum carried him so far over the roof ledge, that only his thighs were resting on it. He still had a firm grasp on the girl's ankles, as she dangled fourteen floors from a certain death. Fulfree, however, began slipping over the edge, and both he and LaShonda were both about to leave this earth, until his partner grabbed his calves.

Hannigan, before becoming a cop, had worked on clam boats in the Great South Bay on Long Island. Every day, for eight hours a day, he had worked a twenty-foot clam rake into the muddy, grassy bottom of the bay. That tortuous physical labor had produced forearms on the cop that resembled those on Popeye the Sailor Man. His grip had become so strong that he was able to tear New York Telephone Books in half.

Thankfully, LaShonda weighed only ninety pounds soaking wet, and although Fulfree tipped the scales at two-hundred-and-twenty five, Hannigan braced his legs against the roof ledge and began to pull his partner and the distraught girl to safety.

By now, dozens of spectators were watching in amazement from the courtyard as the cop and the girl were hanging upside down from the roof. Hannigan, using the leverage from his legs, and an almost supernatural strength from his shoulders and forearms, was finally able to pull both to safety. Then an event occurred that was generally only reserved for firemen. Just about everyone in the projects loved firemen, while cops were viewed as nothing but trouble. Never the less, the mass of onlookers began applauding and cheering the heroic act they had just witnessed, and the street names of "Shock" and "Awe" were bestowed on the two cops by a grateful public.

LaShonda was taken for psychiatric evaluation, and the partners checked on her constantly, making sure she was okay. When she turned eighteen, the cops called in some favors down at Brooklyn Criminal Court, and were able to get LaShonda into stenographer training program. The young woman eventually became an excellent court stenographer and landed a well-paying civil service position in Brooklyn Civil Court. She never forgot what the two cops had done, and named her first born son Shocawe.

The cops had become so well respected, that, if a mother or grandmother knew one of her wayward children was wanted by the police, she would reach out to the them, letting them know where the kid could be located, rather than risk having the child do something foolish, and wind up in a shootout with police. The women knew the partners would deliver their boys safely to detectives.

Hannigan and Fulfree had also taken it upon themselves to check on single mothers and grandmothers whose children had been sent off to war in the Middle East. The cops made sure any repairs to the women's apartments were handled expeditiously by the Housing Authority, and, in some instances, an envelope with some food money would be left on the kitchen table, courtesy of the two cops. That was how they had come to know Adele Simpson.

*

93

"Ty-rell," Hannigan said, "I pray for your brother, risking his life over in Afganistan every day. I pray that he comes home safely, and I pray that you will catch a shiv in the back on your next trip to one of our upstate correctional facilties. Then your grandmoms could finally have some peace." His voice trailed off at the end of the sentence, as he realized who the D.O.A. in the apartment could very well be.

"Oh, shit, no!" both partners yelled simultaneously. They looked down the hallway at Kolitoski, who gently nodded his head.

The two hulking cops removed their hats and walked solemnly down the hallway to the bedroom. They both made the sign of the cross as they stood next to Adele Simpson's bed, silently saying a prayer for the departed woman.

"It look natural to you, Sarge?" asked Fulfree.

"Yeah. No signs of any violence, and the types of medication on her nightstand here indicate she had a heart condition."

"We were here checking up on her not too long ago, and we had to call a bus for her. It seemed to us that she had some trouble breathing. She didn't want to go, but we convinced her to get examined at Brookdale." said Hannigan. "We'll take it from here Sarge. Thanks for responding. We'll get notification to the Army to contact her grandson Thomas, he's over in Afganistan, as soon as possible.

Fulfree had been looking at Linc and finally said, "Hey, brother, don't I know you from somewhere?"

Linc had been prepared for the question, and quickly replied, "Yeah, I seen you in the P.S.A. a couple of times, when I had to pick up some paperwork."

"Maybe. I could swear it was from somewhere else, though."

"See, Fulf, even to other black guys all black guys look alike," said Hannigan.

Kolitoski gathered up his paperwork, in which he had recorded the time he and Linc had responded to the apartment, and their brief interview of Tyrell. He handed the papers to Fulfree. "This here's Linc, fellas. He's my driver, and he seems to be good copper. Linc, these oversized gentlemen are Hannigan and Fulfree, otherwise known as Shock and Awe, the two finest Housing Cops the East New York projects have ever seen. Okay, boys, we're gonna take off. Stay safe."

As Kolitoski and Linc walked past the living room, they noticed that the television had been shut off and Tyrell was sitting on the couch, his face in his hands. He was crying. The young pit bull was sitting in front of his master, patting Tyrell's knee with his paw. It was as if the dog was asking, "What can I do to help?"

The partners walked down the stairs. Upon entering the lobby, they heard the distinct sound of gunfire coming from the front of the building. Linc rushed out the front door and saw one of the males that they had met earlier in the lobby look at him and begin running. The male, still wearing his Yankee Hat, had a black pistol in his right hand. Linc took off after Yankee hat, but as he was about to round the corner of the building, he was pulled back by the collar of his shirt. At that moment Linc heard a shot, and a piece of red brick splintered off the corner of the building, right where Linc had been about to turn.

Linc froze, as Kolitoski stepped in front of him. Kolitoski glanced quickly around the corner of the building and suddenly began pursuing the male. Linc recovered his composure and also began running, trying to catch up to Kolitoski, who had some speed for a white boy. He heard Kolitoski yell to Yankee Hat to drop the gun or he would shoot, and the Yankee Hat then tossed his weapon into a short hedgerow. Linc soon passed Kolitoski, and he raised his gun in order to stop Yankee Hat's escape.

Kolitoski knocked Linc's arm down, yelling, "Don't shoot, Linc!"

Patrol units had responded to the initial calls of "shots fired," and two cars had cut off Yankee Hat's escape. As four cops exited their vehicles with guns drawn, Yankee Hat thought it best that he cut his losses, so he dropped to the ground onto his belly and outstretched his arms. Two cops covered the prone suspect, while the other two handcuffed and then frisked him.

Linc had holstered his weapon, and he ran up to the male who was still lying face down on the ground. "You muthafucka!" yelled Linc, as he began kicking the suspect in the ribcage. Yankee Hat began to scream as Linc's steel-tipped shoes smashed into his ribs.

Kolitoski slammed into Linc, almost knocking him to the ground. "Enough!" yelled Kolitoski. "Do you see all the people out here? How do you know you're not being videotaped? You can be sure the videotape would not include this shit-head firing a shot at you! Once the cuffs are on a perp, all bets are off, Linc. You don't ever beat a handcuffed prisoner. Do you understand?"

A seething Linc stared at Kolitoski and said, "The muthfucka almost killed me, Sarge. You should have let me shoot him."

"First of all, he had dropped his gun. Secondly, you would have shot him in the back. Tomorrow's papers would have had his middle-school graduation picture, with him smiling like a little angel with a graduation cap on his head. All his friends would tell the reporters he had a bright future, because he loved music and was an aspiring rap artist. The paper would have somehow gotten your police identification card picture, and printed it in the paper. You know that picture-- the one where they tell you not to smile, and every cop looks like a Nazi storm trooper. You would have been fucked, my man."

Linc realized that Kolitoski was right. He also realized that Kolitoski might have just saved his life, and he here he was, acting like an asshole towards the Sergeant.

"You're right, Sarge, I apologize. And listen, thanks for what you did for me back there."

"Linc, listen up. I'm gonna tell you something that might just save your life. Never, ever, turn the corner of a building like that without first stopping to peek around it. You never know what is waiting for you on the other side. Another thing-- we're not out here just to execute these scumbags. That makes us no better than them. I've been through it, and you can't imagine what it feels like to take a life. It was either me or him, but not one day goes by that

I don't relive, and sometimes regret, what I did. Linc, I don't want you ever to have to go through that."

# CHAPTER 8

After the shooting incident had occurred at the Pink Houses, Linc had tried to curb his enthusiasm a bit, but he had to admit that he looked forward to those rushes of adrenaline each day he came to work. On this particular Friday night, Linc had pulled the patrol car out of the parking lot and headed east on Sutter Avenue. Linc knew that Kolitoski liked to scoot over the Queens border, where he could get a good cup of Dunkin Donuts coffee. They had just passed Atkins Street, when a call came over the radio for a job in the Cypress Hills projects.

Normally, they would have just kept driving to their coffee destination, allowing the Housing Bureau cops to handle the job, but the call sounded serious. Numerous callers had reported a fire in Apartment 4b at 325 Fountain Avenue, and in addition they had reported hearing screams coming from inside the apartment. To a cop, when numerous calls were coming into 911, that meant the job was probably legit. The first thought in the partners' minds was that there might be children inside the apartment.

"Central, show 7-5 Training Sergeant responding, we are only a couple of blocks out," said Kolitoski into the radio.

Linc hit the lights and sirens, continuing east on Sutter, making a right turn onto Fountain Avenue, and then pulling up in front of 325 Fountain. The cops got out of their car and raced into the lobby of the building. As they entered the lobby, the elevator door opened and a woman with two young children, a boy and a girl, both of whom appeared to be about ten years old, stepped off. The mother had a rolling suitcase, and the children were wearing backpacks stuffed with clothes.

As Kolitoski and Linc jogged towards the stairwell, Linc suddenly stopped. Something didn't seem right to him. He thought he smelled a faint odor of smoke when he passed the woman and kids. More than that, however, he noticed a frightened look in the young boy's eyes. He had seen that look once before, when he first saw his brother, Harris, staring at him from the back of the police car after their father had been killed.

"Sarge, hold on one second."

"Cmon, Linc, calls are still coming in for that apartment."

Linc could not shake the feeling he had. "Excuse me, ma'am, could you hold on for a second," Linc called out, as the woman approached the front door of the lobby. The woman made as though she hadn't heard Linc, and suddenly the boy released his mother's grip and ran towards Linc. The boy wrapped his arms around Linc's legs and began crying.

"Devon, get back here," the mother yelled. Kolitoski had stopped, and as he watched the scene unfold, he too now knew something was amiss.

At that moment, two Housing cops ran into the lobby. "Is everything okay, Sarge?" asked the older cop.

"Yeah. Fine. We just have to check out something here. You guys head upstairs to the apartment." Kolitoski walked over to the woman, who seemed ready to bolt out of the building. He also now smelled smoke on the woman's clothing.

"What apartment are you coming from, ma'am?"

"Umm, Apartment 3b.," the woman muttered.

"That's funny. There was a fire in Apartment 4b, right above you. Did you hear anything?"

"No, officer," said the woman, in a distinct Jamaican accent. "I'm in kind of a hurry. We're going to my sister's house in Crown Heights for the weekend, and I need to catch the bus."

"Let me ask you a question. How come your clothes smell like smoke?" said Kolitoski.

Linc then pulled the little boy aside and asked softly, "You live in Apartment 4b, don't you?" The young boy nodded. Linc walked over to Kolitoski to let him know what the boy had said, and at that point the Sergeant said to the woman, "Ma'am, you're gonna have to come back to the precinct with us."

Over the radio, the officers heard, "7-5 Sergeant, on the air?

"Yeah. Go ahead, unit."

"Sarge, we're up in the apartment. We have a male, D.O.A., from the fire. A couple of witnesses here said they saw the wife holding the door shut on the male, with a clothesline attached to an adjacent apartment doorknob. We found a clothesline lying in the hallway. Neighbors said the woman fled with two kids, a boy and girl. Could be who you have in lobby."

"Is the fire out?" asked Kolitoski.

"Yeah F.D. is on scene, everything under control. As soon as they're out of here we will secure location for Crime Scene Unit."

Kolitoski and Linc then brought the woman and children to the stationhouse and up to the squad offices.

Monahan was the catching detective on the case, and he asked that Kolitoski bring the woman into the interview room while Linc stayed with the two children at Boyd's empty desk. Sgt Dover told Monahan that Dover and another detective, Joe McQuirke, would go over to the apartment and wait for Crime Scene. Monahan could then interview the woman right away, before she thought about getting a lawyer.

Monahan placed a folder he was carrying down on Boyd's desk, and opened one of the drawers of the desk to retrieve some blank pieces of paper. He gave the papers and some pens and pencils to the two children sitting at the desk. "Here you go, kids. We're going to get you guys something to eat, so just wait here with the police officer while I go make sure you're mother is okay."

Sergeant Kolitoski then said, "I'll go downstairs and notify Children's Services, Kevin. I'll leave Linc up here with the two kids."

"Thanks, Sarge, and, hey, good job."

"Wasn't me, Kevin, Linc here knew something was wrong the minute he saw the mother and kids get off the elevator."

"Well then, thanks Linc, for the ground ball." In detective parlance a ground ball was an easy case, one that had been basically solved when the detective received it. Monahan then went into the interview room to question the mother, leaving Linc with the two children. Linc would usually have taken the arrest, but since it was a homicide it was handed off to the detectives. The intricacies of a homicide investigation, at the insistence of the District Attorney's office, dictated that a detective manage a homicide arrest from start to finish.

Within a few minutes, a uniformed cop brought into the squad room some hamburgers, french fries, and sodas for the kids.

Suddenly, a loud bang came from the Lieutenant's office. Shawn, who had been emptying out the garbage cans in Lt. Fisher's room, dropped a garbage can as soon as he smelled the pleasant aroma of McDonalds wafting through the squad office. He ran out of the office and stood in front of Boyd's desk, staring at the kids who were tearing the wrappers off the food.

Shawn stared at the little boy and asked, "Hey kid, you gonna eat all that?"

Linc, who was aware of Shawn's reputation and had heard he could eat like a wolf hound, quickly said, "Step off, son. Let these kids eat in peace." Shawn glared at Linc for a minute, saw that he meant business, and backed off.

Linc looked around the squad office and observed that all the frenetic activity in the room was nothing more than controlled chaos. Phones were continually ringing, prisoners in the cell were yelling about making a phone call, going to the bathroom, or that they were hungry. Two young thugs from Brownsville were in the cells, constantly yelling that Constitutional rights were being violated because they hadn't been fed, and that they were gonna sue "every muthafucka" in the office. Even Shawn, who wouldn't know a lawsuit from a sweat suit, was threatened with litigation, since he was a witness to the torture the two miscreants had to endure.

Their arresting detective, Benny Archer, knew that they had eaten. As a matter of fact, they had probably had four slices of pizza each. The two cretins had been arrested for arson/murder. They had decided to visit a girl who lived in the Boulevard Houses and, being the considerate gentlemen that they were, they had stopped to bring a pizza up to the girl's apartment. They had bought the pie from a place on Stanley Avenue, where a Pakistani made the pizza. The Pakistani could make a pizza about as well as an Italian could make falafel. There was enough grease and oil in it to fill up the crankcase of Volkswagon Jetta.

When they reached the girl's project building, and after extensively discussing the matter, they decided the girl's ass was big enough, and she shouldn't be entitled to more than two slices, so they sat on a bench outside the apartment and devoured three slices each. Carrying the pizza box containing the two slices, they entered the lobby of the building, only to discover the elevator was out of order.

The big-ass girl lived on the fifth floor, and the two discussed whether she was worth a trip up five flights of stairs. Deciding in the affirmative, the two began trekking up the stairs. By the time they reached the third floor, both were in an ornery mood, since the stairwell was hot and stomach cramps began developing from the thirty-weight oil they had ingested with the pizza. When they hit the fourth floor landing, they came upon Darren "T-Bird" Smalls.

T-Bird's mother lived in the building, on the seventh floor. He had stayed in his mom's apartment for the last two days, but once again had overstayed his welcome when his mother caught him lifting twenty dollars out of her purse. Mrs. Smalls had thrown her son out of the apartment more times than the New York Jets have had losing seasons, all because of his drinking. T-Bird had received his nickname not because of his love of the classic Ford car, but rather for his love of the classic, low priced, high alcohol wine, Thunderbird.

T-Birds problems with alcohol had begun after he returned from his second tour in Vietnam with the 101st Airborne. He was an Army Ranger who had returned home having to relive in his mind numerous, unspeakable incidents that he was unfortunate to have witnessed in Nam. After returning home, he was in and out of V.A. Hospitals for what would now be considered Post Traumatic

Stress Disorder, but back then it was simply known as "combat fatigue."

He was unable to hold a steady job, his drinking became worse as the years progressed, and now this American hero was sleeping on an apartment stairwell. He had just consumed three bottles of the 17.5% alcohol rotgut known as Thunderbird when the two sixteen-year-old punk asses from Brownsville, neither whom had ever heard of a land called Vietnam, decided they wanted too have some fun with the bum.

Their idea of fun was to finish the remaining two slices of pizza ("That big-ass girl probably ain't even gonna be home.") and place the oil-soaked cardboard box which proclaimed, "You've tried the rest, now try the best!" on top of the prone T-Bird. Removing a cheap, one-dollar lighter from his pocket, one of the thugs lit the top cover of the box. The box went up in flames, and T-Bird's torn, faded FUBU sweatshirt caught fire as well. T-Bird awoke to thoughts of napalm and burning flesh, but the anesthetic properties of the previously ingested Thunderbird eroded quickly, and now the former Army Ranger was in unimaginable pain. He tried to get up, but one of the teens pushed him back down with his foot, and in less than a minute, T-Birds heart stopped pumping. The fire continued to consume his frail body, but he felt nothing.

The two teens bolted down the stairs and fled the building, running north to Linden Boulevard. On Linden, they caught a bus. They beat the fare by boarding through the rear door, and rode west to safety in Brownsville.

The first two Housing Cops who responded to the scene began retching from the smell of burning flesh and the sight of the skeletal remains of Darren Smalls. The two cops, who had worked the Boulevard Projects for years, knew who the victim was because of the two pieces of metal lying next to him, apparently having dropped out of the pockets as his pants burned.

Lying next to Corporal Darren Smalls was a Silver Star Medal and a Purple Heart, won by the Corporal for his heroic actions in 1970, during a twenty-three day battle in the A-Shau

Valley. There, Darren Smalls, although shot twice in the leg, and under intense fire, had attacked and eliminated a North Vietnamese Army machine gun nest by tossing two hand grenades into it. His actions had saved the lives of a number of his fellow Rangers.

The cops knew it was Darren, as he would pin the medals to his green Army fatigue jacket on Memorial Day and Veterans Day. A Housing Bureau lieutenant, also a Vietnam vet, would assign a car to pick up Darren on those two days to drive him to the New Lots Avenue subway station. In addition, the lieutenant would pull a twenty dollar bill out of his pocket and instruct the cops to hand it over to Darren, ensuring that the former Corporal had money to eat. Before the cops left the command, the lieutenant would gently remind the cops that they had better, "thank Darren for his service to our country."

At the New Lots Avenue subway, Darren would board the train and travel to the Vietnam Veterans Memorial, located on Water Street in lower Manhattan, foregoing the parades up Fifth Avenue. He would always remain bitter about the treatment of returning Vietnam Vets, and since a parade for those that served in Southeast Asia had taken a disgraceful ten years to occur, he had vowed never to march in a parade.

At the Memorial, he would sit quietly on a steel bench in front of the black, granite fountain and silently say The Lord's Prayer seventy-five times, for the seventy five men of the 101st Airborne who were killed during the battle in the A-Shau Valley What the North Vietnamese and Viet Cong could not do in the A-Shau Valley was accomplished by two young hoodlums on a stairwell landing in a Brooklyn project.

The Smalls clan was well known and much loved, with extended families scattered throughout Brooklyn. Rumor had it that T-Bird was related to a favorite son of the Borough of Kings, hip-hop icon "Biggie" Smalls (as with much of the project lore, the rumor was baseless however, as Biggie's real name was Christopher Wallace).

T-Bird's mom had settled into The Boulevard Houses when it had first opened, and she was loved and respected by all within the community who knew her. Those people were now outraged at the horrific murder of T-Bird.

Word soon reached Shock and Awe of the street names of the two thugs. The cops passed on the information to the catching detective, Benny Archer. Detective Archer, who had worked uniformed patrol in Brownsville, reached out to a couple of informants he still knew from his Brownsville days, and now both pieces of vermin were standing in the 7-5 Squad cell, complaining that they were hungry.

"What apartment number you live in?" Archer asked the taller one, as he was filling out the arrest report, commonly known in the N.Y.P.D. as an On Line Booking Sheet.

"I live in Apartment 3."

"3, what?"

"3 nothin. It's just 3."

An exasperated Archer said, "You live in the Tilden projects, right?"

"Yeah, so?"

Archer looked at the ignorant teen and just shook his head. "Listen to me carefully, knucklehead. Each apartment in Tilden has a number and a letter. Think about this for a minute, if your brain can function for that long. If there were no letters for any of the families living on the third floor, how would the mailman know who gets what mail, since everyone would live in Apartment 3?"

"Are you buggin, man? How you become a D.T.? He be knowin cause the family name be on the envelope."

The taller one's partner suddenly chimed in with a brilliant observation. "No, hol up, cuz, that ain't right, cause sometimes we be getting mail that has our apartment number, but was supposed to be going to someone named Resident. And now that I be thinkin about it, cuz, didn't your door used to say 3C?"

The tall one began to scratch his chin, obviously in deep thought, when suddenly a light must have gone off somewhere inside his skull, "Yeah. That's right, but the C fell off bout four months ago. Housing never fixed it. An, you know, some muthafucka stole that C. Hey, big man," he said to Archer. "Ain't that some kind of identity theft?" Mulling over the injustice of his stolen C, he then mumbled to himself, "I catch that muthafucka, I'm gonna smush his ass."

Detective Benny Archer was a weightlifting fitness fanatic, who never touched red meat, avoided processed foods as well as sugar, and never drank alcohol. In other words, he stayed away from everything that tasted good but was bad for you. At that moment, however, the large detective seriously considered walking over to Monahan's desk, opening the bottom drawer, and taking a long pull off that nasty Irish whiskey called Jameson's.

Linc had been sitting at Boyd's desk with the two children, listening to the two academics in the cell, when he spotted the folder Monahan had left on the corner of the desk. He felt the air come out of his lungs, it was a case folder, and written across the top tab was, "Homicide # 2005-18, Thomas "Tarface" Williams".

Linc glanced around the office, saw everyone was occupied with various tasks, and reached across the desk and began to slide the folder towards where he was seated. He looked around once more, satisfied himself that no one was watching, and opened the folder. The first items he saw were the crime scene photos. His hands began to shake as he viewed the detailed color photos of his dead friend lying on the lobby floor. Linc quickly flipped thru the gruesome photos and the crime scene sketches, until he came upon Monahan's D.D. 5's

A detective's investigation into any type of crime he or she has been assigned is chronicled on a form known as a Complaint-Follow Up Informational or N.Y.P.D. Form #313-081A. To detectives throughout the N.Y.P.D., the form was simply known as a D.D.5. Each step of an investigation is detailed on a separate D.D. 5 and maintained in a case folder. The first D.D.5 in a case folder is generally the detective's response to the crime scene, or interview of a complainant, and the last is, hopefully, the arrest of

106

a suspect. Most D.D.5's include interviews of witnesses, canvasses conducted, license plate numbers, names run, etc. A good case folder will have documented each and every step an investigator has taken. It should be so complete that any other investigator, or a supervisor, can read the 5's and know everything about the case.

Monahan's case folders were meticulous. Linc began reading the last D.D.5 that Monahan had inserted into the case folder.

INVESTIGATION: HOMICIDE # 18- 2005
SUBJECT: INTERVIEW OF CONFIDENTIAL INFORMANT
On 12/16/06 at 1030 hrs. the undersigned conducted an interview of a confidential
informant, registered with the N.Y.P.D. as C.I #824. The interview was conducted in
the Rectory Office of Father Michael Fennell at St.Fortunata's church. Father Fennell   was not present during the interview, however, Detective Benny Archer, Sh# 1084 of the 75Pct. Sqd. was present and assisted the undersigned. C.I. #824 stated that he was in Apartment 6A at 765 Stanley Ave. (Boulevard Houses) on the afternoon of 09/12/05. One of the tenants of the apartment and present therein, was Andre Ingram, A.K.A. "Boo". There were no other individuals within the apartment at the time. At appx. 1545 hrs. the C.I. and Ingram heard a banging on the door. Ingram answered the door, and a male known to the C.I. as "Glee" entered the apartment. C.I. stated that "Glee" seemed high, and was sweating profusely. At the time "Glee" was wearing a light gray sweatshirt, blue jeans and a blue bandana. Ingram then asked "Glee" if he "did the deed?"
"Glee" responded by saying they weren't able to get any product, because "Tarface" went for a gun, so he had to "smoke that nigga". "Glee" then produced a black automatic handgun and remarked that the barrel was still hot. He further stated that he thinks he "popped two into the muthafucka's

chest." He stated that when he and "Zeke" ran, another male from the "building across", began popping shots at them. When Ingram asked where "Zeke" was, "Glee" stated he thinks "Zeke" was going to stay with a relative in Bed-Stuy. Ingram then told C.I. #824 to go get some beers. C.I. stated that when he returned to apartment, "Glee" was gone. Case Open.

Linc saw a loose D.D. 5 inside the case folder that Monahan must have just completed but had not yet been inserted into the case file. He read that one:

INVESTIGATION: HOMICIDE #18-2005
SUBJECT : NAME CHECKS

A review of the 75 pct. Sqd. nickname file and a check of the O.L.B.S. system reveals that one Damon "Glee" Miller resides at 725 Stanley Ave (Boulevard Houses), Apt.3 E. Miller, D/O/B – 07/28/1984, had been arrested for two drug offenses and is known under NYSID # 6445527L.
B.C.I. photo of Miller was shown to C.I. #824 on 11/17/06 at 1115 hrs. in parking lot of St.Fortunata's church. Informant positively identified Miller as the individual known as "Glee" that admitted to shooting Thomas "Tarface" Williams on 09/12/05.
A record check for the street name "Zeke" residing in East New York has so far met with negative results. Case Open.

"Hey buddy. You want to help me out with that case, find me a witness," said Monahan.

Linc felt as though his heart would explode in his chest. He dropped the folder onto the desk as Monahan approached him. Trying to regain his composure quickly, Linc replied, "Why not use your C.I. as a witness? He heard him admit it."

"No way. This guy has been a wealth of information for me. I ask him to testify, it's just gonna be one shit-head's word against another's. Nah, I need a legit civilian witness. Besides, I tell him to testify, I wouldn't get another piece of info. from him ever again. I'm lucky I got this from him. The only reason he came forward now was because he's going to trial on a drug charge and he's hoping I can help him out, but all the shit he does give me is right on the money. As long as I now know the shooter, I'll get him. Now the real detective work begins, and, kid, Monahan always gets his man."

Linc looked at Monahan and could see the wheels turning. Monahan said, "I'll eventually identify the other guy, Zeke. Hopefully he gets pinched for something. Then I can squeeze him into giving up Glee, but I still need a legit witness. Shit. It was the middle of the afternoon. Someone had to see something. What I'd really like to know is who the hero was that chased after them and fired shots at their fleeing asses. I would really like to talk to him. Hey pal, you ever worked the Linden Houses? You have anyone that might help me out?"

Linc knew that the hero Monahan referred to was Shortfinger. It was he who had gotten off a couple of shots at the males, now known to Linc as Glee and Zeke. Linc tried to read Monahan's eyes to see if he was being played, but Monahan just stared at Linc, causing him to look away. "Nah, Detective. I never been over to the Linden Houses. Me and the Sarge generally work up north. The only project we might work is Cypress,"

"Well, feel free to read the case folder. See how a homicide is worked."

"Yeah, thanks, but I was just trying to pass the time until A.C.S. gets here for the kids. Thanks anyway." He handed the folder back to Monahan. He still felt a little uneasy about being questioned by Monahan about the Linden projects, and he wasn't sure if Monahan bought it. Linc thought that he would hate to be interrogated by Monahan. Maybe he was just paranoid, but he felt any question Monahan asked him, Monahan already knew the answer. *And he is a sharp son of a bitch,* Linc thought, *interviewing C.I.'s in a church rectory. Nobody would ever think of · a crook going into a rectory.*

Little did Linc know that Monahan's brother, Timothy, had an agreement with a fellow priest and friend, Father Michael Fennell, that allowed Monahan to use the rectory offices for such occasions. Father Fennell was more than agreeable, since like many Irish priests, he had one brother who was a cop, and another who was a fireman. Father Michael's brother was "Patty" Fennell, a legendary Bronx cop who worked out of the tough 4-6 Precinct. Both Father Mike and Timmy knew that as a Murder Cop, Kevin Monahan was doing God's work. They both felt that it was the case-catching detective's responsibility to speak for the deceased. That thought was enough to justify Kevin's utilizing the rectory office.

As Linc finally began to calm down, he heard the booming voice of Detective Joe McQuirke yell, "So, who were the punk bitches that killed one of the Smalls family?" McQuirke and Sergeant Dover had just returned from the crime scene on Monahan's case. A big, ruddy-faced Irishman, McQuirke was the opposite of his partner Benny Archer. McQuirke drank like an English soccer fan, ate his red meat while it was still bleeding, and enjoyed Italian pastries more than sex.

"Ah, man, Joe, don't get these two riled up," said Archer. McQuirke ignored the pleas from his partner and walked over to the cell.

"You didn't know that, heh, you two shitheads. The guy you torched was not only a war hero, but was part of the Smalls family. That means something around here."

"What are you talking bout, you big-headed mutafucka?" asked the taller one.

"What am I talking about? The man you killed was Darren Smalls, get it? Smalls! Even two stupid shit-bags like you should understand. A couple of the boys waiting outside the precinct told me to ask you fuckers what color lip gloss you liked? What you

did ain't no juvenile Spofford time bullshit. You two are going to
Rikers, with the big boys, and I do mean big. Their gonna open up
your assholes so wide the number 3 train will be able to make local
stops inside your rectums."

All the cajoling and threats to keep quiet could not have the
effect on the Brownsville thugs as what McQuirke had just told
them. Both sixteen-year-olds now realized the magnitude of what
they had done, and both sat down on the wooden bench inside the
cell. They remained relatively quiet, except for some occasional
sobbing.

Monahan grabbed Sergeant Dover and explained the results
of his interview with the woman arrested for the arson/murder of
her husband. The woman had told Monahan that the two children
were foster children. She and her husband could not conceive, and
she felt that having children in the house might stabilize their
relationship, but it didn't. The husband would come home drunk
after work and use the woman as a punching bag. When he began
to strike the children for no reason, she had had enough. She had
known she could not just leave him, because he would track her
down wherever she went and, more than likely, he would kill her.

Knowing her only hope was to kill him before he killed her
and the two children, the woman had gone to the store and bought
a can of lighter fluid. She had thought she would never have the
nerve to use it, until today. He came home, drunk again, and he
complained about the dinner she had cooked for him. When she
turned away from him, he hit her in the head with the plate. The
woman had shown Monahan the large bump on the back of her
head.

The children had begun screaming, and the man had
threatened to beat them with the strap he kept in his night-table
drawer. Praying that one of the neighbors would call the police, the
woman begged the man to lie down, promising to cook him
another dinner. He eventually calmed down and lay on the couch
to watch television. The woman knew it would be only minutes
before he was sound asleep in a drunken stupor.

Satisfied that he wouldn't wake up, the woman brought the children into their bedroom and began packing clothes into their backpacks. Instructing them to remain in their room and not to make any noise, she went into her bedroom and packed a suitcase with her belongings. Quietly, she brought them out of their bedroom and led them out of the apartment and into the hallway.

She instructed the children to remain there until she came out of the apartment. She went back inside, removed the can of lighter fluid from underneath the sink, grabbed a bathroom towel, and soaked the towel with the flammable liquid. She then lightly sprinkled the fluid onto her husband's pants and covered him with a sheet that had also been soaked in the fluid.

She opened a kitchen drawer and took out a clothesline she had purchased when she had bought the lighter fluid. She then stuffed the bathroom towel underneath the couch. She set fire to the towel and to the bottom edge of the sheet that lay atop her sleeping husband. The towel underneath the couch immediately went up in flames, and at that point the woman ran out of the apartment and into the hallway.

Quickly, she tied one end of the clothesline to the door knob of her apartment, and the other to the knob of the apartment just across the hallway from hers. She instructed the children to press the button for the elevator and to wait there for her. If the elevator came, she told them, they were to hold the doors until she got there. As she was making sure the knots were secure, she heard a scream from inside her apartment. At that point, her husband's clothes had caught fire and in a panic he ran to the door screaming, looking for an escape from the smoke-filled apartment. He tried to open the door, but the taut clothesline that was now stretched across the hallway made that impossible. The husband then began banging on the door, pleading for help, but not for long.

As she grabbed her suitcase, the woman heard the elevator doors opening on her floor, and she ran to the elevator. Leaving her husband to suffer an excrutiating death, she and the children made it to the lobby, where they were stopped by the two policemen.

She had no regrets about the death of her husband, but she expressed sorrow for the two children, who in their short time on earth would now be resettled with a fourth foster family. Before living with the woman, the brother and sister had been with two other families, both dysfunctional. Drug dealing had been discovered in the squalid apartment of their first family, in Crown Heights, and during their stay with the second family, they had been discovered wandering along Fordham Road in the Bronx at 3 a.m., abandoned by their new "mom and dad."

Linc had overheard most of Monahan's recount of the interview with the woman. Growing up in the projects, too often he had witnessed the same kind of scenario, although never one as violent. He was almost ashamed at himself for not feeling empathy for the two children. To him, it was just the way life was within the tall brick buildings.

A uniformed cop arrived in the squad room to announce that Administration for Children's Services was downstairs, ready to take the children. The brother and sister knew the drill, so they both stood up and grabbed their backpacks that had been stuffed underneath Boyd's desk.

"You all take care of yourselves, everthin gonna be a'ight," said Linc.

The little girl stopped and gave Linc a quick wave with her small hand, but her brother just stood there and looked at Linc with sorrowful eyes. He then pointed at a drawing he had left on the desk and said quietly to Linc, "That's for you, and thanks for the McDonalds." He then ran up and grabbed his sister's hand, and they followed the uniformed cop out the swinging gate to the stairs leading to the front desk.

All the noise in the squad room had stopped, as the street-hardened detectives watched the two youngsters leave the safety of the squad room. Each one silently hoped that the two children would finally find a home, where they could lay their heads at night on soft pillows, be covered by warm blankets, and know that all their tomorrows were going to be just fine.

Linc walked over to the desk and picked up the drawing. It was a crude, stick-figure picture, depicting a boy looking up into a darkened sky. From the sky, rain and lightening bolts descended upon the boy. Next to the boy was written the word ME.

Linc carefully folded the drawing and placed it in his back pocket. As he began walking out of the squad room to find Kolitoski he stopped, feeling an emotional battle raging within him. He suddenly pulled the drawing out of his pocket. Standing above a garbage can, he began ripping the paper into little pieces, watching them drift slowly down into the can. He knew that if he kept the drawing he would dwell on the boy's misfortunes. The miserable fuckin husband was dead. Justice had been served. He had to remain focused. It was time to settle the score for his old friend, Tarface. Glee needed to be paid a visit.

# CHAPTER 9

Johnny McKeefery was sitting comfortably inside the pub that carried his surname. He was in his favorite, strategically placed chair, the one right next to the opening behind the bar. Sipping a cold glass of free Pabst, he was trying to keep an eye on his brother, Tom, who was tending bar. He was also watching the construction workers at the opposite end of the bar from where he now sat. They had been repairing the boardwalk down the block and were now finishing up a late lunch. They had even had something to eat.

They had just squared up the bill with Tom, and Johnny was well aware that, like most working stiffs, construction workers were very good tippers. He knew the timing had to be just right. His luck seemed to be holding out, as four guys from the insurance agency down the block had sat down at a table and ordered some burgers with their beers. Tom had taken the food order from the insurance guys, and he was now walking into the kitchen just as the construction workers were placing their tips on the bar.

Johnny quickly stood up and pulled a bar rag out of his back pocket. He squeezed his oversized stomach past the opening and effortlessly slid behind the bar, wiping it down with his special bar rag. Knowing he had very little time, he glided down to the end of the bar and yelled to the construction workers, "Thanks guy's. Hope to see you boys tomorrow!"

Placing his rag over the forty-two dollars, (Johnny was very adept at counting cash quickly), he began to slide the money along the bar, directing it towards his pocket, when suddenly he heard the booming voice of Detective Matty Boyd yell, "Hey you fat fuck, you ain't allowed behind the bar!"

With that, Tom ran out from the kitchen and screamed at his older brother, "I can't take my fuckin eyes off you for one second!"

"Nah, Tom, these construction guys spilt a shit load of beer on the bar and, knowing you were busy, I was just gonna help you clean it up. Can you imagine these cheap fucks Tom? They didn't leave a fuckin tip! And after all those buy-backs you gave them. I saw the no tip, and I told them they better not come back into our joint any more!"

Tom walked over to his brother, "Open up the rag, Johnny."

Johnny opened the rag, and out fell three tens, two fives, and two singles. Recovering quickly, Johnny said, "I guess when I was cleaning up the beer the bills must have stuck to the bottom of the rag. I guess I owe those guys an apology."

"You sit here all fuckin day, lapping up free beer, eating more hamburgers than Wimpy from the Popeye cartoon, and you still got to steal money?"

Sheepishly, Johnny walked past his brother, and once again took up his position on his barstool, now seated next to Matty Boyd. "Why didn't you keep your mouth shut Matty. I would have given you a ten."

Matty laughed and ordered up a Guinness.

As it was only a few weeks before Christmas, multi-colored strings of blinking lights had been hung across the back of the bar, right above the mirror, giving the place an aura of an underground gay bar. The requisite Christmas songs had been added to the jukebox. Hearing the words, "I'm dreaming of a white Christmas/ Just like the ones I used to know/, further depressed many of the depressed souls, whose only reason for being at the bar was to forget about those long-ago white Christmases.

"Hey Tommy, ain't Dennis supposed to be workin?" asked Matty.

"Yeah, supposed to be, but he's down in Florida on another one of his golf getaways. He plays more golf than Tiger Woods, and still has trouble breaking 100. What brings you down here anyway, pal?"

"I'm meeting your cousin for a pre-Christmas drink. I haven't seen him since I left the squad. Been talking to him on the phone, but this is our first time meetin up."

The early winter darkness had descended upon Rockaway, leaving it a virtual ghost town, a sharp contrast to it on summer nights, when city day-trippers would make Rockaway seem as crowded as South Beach. The winters were a welcome relief to the residents of the peninsula, as the frenetic crowds and noise of summer were an imposition on their normal lives.

Perhaps what gladdened the Rockaway residents all the more was that they once again had unfettered access to their local pubs. Just as the pubs in Mother Ireland were gathering places to discuss all subjects from the weather to world politics, so were places like P.J.McKeefery's to the Rockaway Irish. Following dinner, many meandered down to their favorite watering holes, to enjoy the warmth and comfort only a local pub could provide.

As McKeefery's began to fill up, in walked Monahan, his eyes taking a minute to adjust to the disquieting, blinking lights, while his ears absorbed a rendition of "Frosty the Snowman". He spotted Matty seated next to his cousin Johnny at the end of the bar, but before walking over, he stopped by a table to give his favorite waitress, Deidre, a kiss.

Deidre, originally from the town of Youghal, a port city in county Cork in Ireland, had been coming to Rockaway every year since 1993, to work the summer bars on a work visa. Five years ago she had finally gotten her citizenship and decided to remain in Rockaway. Deidre Killeen was fast approaching forty, and her jet black hair was slowly being invaded by gray roots. Years of working tables and tending bar had kept her body firm and her tongue sharp.

While growing up in Ireland, Deidre had married a childhood sweetheart. Her young husband had worked the fishing boats out of Youghal. Soon her husband's love for the sea had outshone his love for Deidre, so after two years of marriage they separated and finally divorced. A year after her divorce Deidre made her first trip to Rockaway. During that first summer in Rockaway, she fell in love with the place. Born on the water herself, the Irish lass had saltwater coursing through her veins. Along with her black hair, Deidre had dark eyes making her what was commonly called "black Irish."

In her early years of working in Rockaway, she had never wished for a long term relationship, as her love for Erin pulled her back after every summer. When she finally decided to settle in Rockaway, she was in her mid thirties, and the good men had been taken, all but Kevin Monahan. She and Kevin had tried to make a go of it, but after a few months of living together, she knew it would never work.

Just as her first man loved the sea, so Kevin loved being a cop. Experience had taught her not to attempt to compete with a man's passion, so they parted amicably, and still would get together occasionally, when primal urges surfaced. She often thought that perhaps when he retired, if he ever could, they would get together once again and while away their golden years together, sitting in sand chairs on the beach, enjoying the beautiful salt air and their love for one another. Until then she would just have to satisfy her self with the quick, soft kisses he gave her when entering and leaving the bar.

"You look particularly lovely tonight, darling," Kevin whispered, after the kiss and a warm hug.

"Don't you be givin me any of your Rockaway blarney bullshit, Kevin Monahan. I've much work to do, so go down to the end of the bar and sit with your pain-in-the-ass ex-partner. And while you're at it, see if you can get your fat cousin out of here as well. He doesn't think I see him eyeing me tips."

Kevin laughed, giving Deidre a gentle slap on her firm rear as he walked over to Matty. His cousin, Johnny, turned to him and asked, "Hey, Kevin, do you fill up your car a lot?"

"Yeah, I guess so, why?"

"Well, like I was just telling Matty, what if you got into an accident and you're car gets wiped out. With the price of gas you could be out forty or fifty bucks at least, because you know the insurance company ain't gonna pay for that gas. That's why I never put more than a quarter of a tank in my car. Makes sense, right?"

"Yeah, Makes sense. But that means you have to stop for gas all the time!"

"So what? What the fuck else do I have to do?"

Matty glanced over to Kevin and shook his head. "It's this type of scintillating conversation I have been having with your esteemed cousin for the last fifteen minutes. Thank God you're here. I actually feel my brain turning to mush."

After ordering a Guinness from Tom, Kevin said, "So, talk to me, Matty. What's been going on? How is the new job?"

"Kevin, the place is totally fucked up. I can't complain about the overtime, but I never stop. They are now trying to play catch-up with the background checks for the class that graduated in July. Some of these graduates are living all over the place: Jersey, upstate, a couple still in Pennsylvania. They signed those bullshit, "I promise you" forms, but quite a few never moved into the boroughs or adjoining counties. Now that we're doing complete records checks, we're finding more and more with active warrants.

"They let some of these guys in that had gang tattoos on them. That's what I'm doing now, doing residency checks and interviewing neighbors, shit that should have been done before these people raised their right hands. At least I get a car, and my background checks are mostly in Brooklyn and Queens."

Matty stopped and took a long gulp of Guiness. "To make matters worse, my partner is a career Applicant Investigation guy, and he has about as much balls as Lieutenant Fisher. Speaking of which, how is, 'Anybody-seen-my-gun' Fisher?"

Kevin laughed. "Well, you'll be happy to know not much has changed in that department. The other night shots were fired around the block from the precinct, and McQuirke saw Fisher dive underneath his desk. Other than that, everything else is still the same. Place is still a madhouse.

"One of those July graduates made a good collar the other day, got me plenty of overtime. It was an arson/murder. Kid named Linc. I think his last name is Watson or Wilson, something like that. Anyway, seems like a good kid, has some good street sense, but there's the rub. There is something about him, can't put my finger on it. He's always looking around, at any papers on desks, photos on walls, shit like that. The day of the collar, I found him going through one of my case folders that I had stupidly left on your desk, and when I talked to him about the case, he wouldn't look me in the eye. I don't know. Maybe I'm just being paranoid."

"Hey, that's one of a detective's greatest assets, being paranoid. Kevin, when Fisher came out from underneath the desk, did he have a garbage can on his head?" They both began laughing as they faced the bar to down the remainder of their Guinness, when someone came behind them and banged their heads together.

"Now is this any way to celebrate the upcoming birth of our savior, the Lord Jesus Christ? That's the problem with you Irish. You find any excuse to drink. Someone dies, you drink. Someone is born, you drink. Someone takes a good shit, you drink." They both recognized the voice of Kevin's younger brother, Father Timothy Monahan.

"Now this is what I want to know." said Boyd. "You, Father Monahan, just uttered a profanity, I think the word was *shit*. Now who do you confess that venial sin to, I wonder? And what would your penance be? I'd bet you wouldn't even have to say one Hail Mary, because you priests are just like cops. You all stick together."

The tall, lanky priest quietly replied, "Penance, Matty? Don't talk to me about penance and the Catholic Church."

*

Right after Father Timothy had been ordained, he had been sent to his first parish, St. Bridget's, located in a quiet little town called Leeds, in the upstate Catskills. Leeds and the surrounding communities were populated mostly by Germans and Irish. The Germans had their Lutheran church, while the Irish flocked to St.

120

Bridget's. Many of the Irish had originally come, during the late 1950's and early 1960's, from Rockaway and certain sections of Brooklyn, such as Flatbush and Crown Heights. Irish from Woodside in Queens and the University Heights/ Fordham sections of the Bronx were also well represented.

Each summer, buses would leave from the neighborhood pubs and transport families up to what had become known as the "Irish Alps," to vacation in the many hotels that dotted the bucolic countryside. Places like Duffy's, The Sligo House, Gilfeather's, and O'Shea's would post No Vacancy signs throughout the summer. Many of the vacationers fell in love with the rolling green mountains and cold, clear streams and decided to take root in the small towns. There was plenty of work in construction, as the giant Albany mall was just breaking ground and the University of Albany was expanding its large campus.

Father Timothy was assigned to St. Bridget's in 1984, after two years of missionary work in East Africa. Leeds seemed like heaven to Father Tim. He embraced the cold, Catskill winters as well as the hot summers, because he loved the quiet serenity of the area.

An intelligent, affable young man, Father Tim was one of three priests who served St. Bridget's. They were supervised by Monsignor Walsh, who was responsible for all the Catholic parishes in the Leeds, South Cairo, and East Durham areas. Almost as adept with numbers as his cousin, Thomas McKeefery, Father Tim was charged with maintaining the accounting ledgers for the small parish.

After examining the books for the first quarter, Father Tim noticed quite a bit of the collection money and other donations was being entered as "miscellaneous" by one of the other priests, Father Rutherford. At year's end, when he went to balance the books, Father Tim discovered that almost forty-percent of the monies collected had made their way into the miscellaneous fund. When he asked Father Rutherford what exactly the miscellaneous fund consisted of, he was told not to worry, that it was no concern of Father Tim's.

Father Tim's conscience began to bother him. So one Sunday, after Mass, when Monsignor Walsh had stopped by St. Bridget's, Father Tim confided his concerns to the Monsignor.

"Father, I will be sure to investigate the matter thoroughly," the Monsignor said. "Good work, and thank you for bringing this to my attention,"

One week later, Father Timothy was sent on a missionary assignment, to a remote area of Chile. There he remained for another two years before being sent back to the Diocese of Brooklyn to serve in the St. Jerome parish in East Flatbush.

There wasn't much concern about money manipulation at St. Jerome's, as many of the parishioners lived just above the poverty line. The East Flatbush community was over ninety-percent black. A majority of the inhabitants traced their roots to the West Indies. Catholicism had been introduced to the islands by the French and Spanish invaders, and it still remained the predominant religion for many of the people.

The Sunday masses at St. Jerome's drew a great many of the faithful, but they had little money to give, and needed so much. Father Timothy was constantly busy consoling mothers whose sons had been lost on the violent streets of the gang-infested community. Many times he took money out of his own pocket to help defray the cost of a burial. He prayed with mothers whose sons and daughters had succumbed to the sinister call of the crack pipe.

Walking down Rogers Avenue or Newkirk Avenue, Father Timothy would make sure his white collar was visible, in hopes that he would not be set upon by the gangs of thugs that inhabited the corners. From his bedroom in the rectory, he was often awakened by sharp cracks of gunfire, and he would pray that another mother's son had not met his end on these hard streets of Brooklyn.

Father Timothy would often reflect on his time at St. Bridget's, when he had taken long, leisurely strolls down tree-lined country roads, sometimes not seeing another human being for hours. In the lush, green fields he had sat and watched deer peacefully grazing against a beautiful mountain background. The air had been so fresh and invigorating, the only noise coming from birds or the rushing water of a mountain stream.

Now, walking down Flatbush Avenue, he would be wading through a sea of humanity, hearing the cacophonous sounds of livery van drivers blowing their horns, sidewalk vendors yelling, and the loud, hissing sounds of bus doors opening and closing.

And the smells! The favored ingredient in many of the West Indian dishes, curry, floated through the air, invading the nostrils of every person walking along Flatbush Avenue. The sidewalk vendors offered steaming pots of oxtail, curried goat and chicken, and Father Timothy's favorite, the spicy Jamaican Roti. As bucolic and pleasant as St. Bridget's was, it was on the hard streets of East Flatbush that Father Timothy felt he belonged, among people who needed his direction and guidance more than he could ever imagine.

*

As he stood, sipping his Guinness and chatting with Kevin and Matty, he felt a gentle pull at his elbow. Deidre said, "Now, don't you be talking to these two for any length of time, Father Tim, for sure they will be leading you down a dangerous path."

"I'll try not to, Deidre, but it's difficult to walk away from two lads who won't let me take a dollar out of my pocket."

"Ah, even Jesus himself was tempted by the devil. Just make sure you reject the temptations, just as he did."

"I always do, Deidre. I always do."

Deidre stared at the tall, handsome priest and said, "Now, when is the church gonna give up on this foolish celibacy thing? It's a cryin shame that a lovely lookin man such as yourself has to spend his nights alone. You know that St.Peter himself was married, and for hundreds of years after Christ died, priests had been married and many even had children. Do you know why it all of a sudden changed?"

"I have a few ideas, but let me hear the Killeen version."

"Money, Father Tim, money. The Church wanted all the property and any money a priest owned. They didn't wish to see it left to the man's wife or children. So the edict was proclaimed, stating no man would be allowed into the priesthood if he had a wife. I'm hoping they end it, so I can finally walk down the aisle with a Monahan," she said, slyly glancing at Kevin.

Kevin ignored the dig and ordered a shot of Tullamore Dew to go with his beer.

"Deidre, please, let's not talk about money and the Church, for the next thing I know, I'll be on a plane to Somalia," said Father Timothy. Deidre laughed and walked away to tend to the crowded tables. Father Tim also walked away from Matty and Kevin, letting the two partners catch up on department gossip and rumors. He made his rounds, greeting old neighborhood friends, making sure everyone was still attending mass regularly.

After another couple of hours of drinking and bullshitting, Matty finally said, "Well, pal, I know you're swinging into your days off, but the rest of us aren't so lucky. I got to get up early to start my background checks on the young ones. For the next week or so I'll be out in Queens, plus Bayside ain't within walking distance from here. I better get going."

Kevin, although feeling no pain, knew better than to say, "C'mon, have one more." He knew he could never forgive himself if his partner got jammed up with a D.W.I. rap, or worse, a fatal crash. Kevin stood up and gave Matty a hug, "Don't be a stranger, boyo."

Matty bid all a good night and walked out into the cold Rockaway air.

Father Tim then made his way over to Kevin, "Take it easy on the Tullamore, brother. You know it summons the demons inside that thick skull of yours. I'm going to get going, Kev, and

I'm gonna take an Irish exit. If I had to say good night to everyone in here I'd be here for another hour, at least."

The brothers gave each other a hug and Kevin gave Father Timothy a drunken kiss on the top of his forehead, "I don't know what I would do without you," said Kevin, slurring his words. Father Tim said goodbye to his cousin Tom, and left the bar out the back door from the kitchen.

Kevin stayed for almost another hour, and after being rebuffed by Deidre when he asked her to sleep at his place, he also made his exit out the back, no longer wishing to speak to anyone. He staggered down 116th Street to the promenade, where he stopped to listen to the ocean waves pound the fragile shore. They always sounded much louder during the winter.

Kevin began taking deep breaths, in order to clear his head of the thoughts that began to seep slowly into his brain. He knew quite a few cops, who had had too much to drink the night before, would pull up to E.M.S. trucks and ask for hits on the oxygen tank. The oxygen seemed to rejuvenate the alcohol-damaged cells within the body, and the cop would feel like a new man, but alas, like most good things, the fix was only temporary. After fifteen or so minutes, the cop would feel like shit again, realizing he needed to suffer through it. Either that, or chase E.M.S. trucks around all day.

Kevin continued to walk home, fumbling for the house keys in his pocket. After spending a couple of minutes attempting to get the key into the keyhole, Kevin made it inside. He made it into his bedroom, kicked off his shoes, and placed his holstered off-duty .38 caliber Smith and Wesson in his nightstand drawer. Flopping down onto his bed, fully clothed, Kevin did not wish to close his eyes. Once he did however, he was sleeping inside a pickup truck on a rural road in South Carolina.

He fought to open his eyes, in order to get out of the pickup truck, but it was just no use. Looking out the front window of the pickup truck, he saw the lifeless body of Thomas Mickens lying on the dusty road. Suddenly, Kevin was driving the pickup straight at the twenty-three-year old black man. Kevin could see the contorted face of the male, his left arm hanging limply by his side, his skull split open, with blood seeping out of the wound. But it was the eyes. Kevin had seen those eyes at close to a hundred crime scenes. They stared blankly into the abyss, unable to blink or move from side to side. They looked straight ahead, as if they were now focused on a new path.

Kevin raced towards him in the truck. As he was about to run over the male, he awoke and sat up, his clothes drenched in sweat, his heart pounding like a jackhammer within his chest. "Please God, no! No more!" he screamed. He reached over to the nightstand, picked up the phone, and even in his drunken state, he remembered the number.

"Hello," answered the sleepy voice on the other end.

"Bless me, Father, for I have sinned. It has been eight days since my last confession. I watched and did nothing as an innocent young man was beaten to death. After he was beaten and later died, I failed to report the crime to the authorities. That is my sin."

"Kevin, you had me worried. I thought it was one of my parishioners. Before I fell asleep I heard five shots go off. They were close. Had to be down the block on Newkirk Avenue. I knew the demons would appear again when I saw you start with the Tullamore. Why do you do this to yourself? Every time you start with the Irish firewater, be it Tullamore or Jameson's, I know I can expect a confession call in the middle of the night. You've done your penance, Kevin."

Father Timothy was silent for a few moments, and then he said, "You've brought many a murderer to justice. Its God's work you're doing, man. There is nothing you can do to bring the poor Micken's boy back, and the two lowlifes that did it are gone, serving their time in hell. Kevin, you're a cop, and a very good one at that. Remember what Jesus said to his disciples: "Blessed are the peacemakers, for they shall be called the children of God." That is you Kevin. You're a cop, a peacemaker. Now go to sleep, and for my own health, please lay off the whisky. Then I might get a good night's sleep. The whiskey opens up doors inside your mind that should remain locked."

As always, Kevin absorbed the comforting words. "Thanks, Father. Sorry to have wakened you." Tim hung up the phone and Kevin lay back down in bed, staring at the ceiling, the phone still in his hand. Kevin began to doze off when he was suddenly awoken by a voice instructing him that, if he wished to make a call he needed to hang up and dial the number again, or if he needed help he should dial the operator. Kevin thought to himself, *maybe that's what I need to do, call the operator instead of my brother, I'm sure he would agree with that.* He hung up the phone, stood up and removed all his clothes. Slipping on a new pair of boxer shorts, he opened one of his bedroom windows, and he lay back down on his bed. Kevin knew he would have to get to sleep soon, because within a few hours, the alcohol in his system would be converted into sugar, and he would suddenly be wide awake. The black crow would be perched on his headboard, cawing, seemingly laughing, at the tormenting thoughts flying through Kevin's mind.

Kevin knew that he could not continue like this. He knew he would eventually have to do something to erase the pain.

# CHAPTER 10

Linc had enjoyed his day off. He had loaded the sled into his car after breakfast, and he and Harris had ridden the hills at Highland Park all afternoon, just as they had done with their father when he was still alive. The fresh, clean white snow seemed to erase all the dark thoughts inside Linc's head. Dark thoughts brought on by some of the horrific jobs he had responded to while on patrol.

Just two nights ago, he and Kolitoski had responded to an aided call, a child in distress, but it turned out to be much worse than a child in distress. A crackhead mother who had just hit the pipe, decided that her four-month-old baby daughter needed a bath, so she filled up the kitchen sink with water. Unfortunately, the water was hot enough to kill a live lobster, and, without testing the temperature, the mother slipped the baby into the sink. The baby's screams alerted a concerned neighbor, who dialed 911. When the officers responded to the apartment, the door was open, the mother had fled, and the baby was lying on the floor in the kitchen, in shock and near death, with second and third degree burns throughout her body. Her once black skin was now white, as the black epidermis had been burned away.

Linc had wrapped the child in a wet towel and run down to the patrol car with the baby in his arms. Rather than wait for E.M.S, the cops sped, with lights and sirens, to Brookdale Hospital. The doctors at Brookdale did what they could, but ultimately, they wound up sending the baby to the Cornell Burn Center in Manhattan. Linc could not imagine how some cops could witness those kinds of atrocities for twenty years.

Sleigh-riding with his brother was a welcome relief from the pressure he was beginning to feel. Between work and school and trying to provide Silky with intelligence, he was burning himself out. Regretfully, he never got to spend much time with Harris, something he always enjoyed. Today, however, was different.

128

Days like today, made him remember just how much he loved his brother. After a full day on the hills, both were looking forward to the hot meal of roast beef, roasted potatoes, and corn, promised by their mother.

It was just after 5 p.m. when they entered their apartment and Linc's phone rang. He walked into the bedroom he shared with his brother and shut the door. It was Shortfinger, "Yo, what's up, Shorty?"

"Listen up, cuz, I been clockin that muthafucka Glee, and I got his shit down to the minute. We got to do this tonight though. Word on the street is he be goin down to North Carolina to live with his people. He heard 7-5 D.T.s be onto his shit."

Linc was suddenly in turmoil. He knew what had to be done. He had even gone so far as to *borrow* a bubble light out of one of the unmarked cars from the precinct. He had also begun bringing his assigned police radio home each night, making sure he had a freshly charged battery for the radio before he left work, just for this occasion. There was a long pause before he answered, "Yo, B, you don't even got a car yet."

"Nah, man, I got that covered. One of the spanny men in my building be parking his Crown Vic right on Wortman. I got it scoped out. It's a livery, bro, all dark colored and shit. Looks just like a po-po unmarked. We all good. You sound like you goin soft on me, cuz. You a'ight?"

"Soft? What the fuck you talking bout? I'm the one tol you who the muthafucka was, didn't I? We gonna go hard on that bitch! You got your burner?"

"Yeah, cuz, got a 9, just like you. You sure we shouldn't let Silky know what's goin down here, bro?"

Linc had thought about it, and he figured the less Silky had on him the better. Besides, Tarface was his and Shortfinger's boy. To Silky, Tarface was nothing more than an employee. "Nah, cuz. This is our bizness. Somethin only me and you gots to know about. You feel me?"

"True-that, true-that. Listen up, at bout 10 o'clock the muthafucka be hangin with his boys on Wortman and Ashford. Ain't nothing happening, he carries his stink-ass down to Shepard and Cozine. Be looking for some pussy down there. You meet me at Cozine and Vermont bout ten thirty, a'ight?"

"That can happen, Shorty. Catch you later." Linc was a bit apprehensive after hanging up the phone. He knew Monahan was a very good detective, but he also knew that it had been over one year since Tarface's murder and no witnesses had come forward, and Linc doubted that any would, meaning that muthafucka Glee would get away with murder.

Linc had held off telling Shortfinger about Glee, or how he had come to find out that Glee was the shooter. Knowing how sharp Monahan was, he wanted to wait awhile before he made a move on Glee. It would have looked much too suspicious if Glee wound up dead not long after Linc had been caught reading Tarface's case folder.

Now it was a little since over two months since he had read the folder. *Enough time*, thought Linc. When Glee was found dead, it would be just another crack-selling project punk that had succumbed to one of the hazards of the job.

He washed up, and sat down at the dinner table, with his mom and brother. He had suddenly lost his appetite, and his mother noticed it right away. "What's bothering you, boy? You would never leave one roasted potato in that bowl, never mind a half a dozen."

"Just not that hungry, moms."

"Since when? I don't know, Linc, but I think the police job seems to be getting to you. You don't eat right, don't sleep right, and your mind always seems to be somewhere else. You get up, go to school, come home, go to work, come home, go to bed. We hardly ever see you. You're wearing yourself out, boy."

*You should only know*, thought Linc.

Noticing that his brother was becoming upset, Harris chimed in, "D- D-Don't worry, mom, I'll e- e-eat the rest of them p-p-potatoes, okay?"

Linc smiled and playfully slapped his younger brother on the back of the head. "Listen, mom. I just got to put a little bit more money away to pay for school. Then I'll quit the police job, I promise. I always told you I'm gonna be a teacher, and I mean it."

"Allright, baby. I know. I'd feel a whole lot better if you were a teacher. I know you work in a quiet neighborhood in Queens, but there still got to be some danger there. I just worry that you look tired all the time. Sometimes I see you sitting on the couch, watching T.V., but I can tell you ain't really watching it. You seem to be just staring off into space, like you got a lot of troubles on your mind."

"You right, mom. I am tired. Matter of fact, I'm just gonna lay down for a little while. I'm hooking up with Shortfinger later. I haven't seen him in a while."

"Okay. That's good. You got to keep in touch with your old friends. You can't forget them. Make sure you tell Devon I said hello, when you see him. You got to invite him up so I can cook a nice dinner for you boys. Now you go lie down and get some rest."

Linc stood up from the table, thinking about what his mother said. He placed his dish and silverware into the sink. He walked into his room and, too tired to remove his clothes, he lay down on his bed. Linc was glad he had told his mother he was assigned to a quiet Queen's precinct. He knew that she would be worried sick if she ever discovered that he was actually patrolling sections of East New York.

It wasn't long before Linc descended into a fitful sleep, dreaming of scalded babies and little boys upon whom rain constantly fell.

*

Linc had to admit, Shortfinger did well with the car. It was a black Crown Victoria, very similar to the vehicles used by the anti-crime teams and the detective squad. Shortfinger was seated in the

131

front passenger seat of the vehicle, while Linc was outstretched in the back. Linc had learned this tactic by watching the anti-crime and S.N.E.U. teams on stakeouts. A lookout might very well spot a police type vehicle, but all he would see would be one person sitting in the front. Lookouts knew that cops worked in pairs, and hit teams would surely have more than one person to carry out the deed, so the lookouts' suspicions would be lowered. More often than not, they figured it to be a livery car.

Shortfinger had been impressed. "Boy, you even thinking like 5-0 now!"

The two friends had the car parked on Ashford Street, between Wortman and Cozine Avenues. The nighttime temperature had dipped into the upper twenties, and the heater was on full blast. A light snow began to fall, which made it all the more difficult to clock Glee's movements.

Shortfinger had done a quiet recon about one-half hour ago and Glee, as was his habit on cold nights, was standing in the lobby of the 920 building. Glee was bullshitting with two other members of the Boulevard Houses gang, but business was slow. Shortfinger didn't figure Glee would be hanging out much longer. What concerned Shortfinger, however, was that because of the cold and the snow, Glee might not go out for his daily booty-call with his favorite crack whore down on Fountain and Flatlands, but Shortfinger knew Glee was a fiend. At the very least he would have her bobble-head on his junk.

Outstretched in the back, Linc felt his knees begin to stiffen up, so he decided to step out of the car to get a good stretch. The snow had just stopped falling, and it had left a blanket of white on the grass skirts that bordered the sidewalks along Ashford Street. Before exiting the vehicle, Linc did a quick surveillance, and all he saw was what appeared to be a bum, wearing a green army fatigue jacket and a black knit cap, walking on the opposite side of the street. The bum appeared to be walking toward the Boulevard Houses.

Linc stepped out of the car, eyeing the bum as he just kept walking with his head down, his hands in his pockets. Realizing he was standing underneath a streetlight, Linc moved a few steps into the darkness because, for some strange reason, Linc began to get an uneasy feeling about the bum. He thought the man looked familiar.

*

Shawn loved to walk. Every day, as long as he didn't have a doctor's appointment, he walked to the 7-5 Precinct and did his "tour." Then he would walk back to his apartment at 920 Stanley Avenue. At night, as long as he ate everything on his plate, his mother would give him two dollars, and Shawn would walk from his apartment down to Cozine Avenue.

He would then stroll west along Cozine, until he reached the stores along Pennsylvania Avenue. There he would buy some Devil Dogs, or Suzy Q's, and sit on a bench, watching all the shoppers walk by. Shawn saw and heard everything. He could hear whispered conversations of the passersby. The problem was that he had difficulty understanding what the people were saying. It was the same with his eyesight. Although he had the mind of a child ten or eleven years old, he also had the sharp eyesight and the keen hearing of a boy that age.

Thankful that it had stopped snowing, Shawn began walking back from the stores. He had taken his usual route, walking east on Cozine Avenue, then turning north to walk along Ashford Street back to his apartment. He suddenly heard a car door open. Shawn glanced up quickly, and he saw the face of a kid he knew. He had difficulty processing where he recognized that person from.

Shawn continued walking to his building, and once inside the lobby he waited for the elevator. Three kids were standing in the lobby. Shawn's mother had told him numerous times never to speak to the boys hanging out in the lobby, but Shawn had never understood why. The boys were buttoning up their jackets, looking like they were getting ready to leave. *Their moms probably want them home too,* thought Shawn. The elevator arrived, and Shawn rode it up to the fifth floor, where he entered his apartment, safe for the night.

*

"Yo Linc, get back in the ride, he's comin out of the lobby!"

Linc jumped into the driver's seat of the car, made a quick u-turn on Ashford and headed down to Flatlands Avenue. He parked the car on Flatlands, a little west of Ashford, and the two friends waited. Within a few minutes they spotted Glee at the corner of Flatlands and Ashford. He stood on the corner for a good minute, looking up and down Flatlands Avenue. Linc and Shortfinger both slid down under the dashboard.

"Muthafucka is on point!" whispered Linc.

"I tol you that, cuz, he know the 7-5 D.T's be lookin for him."

Linc slowly slid up, and glancing over the dash board, he saw Glee walking east on Flatlands towards Fountain Avenue.

"He on the move, Shorty."

"See. I tol you that muthafucka be a sex fiend, every night, could be raining, snowing, any muthafuckin thing, that boy gotta get some. That crack–ho must have some kind of evil spell over that nigga. Muthafucka must be taken that Niagara shit or something, man."

"Viagra?" asked Linc.

"I don't know that bitch's name, man. All I know she be skanky. Hey, how you find out her name?"

"Never mind," said Linc, shaking his head. "Yo, listen up, we got to have our shit wired tight here, cuz. You remember the plan?"

"Yeah. I do nothing. I let you do all the talkin."

"That's it, cuz. Now let's do this." Linc slipped on his blue windbreaker, a jacket that had N.Y.P.D. written in large, white letters across the back of the jacket, along with the official N.Y.P.D patch on both sleeves. He then pulled the car slowly out onto Flatlands Avenue, making sure to keep the headlights off, lest they spook their target. The cold weather had swept the streets clean of people, and no other cars were driving on the dimly-lit street. They could not have asked for better conditions.

*

Glee was walking east on Flatlands towards Fountain Avenue, and he had just passed Berriman Street when the black Crown Victoria with the red flashing dashboard light pulled up in front of him. *Just my fuckin luck,* he thought to himself. He had planned on heading down to North Carolina in two days to stay with his cousins, as word on the street was the 7-5 detectives were looking for him for the Tarface shooting. To make matters worse, he had a 9mm Beretta tucked in his waistband at the small of his back.

Glee froze, and was about to run, when a tall black cop with an N.Y.P.D jacket jumped out of the car and pointed a black gun at him.

"Police! Don't move, muthafucka, or I will light you up!" yelled Linc.

"A'ight, a'ight officer. I ain't goin nowhere," said Glee, raising his hands in the air. "Yo, what's this all about? I ain't done nothing. Just walkin over to see my girl."

Linc had his police radio on, so Glee could hear the radio transmissions, which would hopefully prove to Glee that Linc was a cop. "Yo, listen up homeboy. A call just came over the radio for a robbery over on Pennsylvania Avenue, and you fit the description. We just want to ask you a few questions," said Linc.

Glee felt some relief, as he knew he wasn't involved in any robbery on Pennsylvania. He might still get down to North Carolina after all. At that moment though, he saw a second black male exit from the passenger side of the Crown Vic, this male had no radio or Police jacket, but he did have a gun in his hand.

Linc made his way around the back of the vehicle and approached Glee, his 9 mm Glock 17 trained on Glee's chest.

"Yo, officer, you makin me nervous. I ain't done no robbery. I been in my building over at Boulevard all night. Got witnesses." Glee glanced over at the second male, and suddenly recognized him as the punk who had shot at him when he smoked that boy Tarface. Now he was beginning to recognize the cop that had the gun on him. He had seen him steerin on the bench outside 180 Wortman when they recogged the buildings before the shooting. *Both these muthafuckas work for Silky,* he thought to himself. Glee slowly began to put his hands down. "You ain't no muthafuckin cops. You punk asses be from Linden."

"Linc, shoot the muthafucka!" yelled Shortfinger.

Everything was going on in slow motion. Linc saw Glee's arms begin to drop to his sides, and he knew he should pull the trigger, but his hands began shaking, and, despite the cold, sweat began forming on his brow. He saw Glee's lips moving, but he could not hear a thing, and all he saw was the face of his father. Glee's right arm reached around his back, and suddenly Linc heard an explosion from his left side, then another and another. Glee fell back into a parked car, slowly sinking onto the cold street. Linc turned and looked at Shortfinger, whose outstretched arm still held his 9mm Llama. The smell of gunpowder hung in the cold night air, like the smell of Roman candles at a July 4th fireworks display.

"Linc, let's jet, man, 5-0 be coming soon!" screamed Shortfinger, as he grabbed Linc by the elbow. The mention of 5-0 awoke Linc, and he and Shortfinger began to run to their car.

"Wait, holdup, Shorty. The casings!" Linc ran back to where Shortfinger had been standing, and he pulled a mini-mag lite out of his windbreaker pocket. He found himself extremely focused, as he began to search for the three casings that had been ejected by Shortfinger's gun. He knew it was important to find the casings, since they could be matched up to the weapon. There would be ejector marks on them, as well as impact marks on the bases of the shells from the firing pin.

He located two casings right away, and was frantically searching for the third, when he heard the words he had been dreading, spoken by the Communications operator over his radio: "All units, be advised, in the 75 Precinct we are receiving numerous calls of shots fired. Vicinity of Flatlands Avenue and

Sheppard, Flatlands and Berriman, and Flatlands and Atkins. Need a unit to respond."

Linc knew that every sector car that wasn't on an important job would be responding. He only had about three minutes to find that last casing. He dropped to the ground and shone his light under the parked vehicles.

"7-5 Frank, Central. Do we have any description?"

"Negative, Frank. Checked the callbacks. All callers stated they heard anywhere from three to seven shots fired from that area. Are you responding, Frank?"

"4, Central, about two minutes out."

Linc then heard the voice he hoped he would not hear. "7-5 Training Sergeant. Show me responding, also about a two minute ETA."

"10-4, 7-5 Sergeant. First units 10-84, please advise."

Linc knew that Big Gino Williams would be driving Kolitoski, which was not good. Williams was one of the craziest, yet most proficient drivers in the precinct. He loved speed. Williams would drive 100 miles per hour to respond to a drunk and disorderly.

Linc finally spotted the casing underneath a white Nissan Sentra. He dropped onto his stomach and crawled as far as he could under the vehicle, but the car was too low for him to get very far underneath. He heard the approaching sirens in the distance.

"Any units 84 on Flatlands?" It was Kolitoski.

"Sarge, 7-5 Charlie will be 84 in about one minute."

Linc stretched as far as he could under the Nissan and touched the casing. As soon as he touched it, it rolled further away. *No more time,* he thought to himself.

Leaving the casing underneath the Nissan, he jumped to his feet and ran to the car. Shortfinger was in the driver's seat. Linc could see the stobe lights from the approaching police cars dancing off the Boulevard Houses project buildings, just a short distance away. Shortfinger began to make a u-turn on Flatlands, to head to Canarsie, which was covered by the 6-9 Precinct. The 6-9 was on a different radio frequency, so their cops would have heard nothing about the shooting on Flatlands Avenue.

"No. Fuck that," said Linc. "They're gonna have us boxed in. Go down the block to Fountain, make a right, then go right on Vandalia to Erskine. Erskine will take us onto the Belt Parkway. They won't have anyone coming from there. We'll be safer. Keep your headlights off until we reach Vandalia."

Shortfinger floored the Crown Vic, racing the five blocks until he hit Fountain Avenue. As he made the right onto Fountain, he took the turn too fast, and the vehicle caught the corner curb. The car bounced off the curb, and Shortfinger momentarily lost control of it, righting it just as it was about to plow into a Ford Explorer that was traveling north on Fountain.

The Explorer driver lay on the horn of his car, honking at the crazy driver with no headlights on.

"Okay, okay," said Linc. "Start to slow down. Last thing we need is to get in a fuckin accident. We're comin up on Vandalia. Turn on the headlights." Linc gripped the dashboard for dear life.

Shortfinger made the right on Vandalia, and the quick left onto Erskine Street, which put them on the Belt Parkway heading westbound. Shortfinger got off at the next exit, Pennsylvania Avenue, and proceeded north, back to the Linden Houses. He pulled up in front of Linc's building.

Shortfinger hadn't said a word since the shooting, but now he said, "Man, what the fuck happened to you back there, cuz? You fuckin froze on me. That muthafucka almost drew down on us B."

Linc looked at his lifelong friend and really did not know what to say. How could he explain that he didn't think he had the balls to carry out a cold-blooded murder. As Kolitoski had told him, "We execute them, we're just as bad as they are." Linc was in turmoil. Sure, he hated Glee for what he had done to Tarface. The more he thought about it, however, Tarface had known the dangers of the business in which he was involved, a business Linc no longer wanted any part of. *Bottom line,* thought Linc. *Unlike his father, Tarface didn't die an innocent.*

"Answer up, cuz, what the fuck happened? You can't shoot the muthafucka, then you go all Bruce Willis, Die Hard, tryin to find a casin while the po-po be bearin down on us. I was hearin those sirens and seein those lights. Yo, my balls were up in my stomach, an I look, an you still tryin to crawl underneath that car. That was some crazy shit, man. Boy, you one complicated muthafucka, Linc."

"Shorty, I can't answer you up. You right, shit is gettin complicated. Hear me, bro. You got to get rid of that gun. I couldn't get that last casing, and I know they probably gonna recover some lead out of our boy Glee. They can't match it to a gun if there ain't no gun. You feel me? You got to get down to the Canarsie Pier, down by the Bayview projects, and toss that gun into the bay, a'ight?"

"Ah, man, I be havin this Llama since I was a young pup. Yo, we got away clean an shit. No sense losin a good piece."

"Shorty, no fuckin around. Promise me you gonna dump that burner. And make sure you wipe this car down before you dump it." Linc stepped out of the car and began walking towards his lobby, leaving Shortfinger almost in tears at the thought of having to part with his most prized possession.

*

"7-5 Sergeant to Central K, be advised I am 10-84 at Flatlands and Sheppard Ave. We have one male shot, likely. Have EMS respond. Also notify the 7-5 Squad and the Duty Captain. Also be advised, Central, I am calling a Level One mobilization at this location for Brooklyn North Task Force to respond as well."

"10-4, 7-5, Sergeant. Do we have any description on the shooter?"

"Negative, Central. Be advised that a dark-colored Crown Victoria was observed leaving the scene immediately after the shooting. All we have right now is a dark Crown Vic, no plate number. Vehicle was being operated with no headlights."

After relaying his transmissions, Kolitoski began directing the cops at the location to begin to establish a crime scene. He knew his transmission had stated that the victim was likely to die, but Kolitoski also knew the victim was already dead. He needed EMS however, to verify that fact and give a time of pronouncement. As he began to walk toward the body he saw a flash from a camera go off. Shock and Awe, the two Housing cops, were one of the first units to respond to the scene, and now they were adding to their photo collection.

Officer John "Awe" Fulfree was crouched down in a catcher's stance right next to the lifeless body of Glee. After being fatally shot, Glee had slid down the side of a white Toyota Camry, and now his legs were outstretched onto the street. His back was being supported by the rear driver's side door, and his head was tilted, lying on his right shoulder. If one did not know better, it would appear that Glee had just decided to lie back against the car in order to get some sleep, which in a way he was, permanently.

Fulfree had his right hand on Glee's shoulder while flashing a gang sign with his left hand. His partner, Officer Steve "Shock" Hannigan, was taking pictures of the couple with an old, yet reliable, Polaroid One Step camera. This allowed the two photo collectors to view their handiwork immediately. Many of the younger cops at the scene had never seen such an odd contraption, and were amazed that a picture was developed instantaneously!

The two big Housing cops then switched positions so that neither one's feelings were hurt. With Glee's picture, that brought the partners' homicide photo album up to twenty-eight pictures. They would only take photos with victims that fit their community service homicide profile, that is, murderers, drug dealers, robbers, rapists, and gun-carrying thugs.

Kolitoski knew of the two Housing Cop's wild reputation, and also knew he had to end the photography session, as the Duty Captain and the squad would be at the scene shortly. He also saw that the E.M.S. truck had just pulled up. "Hey guys, finish up. EMS is here."

"Well, they're just gonna have to wait their turn, Sarge!" yelled Hannigan. The two cops looked at Kolitoski and saw he was not laughing, so Fulfree quickly said, "Sorry, Sarge. We're all done, we'll be right there. Hey, Sarge, I think the squad is here."

Kolitoski turned, and walking towards him were Sgt. Dover and Detectives McQuirke and Monahan.

Sgt.Dover was the first to speak the traditional opening line, used by countless detectives throughout the ages when coming upon a homicide. "Hey, John, so what do we got here?" he asked Kolitoski. Monahan and McQuirke each pulled out the standard detective notepad, and McQuirke left the group to speak to EMS and the first officers who had responded to the scene. Monahan remained to hear Kolitoski's version of events.

Kolitoski said, "As of right now we have an unidentified male that was shot. It appears he was shot three times in the chest. The shooter must have been fairly close as the bullet grouping is all in the center mass. The 911 calls that brought us here were all the result of hearing gunfire. No one provided any type of description of the bad guys.

"We do have a possible witness, standing over there. He was driving that white Ford Explorer, coming northbound on Fountain, when a dark-colored, what appeared to be a Crown Vic, made the right off of Flatlands up there, to go southbound on Fountain. Witness stated that the vehicle was traveling at a high rate of speed, with its headlights off. The driver of the Crown Vic couldn't negotiate the turn and bounced off the curb, almost colliding with the witness's Explorer."

"That would have been a shame," said Monahan. "Did he get a look at the driver, or how many were in the car?"

"He is sure he saw two male blacks, seated in the front. Couldn't tell if there was anyone in the back. As far as evidence, I got the Emergency Service guys from Truck 7 looking for anything and everything."

"Victim had no I.D. on him?" asked Dover.

"No. We did a quick search of accessible pockets and couldn't find anything. Might have something in the back pocket, but we weren't gonna move him until Crime Scene is done with him."

"You sure you didn't find a library card on him? Glee was known to spend a lot of time at the library" said a chuckling voice from behind Kolitoski. It was Fulfree. The big, black cop then said, "Only kiddin of course, Sarge. Me and my partner here will give you nothing but love. We can help you out identifying that puddle of piss sitting in the street like he's waitin for a bus. That there is Damon Miller, also known to all that love him as "Glee." Only he ain't showing much glee now, is he?"

Almost on cue, Hannigan took over the conversation, "Miller is from the Boulevard Houses, think he lives at 725 Stanley, but that will be easy enough to find out, since Miller has been taking collars since he was about fourteen, mostly for drugs, some strongarm robs when he was younger. I'm sure you're gonna find a gun on the muthafucka when you do a complete search. This here was truly a misdemeanor homicide. Gonna be a lot of happy residents in Boulevard tomorrow, when they hear Glee is on the non-stop flight to hell."

Monahan had been writing everything down in his notepad, but stopped at Fulfree's mention of the name, Glee. "I had this guy marked for a shooting, I think it was in the Linden Houses, over a year ago. I can't remember the vic's name though. Before you ask, Sarge, I hadn't collared him because I had no legitimate witnesses. My only I.D on him was from my C.I."

"Makes sense," chimed in Hannigan. "Boulevard and Linden have always had a longstanding beef. Boulevard has been trying to muscle in on Silky's drug sets forever."

It bothered Monahan when he could not remember a victim's name, but there were just so many, and as he had become older he had found his memory ebbing. Another issue was bothering Monahan about Glee, but now was not the time to mention it.

*

After Shortfinger had dropped him off, Linc rode the elevator up to his apartment. It was almost eleven-thirty p.m. when he quietly opened the door. As he did every night or early morning, after returning home, he glanced in to check on Harris, who was sound asleep. He was about to go into the bathroom when he saw a light shining from underneath his mother's door. Slowly opening the door, he saw his mother lying on her bed, tucked under the covers. The lamp on her nightstand, was on, and she was engrossed in her newest novel from the Oprah Book Club, *The Road*, by Cormac McCarthy. She was so intent on her reading she never heard Linc enter the room.

"Hey, Moms," he whispered.

His mother dropped her book and placed her hand over her heart. "Oh my God, baby. You almost gave me a heart attack!"

"Sorry, Moms. Good book?"

"Oh, yeah. I haven't gotten one bad book from Oprah's club. How you doin baby? Hey, how was Devon? You told him I promised him a meal, I hope."

"Yeah, Moms. Said he couldn't wait. He doin good, stayin out of trouble. Lookin for work, you know."

"Well, I hope so. Hope he don't take after that no-count Uncle Bernard of his. Unless he gonna get paid for sleeping on a couch all day, that man ain't never gonna find work. I just feel so bad for the mother. Baby, you still look exhausted, you got to work tomorrow night, why don't you go in and get some good sleep."

Linc walked over to his mother and gave her a kiss on the top of her head, "I am, Moms. See you in the morning." As he walked out of his mother's room, he suddenly stopped, "Mom, can I ask you a question? Did Pops ever talk to you after he was gone? You know, you ever see his face, or hear his voice?"

His mother put her book down once more, "Lincoln, every night after I reach out and shut off this light I speak with your father. I tell him what happened during the day and how proud he would be of his two sons, especially you, Linc. And sometimes when I'm troubled about something, you know, not sure what to

143

do, I can hear your father's voice, clear as a cold winter morning. He guides me, Lincoln. Why you ask that, baby? Did your dad speak to you? Did he give you guidance?"

"Yeah Moms, I think he did.

# CHAPTER 11

Detective Matty Boyd had just turned off the Belt Parkway and was headed north on Cross Bay Boulevard. The gold Caprice's heater was operating just well enough to send his partner, Detective Joe Angelo, into one of his frequent slumbers. It was the beginning of March, and Matty hoped the heater would not be needed much longer, but then again, his partner might stay awake, which wouldn't be good. They only had a couple of more checks to do for that day, and both checks were in the Ozone Park section of Queens. Matty looked over at his snoring partner and shook his head. *Imagine if this guy had to do some real police work,* he thought.

Angelo had been assigned to Applicant Investigation for almost eighteen years and had actually received the coveted detective's shield. Years ago, Applicant Investigation was part of the career path, which, like most things about the job, irked Matty to no end. Remembering how he and Monahan had received their gold shields by locking up bad guys in the Robbery unit in the 7-5, or other cops had to work undercover narcotics to get their shield, it bothered the hell out of Boyd that his new partner had received his by checking on prospective candidates for the N.Y.P.D.

Matty knew there was some career liability in reviewing prospective candidates in the Applicant Investigation Unit. For instance, if you stamped "Recommend for Hire" on a candidate's case folder, and he or she wound up get locked up while on the job, the bosses would immediately try to find out who recommended the candidate. Angelo never had to worry about that, however, because if there was any hiccup in a candidate's background check, Angelo automatically rejected the hire. *And that was a shame,* thought Boyd, *as quite a few potentially good cops were rejected by sleeping beauty because they had not cleared up some parking tickets.*

Boyd made a right turn onto Liberty Avenue, and the noise from the train on the overhead el awakened Angelo. Angelo shook the cobwebs from his head and looked out the passenger side window.

"Where are we Boyd, Liberty Avenue? Oh, man, this street is a fuckin horror with traffic. We're gonna wind up getting done late. Let's do these two tomorrow."

"Hey, Joe. The only reason I'm in this fuckin unit is to make overtime. If I get stuck, so be it. How the fuck can you pass up easy overtime like this? There are squad guy's doin homicide canvasses in piss-smellin apartment buildings, buildings where you need to wear two vests to feel safe. They would kill for O.T. like this."

"I'm not gonna hear one of those, "When me and Monahan were in the 7-5" stories again, am I?"

"Joe, I only tell you those stories so that when you have one of your infrequent barbecues, you can tell your neighbors, Biff and Chad, some real police shit. You can even make believe you were there. I can just imagine the stories you have to tell, like, "Yeah, Biff, I had this candidate come into my office and, would you believe, he admitted right to my face that he had smoked pot. I threw him out of my office, right then and there!""

To conduct neighbor and past employer interviews, the N.Y.P.D had recently instituted a program in which they hired, on a per-diem basis, retired Applicant Investigation supervisors to conduct those interviews. The caseloads however, were backed up, so Applicant Investigation detectives were assisting with the interviews. Otherwise many Applicant detectives, like Joe Angelo, were content never to leave their office but to do all of their business over the phone.

Boyd made a right turn onto 114th Street, and continued south until he came to the corner of 107th Avenue, where he pulled over. He pulled a folder out of his briefcase and began reading the particulars.

"Jesus, this kid has been out of the academy nine months, and we're only now getting around to checking him. Lincoln Watson, currently assigned to the 7-5 Precinct. Did I ever tell you I used to work there, Joe?"

"Only every fuckin day! Come on. Let's get this over with."

Boyd sat there, silently thinking to himself, *Lincoln Watson. Where did I hear that name?* Boyd had sharp recall when it came to names, and he suddenly remembered that when he was with Monahan, right before Christmas at McKeefery's, the kid had given Monahan a ground ball homicide collar. This should be a slam-dunk. The kid seemed as if he was going be a good cop.

"Don't get your balls in a bunch Joey, my boy. This one should be a piece of cake." Boyd exited the car, and wasn't surprised to see that Angelo remained inside the vehicle. Walking south on 114th Street, he located the address Linc had listed as his residence, 107-06 114th Street. Boyd knew that most of the kids worked nights, so there was a good chance he would be home. Maybe the kid could catch Boyd up on some 7-5 gossip.

The house was a single family residence, with white vinyl siding and a black roof. Black vinyl shutters bordered the front windows, and a brick walkway intersected two sections of a manicured lawn. Walking up the five brick steps to the front door, Boyd noticed that the front evergreen hedges were also well taken care of. Boyd could look right into the front windows. To the right, he looked into a kitchen area, while on the left he viewed a small living room. He rang the front doorbell.

A large, older black woman answered the door. Dressed in a pale blue housedress, she stood on the inside of the glass door, and she looked at Boyd from head to toe, trying to determine if he was going to try and sell her something, or if perhaps he was a Jehovah's Witness. She pushed her black-rimmed glasses down from the bridge of her nose to the tip, in order to get a better read on the stranger at her doorstep.

"I ain't lookin to buy anything, and I'm a church-goin Baptist, so don't be wastin my time, or yours, mister." As she was about to shut the door she noticed the gold shield being displayed in the good-lookin white man's hand.

"I'm Detective Boyd ma'am, from the N.Y.P.D. Sorry to bother you, but I was looking for Lincoln."

Boyd noticed right away that the woman seemed taken aback, as she said, "Um, well, Lincoln ain't here right now. You have to come back another time."

"Doesn't he work nights?"

"Uh, yeah, he does, but I think he be at court right now"

"Well, it's you I really would like to speak to. Would you mind if I came in?"

The woman slowly opened the door, "Where are my manners? I'm sorry, officer. I was just a little surprised. Lincoln ain't in any trouble, is he?"

Stepping into the well-furnished house, Boyd smelled the delicious aroma of chicken cutlets frying on the stove. "No, he's in no trouble. This is just a routine check of his residence, something that should have been done months ago. He has listed on his residence report that he lives with his grandmother. Is that you, ma'am?"

"Well, um, he really is my godson. Him and his moms never got along, and when she heard he was going to be police, she didn't want anything to do with him."

"Where does his mother live?"

Nervously, the big woman said, "Um, I think she lives in Brooklyn somewhere, you see she ain't no kin to me, I'm closer to Linc's father's side of the family, but he took off a long time ago, so when Lincoln needed a place to stay, he asked if he could live with me."

Boyd noticed beads of sweat forming on the woman's forehead. "Are you okay ma'am? By the way I didn't get your name?"

"Well, I gots the hypertension, besides some diabetes."

"Your name, ma'am?"

"Oh, I'm sorry officer. Um, my name is Dorita, Dorita Tucker. I'm not feelin real good right now, officer. I think I got to take my medicine and rest. You be needin anything else?"

Boyd glanced at Linc's resident sheet, and saw that Dorita Tucker was the name Linc had listed on his residence form, only he listed her as his grandmother. Something was just not right, "Would you mind if I took a quick peek at Lincoln's bedroom?"

"Oh, no. I'm sorry, officer. His room be locked all the time, you know, cause he have his guns and whatnot in there. You got a card or something I can give him when he gets home, so I can have him call you?"

Boyd reached into his shield and I.D. Card case, and pulled out one of his cards. "Here you go. Have him give me a call, and if there is anything you want to speak to me about, you feel free to call me also. I hope you feel better, Ms.Tucker. And those chicken cutlets smell delicious. You cookin them up for Lincoln?"

"No, actually, I got a man friend comin over a little later. Lincoln always be going out on dates. He got plenty of girlfriends, he's hardly ever here."

"I see. Okay. Well, again, I'm sorry to have bothered you. You get some rest now."

"I sure will," she said, as she quickly led Boyd to the front door. Boyd walked down the steps and out into the street, and he could feel her eyes watching his every step. He opened the door of the Caprice and slid into the driver's seat.

An agitated Angelo said, "I thought that you said the case would be a piece of cake? What the fuck took you so long? You tryin to make time with the kid's grandmother, you fuckin degenerate!"

Boyd started the car, put it into drive, and made a quick u-turn on 114th Street, even though it was a one-way, but he wasn't going far. "Will you shut the fuck up for one second?" he said. He pulled up onto the corner of 107th Avenue and put the car in park. "I know I don't have to say this, but stay in the car, I'll be right back," he told Angelo, as he opened the door and got out of the vehicle.

In order not to make any noise, he did not shut the door completely. He began jogging back to the address. When he got to the property line, he ducked down and hurried up to the front of the house. Crouched down behind the evergreens, he slowly lifted himself up and peeked through the window that opened to the kitchen. Sure enough, he saw Dorita Tucker on the house phone. *She could be calling Linc,* he thought, *but why not do that while I was inside with her?* Something just did not feel right to Boyd.

*

"You never tol me I be getting a visit from the fuckin police!" she said. "Blue eyed mother-fucka scared the shit out a me, asking me all kinds of questions I ain't had no answers to!"

"Chill, Aunt Dorita," said Silky. "I'll take care of this. I'm gonna send Bam-Bam out there to get the D.T.'s card, then I'm gonna have Linc call the muthafucka. You gotta relax. You know how your blood pressure get when you get all anxious and shit."

"Anxious? The top a my head was bout to explode! That sharp-eyed muthafucka seen me sweatin, him lookin around the whole house, like he some kind of Jew landlord or something. I should have never let the bitch in."

"You ain't got no choice, you had to let him. Linc'll call him, and you won't see the D.T. anymore."

"I better not see that heart-attack maker again, or---."

"Or what? You old bitch! Who's payin half the rent on that muthafuckin house, heh? Me, that's who. When Housing throw your fat ass out of that shit project apartment and into the street, who took care of you? I ask you for this one favor, an you cryin like a little bitch!"

"A'ight, Silky, a'ight. You right, you right. Just that the muthafucka got them eyes stare right through you, eyes that be sayin, "I know you lyin to me bitch."

"You all paranoid and shit. Just give Bam-Bam the card, I take care of everything."

150

Boyd jogged back up to 107th Avenue and got back into the car. Angelo, who was very annoyed that he probably would not be getting onto the Long Island Expressway until after 4 p.m, said, "You all done with your covert ops shit. Its' gonna be two fuckin hours now for me to get home. You gonna tell me what's going on?

"I don't know, Joe. Something just doesn't seem right. The kid is supposed to be livin there, but I saw no signs of a male livin in that house. No sneakers or shoes layin around. The washer and dryer room is right off the kitchen, and the door was open. She had a full clothes basket on top of the washer, and I didn't spot one item of men's clothes. No dirty socks, no underwear or T-shirts. What guy doesn't have a dirty pair of socks that need to be washed? And there was no smell."

"Smell? What the fuck are you talking about, smell? What are you, a fuckin deer?"

"Listen, I've been in hundreds of homes and apartments and I can always pick up a scent if a male is living in the house."

"So, now you can smell men? You want me to pick you up an application for the Gay Officer's Action League?"

Ignoring the comment, Boyd pulled a photo of Linc from his case folder. It was the black-and-white passport style photo that every candidate is required to submit to the Applicant Investigation Unit when they are called for candidate screening. "There's one more thing I want to do, Joe."

Ignoring Angelo's groans, Boyd drove past Dorita Tucker's address and pulled the Caprice over to the curb, about two houses south of 107-06. Boyd noticed the shades were pulled down at the Tucker address. *She thinks we might be coming back, and with the shades drawn she can pretend she is not home,* thought Boyd.

He exited the vehicle and walked up the small stairway to the house directly to the left of 107-06. Immediately spotting the shades on the front window being closed, Boyd rang the doorbell.

151

*This woman, if it is a woman, doesn't miss a trick,* thought Boyd. *A woman that knew everyone's business.*

A frail, light skinned black woman of about sixty slowly pulled the door open. She looked up and down the block in order to see if anyone was watching her talk to the man in her doorway. "Can I help you?" she asked in a whisper, as if someone could hear their conversation.

Figuring he would make her feel more comfortable, Boyd whispered back, "Hello, ma'am. My name is Detective Boyd with the N.Y.P.D. Just want to take a second of your time. If you could please look at this photo and let me know if you have seen this person in the neighborhood."

The woman opened her glass door a crack, and reached a skinny arm out the door to retrieve the photo. She studied it for quite a while and said, "What a good looking boy! And all dressed up in a suit and tie. Is he in some kind of trouble?"

"No. Absolutely not, ma'am. He might have witnessed something, and we just need to speak to him a bit."

"I saw you parked in front of Ms. Tucker's house next door. Did she ever see him?"

*Well*, thought Boyd, *she just answered my question.* "I can't disclose that, ma'am. Just like I would never tell anyone what you tell me. Everything is strictly confidential."

"Well, that's good to know. Everybody is so nosy around here. No officer, I have to say, I've never seen this young man around here." She handed Boyd back the photo.

Boyd thanked her for her time, and gave her one of his cards, asking that she call him if she did spot the male in the area. He then crossed the street to the house directly across from 107-06, knowing that Ms. Tucker might be watching his every move. As a detective, he knew that stirring the pot sometimes produced unexpected, yet beneficial, results.

The gate to the walkway at 107-05 114th Street was off its hinges, and an old brown Ford Torino sat neglected on one side of what might generously be called a lawn. Boyd climbed the broken steps and knocked on the wooden door. The screen door had apparently been ripped from its jamb some time ago. After five loud knocks, Boyd was about to leave, when he heard the door being unlocked.

A skinny, Hispanic male with wild eyes, wearing a ripped sweatshirt, peeked out the crack of the door, "What you want?"

"Police. Just want to show you a photo. See if you recognize someone."

The agitated male yelled at Boyd, "I want an attorney! You can't arrest me unless I speak to an attorney. I don't have to say anything to you. Am I free to go?"

Boyd stared at the apparent lunatic and thought to himself, *why me?* "Yeah, amigo, you're free to go. Just don't come back here any more, comprende?"

"Okay. I won't. You had to let me go cause you didn't read me my rights!"

"Yeah, that's right. Listen, I'm gonna give you a card with my phone number on it. If you have any money problems or hear any strange noises, you call the number and I'll take care of it." He then handed the loco Hispanic one of Detective Angelo's cards, one of the many that he had taken from Angelo's desk for occasions such as this.

Boyd walked down the steps figuring he'd better quit while he was ahead and before Angelo had a nervous breakdown, knowing that his two-hour ride was increasing exponentially one half-hour for every fifteen-minute delay. Boyd pulled off his sports jacket and opened the door of the car. He then threw Linc's case folder onto the back seat before sliding into the driver's seat.

"My ride will be completely fucked, you know that, Boyd? I hope you got something after your complete canvas of the whole fuckin neighborhood. You get anything?"

Pulling out his phone, Boyd said, "I think we might be hearing from the Spanish guy in that house over there. Nice man. Seems like he might be very helpful to me." Boyd dialed the 7-5 Precinct desk.

"7-5 Desk. Officer Keavney. How can I help you?"

"Hey Kevin, Matty Boyd here. Wondering if you can do me a favor?"

"Do you a favor? After you loosened the fuckin straps on my golf cart at the last outing, and my bag flew onto the cart path? I haven't been able to hit the ball straight off the tee since that happened, you miserable fuck."

"That wasn't me. That was Monahan."

"Yeah, and professional wrestling is on the level. What do you need?"

"Check the day-tour roll call and tell me if Officer Linc Watson had court. I'll hold."

Boyd only had to wait one minute before Keavney came back on the line, "No scheduled court for him today, matter of fact he's due in for a 6 p.m. by 2 a.m. tour tonight. Want me to tell him to call you?"

"No. That's okay, Kev. Do me a favor. Don't even mention I called. Okay pal?"

"You got it, Matty. Be safe."

*The plot thickens,* thought Boyd, as he put the car in drive. *The plot thickens.*

# CHAPTER 12

His whole day had been fucked up, and Silky was in a foul mood. First, he had received that phone call from that fat bitch aunt of his, and then he got the call from his cousin Nigel.

Nigel had arrived from Jamaica almost eight years ago, and hooked up with the Cargill Posse, a Jamaican drug organization whose roots traced back to the slums of Kingston. A vicious, fearless gang, the Cargill Posse originally controlled the drug trade in East Flatbush, and now they were expanding their tentacles throughout Brooklyn. Word on the street was that the murderous gang was even attempting to take over spots in Harlem and the South Bronx.

Silky was to be the point man for their expansion into East New York and Silky, who wished to reach Social Security age, knew better than to resist his cousin's overtures, as he had viewed firsthand the torture inflicted on non-compliant dealers. Just to work with the posse, Silky had to do a "piece of work" to earn the trust of Nigel and his boys.

\*

A stubborn crack dealer had said no to the posse, when they had asked to buy his lucrative drug corner spots on Beverly and Nostrand Avenues. To convince other dealers in the area that they did, indeed, mean business, it had been decided by the posse bosses that an example should be made of the recalcitrant drug peddler. Silky was given the job. He had been instructed to gun down the dealer and his girlfriend, who was two months pregnant, while both were coming out of their favorite Roti shop, a shop which they visited daily. The shop was on Church Avenue, and Nigel had insisted the job be done in broad daylight, just to send a message.

Silky remembered standing outside the Roti shop, waiting for the couple to exit, for so long that he smoked half a pack of Newports. When the dealer and his girlfriend had finally come out,

Silky had stepped up behind the two and put three bullets into the back of each of them, as they were crossing Church Avenue. As soon as the two bodies dropped in the street, Nigel pulled up in his black Hummer, but before spiriting Silky away, he ran over both bodies with the big truck. It wasn't the first time Silky had killed someone, but a pregnant girl? *These muthafuckas are insane,* thought Silky at the time.

*

At tonight's meeting, Silky figured that Nigel was going to present him with a timetable of the takeover of the various East New York drug spots. This was no problem, but Silky was pissed off that he had had to drive over to East Flatbush by himself. Bam-Bam would have normally driven him, but he had to send his bodyguard out to Ozone Park to get that stupid fuckin detective's card from his pain-in-the-ass aunt. This Linc shit was beginning to be more trouble that it was worth. *Shit,* thought Silky, *that college-goin muthafucka hasn't been givin up much info lately. He'd be just as valuable back steerin on the bench.* He had to have a talk with that boy, real soon.

Silky was making good time for the meet, but he knew that to be right on time made a big time gangsta like him appear soft, so he decided to stop and get some ribs at a Chinese takeout on Rodgers Avenue. Pulling up in front of the Sweet Mandarin, Silky had to double-park, since no spots were available in front of the restaurant, unless he wanted to walk a half a block, and that wasn't about to happen.

Silky locked the car and entered the small restaurant. He walked up to the counter. The counter had more plexiglass than one would find at a Las Vegas cash-chip exchange window. The owner, Duk Thien, had had it installed after the third robbery. One bullet ding was in the thick glass, a result of an unsatisfied customer's complaint that he had not received enough pieces of shrimp in his shrimp lo-mein.

"I want a large order of ribs, and put some extra sauce on em. And don't short me on the count, Chi-nie man," said Silky.

156

Duk Thien, who was not actually Chi-nie, but rather Cambodian, had arrived in the United States eight years ago. He now worked sixteen-hour days, six days a week, so that his two daughters would not have to when they became adults. Mr. Thien had been a structural engineer in his native country, and he knew the importance of a good education.

Although he had held a position of some standing in Cambodia, and had earned a comfortable salary, he knew his two daughters would not have the same chance when they grew up. In the male-dominated Cambodian society, all that was expected of adult women was that they marry and have children, preferably sons. The Thiens had used all their life savings to come to America, truly the land of opportunity, to ensure that their daughters could become whatever they wished. A position as a doctor, scientist, teacher, or maybe even an engineer was not out of the realm of possibility for a female in America.

Thien felt nothing was out of reach, as long as one was willing to sacrifice, and sacrifice he had. A man who at one time had helped design buildings and roads was now reduced to taking food orders from oftentimes rude, ignorant, and sometimes even violent people. Thien put a majority of his earnings towards the Asian school that his children attended. The school taught the children how to speak and write proper English, placed an emphasis on math and science, and also instilled in the children the cultural and historical importance of their ancestral countries.

"Chop, chop, Charlie Chan," Silky yelled. "I'm double-parked out there, and if I get a ticket you gonna be payin for it. You understand English?"

Thien, who was not only fluent in English, but could speak Vietnamese and also had a passable knowledge of Cantonese, placed Silky's order under the plexiglass opening.

"That's six-dollars and eighteen-cents," said Thien.

Silky opened up the bag and counted out the number of ribs inside. Satisfied, he took a wad of bills out of his pocket and counted out six dollars. "I don't got the eighteen cents, I had to wait too long, anyway."

Thien, shaking his head, knew better than to argue. He took the six dollars and placed it in the register.

As Silky was about to exit the restaurant, a black male about thirty-five-years old opened the door. "Anybody own the black BMW double-parked?"

Silky thought to himself, *those muthafuckin traffic agents.* "Yeah. That my car. What happened? I get a ticket?"

"No, man, but you got me blocked in, I been sittin in the car for five minutes, waitin."

"Don't blame me, blame the Chi-nie man. He took his time getting me my ribs."

"Yea well, the Chi-nie man didn't park your car, cuz. I got to go to work, so get busy and move the car."

Silky could feel himself beginning to get hot, "Chill, old man. You don't know who you be talking to, feel me?"

"No. I know who I'm talking to. I'm talking to some rude muthafucka."

Silky knew he could not miss the meeting with Nigel, and yet he knew this punk was disrespecting him and needed a beat-down. *No man, it ain't worth it,* he thought to himself. He pushed past the male, and walked to his car. As he was about to open the vehicle door he heard, "That's right, you soft muthafucka. Move that piece of shit."

Silky slowly opened the car door and placed the bag of ribs on the driver's side floor mat. Then he closed the door. He clenched the car keys in his right fist and began to walk slowly towards the male.

The male saw Silky approach, and clenched his hands into fists, letting his arms hang down his sides, "You got something on your mind, brother?"

Silky stopped in front of the male, "No, brother, just wonderin why you would wanna call my BMW a piece of...," said Silky, his voice trailing off as he launched off his feet, landing a solid right to the male's jaw. The male's head snapped back, as he fell against his car. Silky grabbed him by his dreadlocks, and began slamming his head into the driver's side doorframe.

At that moment, two rookie cops assigned to Operation Impact in the 6-7 Precinct, turned the corner off Beverly Road. The two young cops heard a commotion, and saw a group of young males urging Silky to "beat down the punk bitch."

Running up to the scene, the larger of the two cops hit Silky, lifting him off the ground with a tackle that would have made Michael Strahan proud. The tackle brought a series of, "Oh shits!" from the interested onlookers. The smaller cop called for an ambulance for the dazed and battered victim, while his partner cuffed Silky up. After calling for the bus, the cop then called for the Sergeant, and for a car to transport Silky back to the 67th Precinct.

*

With names like O'Laughlin and Reeny, one would have thought the two detectives would have been card-carrying members of the N.Y.P.D. Emerald Society. Perhaps they would have, except for the fact that both were as black as a starless night. The two partners had been assigned to the 6-7 Squad for five years, and they specialized in Jamaican gang homicides. A rather quiet night tour, which was unusual for the 6-7, had suddenly turned quite interesting, when young Police Officer Brian Russell brought up a de-briefing sheet for the detectives.

In the mid-1990's, mandatory detective debriefings of prisoners had been one of the many strategic initiatives instituted by Commissioner Bill Bratton and his eccentric yet brilliant Deputy Commissioner, Jack Maple. Detectives were required to debrief every prisoner brought into the precinct by the patrol cops. It did not matter if the prisoner had been arrested for disorderly conduct or armed robbery. He or she was to be debriefed.

The theory was that detectives, who were generally excellent interviewers and interrogators, could elicit information from the arrestee about chop shops for stolen cars, anyone who was carrying or selling guns, and any kind of intelligence or information that would aid in decreasing crime within the city.

The problem however, was that in the busy detective squads, such as the 6-7 and the 7-5, as well as many others throughout the city, the squad detectives were so bogged down with their own caseloads that proper debriefings were almost impossible. A proper debriefing would generally last up to a half hour, and on a busy patrol night a detective could conceivably wind up conducting five or six debriefings. They just did not have enough time.

Many squad bosses would have liked to have designated one detective, perhaps their best interviewer, to conduct all debriefings, but again there was the problem of manpower. Consequently, in busy squads, the detective would just ask the arresting officer if the prisoner was willing to talk. The arresting officer, who wanted to get down to Central Booking as soon as possible, would just say "no". There would be a wink and a nod, and the detective would sign his or her name to the debriefing sheet, indicating that the prisoner had been interviewed by the detective and was not willing to provide any information.

That was why Officer Russell was quite surprised when he heard Detective O'Loughlin yell, "Well, I'll be a muthafucka! Hey Reeny, don't we have a Want Card out for a Gary "Silky" Pitt?"

"Yeah. We dropped it about two months ago. Remember, one of Nigel's boys, Trevor, cut the deal with the D.A's office, told us that he heard someone by the name of Silky was the shooter on the double homicide on Church, about a year ago. The female vic was pregnant."

"Well, we can cancel the Want Card, my brother. Silky is in the house!"

A Want Card, or as it is officially known, an Investigation Card or I Card, is a card filled out by detectives when they wished to be notified that a particular person had been arrested. The detective might wish to speak to that person for one of three reasons: The person sought had been positively identified as having committed a crime, and therefore could be arrested on

160

contact. The person might be a suspect, but there was no probable cause for arrest, yet the detective, as in Silky's case, wished to have a tete-a-tete with the individual. Finally, a Want Card could be issued for a witness.

For example, if the detectives discovered that a particular individual was a witness to a shooting, but that individual did not wish to come forward, they might issue a Want Card for that person. If that person was arrested, he or she might be forthcoming about what they had witnessed, especially if the detective could talk to the Assistant District Attorney who would be handling the case that the witness had been arrested for.

In relation to Silky's shooting, the informant had only heard that the shooter involved in the double homicide went by the street name of Silky, and that he was from East New York. Silky had only been arrested once in his long criminal career, when he was eighteen years old, for Assault 3rd degree, a misdemeanor. While on the #3 train, he had punched out another teen who had had the audacity to accidentally step on Silky's new Air Jordans. A Transit Cop had walked into the subway car before Silky had managed to do further damage to the unlucky teen's face. Silky was quickly collared, and during the booking process he unwisely, as first time arrestees often do, gave the officer his street name.

When O'Laughlin's informant, Trevor, provided the 6-7 detectives with the street name Silky, they dutifully ran the name through the nickname database. A number of Silkys appeared, but only one lived in East New York, one with the government name of Gary Pitt. Unfortunately for the detectives, Silky's earlier assault case on the train had been A.C.D. (adjourned contemplating dismissal). The agreement on an A.C.D. was that if the defendant stayed out of trouble for a period of time, in Silky's case, six months, the case was sealed, and along with it the always-valuable booking mug shot. Silky somehow had managed to stay out of trouble.

O'Laughlin asked, "So Officer Russell, what was our friend Mr.Pitt collared for?"

"Me and my partner came around the corner from Beverly onto Church and we saw Pitt bouncing another guy's head off the door frame of a car. The guy might have a broken jaw and he will definitely need some stitches to the back of his head. Witnesses said the victim actually started it, he got up in the grill of our perp and said something nasty about the perp's car."

"Well, we surely can't be going hard on a man's ride now. What are you charging Pitt with?" asked O'Laughlin.

"He had no weapons," said Russell. "But because of the injuries we charged him with Assault 2."

"Yeah, but with no weapons and because of the witnesses statements, the D.A. will probably drop it to Assault 3. Unless he dies, then the Brooklyn D.A. might keep it at Assault 2," laughed O'Laughlin. "Sorry, Russell, but I can't sign the de-briefing sheet right yet. We're gonna conduct an honest-to-goodness debriefing on our boy Silky. So bring him up, my brother!"

Detective Reeny, meanwhile, was perusing the double homicide case folder, "We really ain't got shit on this case, partner. A week of canvassing only came up with one witness. At least now, with this collar, we have a photo to place in a photo array for the witness to look at. They had the T.I.P.S. van out there for a week, and a couple of calls came in, but nothing panned out."

Reeny continued to read, and suddenly said, "Wait. Hold up! It looks like Crime Scene had seven Newport cigarettes vouchered as Investigatory Evidence. Buono, who caught the case, requested DNA testing on the butts. The smokes were found next to the front door of the Roti place, and they all appeared to be fresh. Bet you the muthafucka was all nervous and shit, smoking up his NewPs, waitin for the vics to come out."

At that moment Officer Russell approached the gate to enter the squad room with a handcuffed, sullen Silky in tow.

"Man, what the fuck am I doin up here," said Silky. "I ain't done shit! That muthafucka attacked me, man, I was just defendin myself!"

162

"Now, now, Mr.Pitt," said O'Laughlin. "Chill, my brother. The 6-7 Squad room is a serene place, a place for relaxation and contemplation, and you are our honored guest."

"Constipation!" said Silky. "Listen, I don't know what you muthafuckas are into, but I ain't pullin my pants down for nobody!"

O'Laughlin shook his head and laughed, as he opened the gate and brought Silky into the interview room. The room was painted a light blue, and a large, brown table was in the middle it. The detective removed the handcuffs and sat Silky in the chair against the back wall, the chair farthest from the door. The detectives would occupy two chairs opposite Silky, giving him the feeling that he was trapped and his only hope out of the room was the two detectives sitting in front of him, but they didn't know Silky.

As O'Laughlin walked out of the room and shut the door behind him, Reeny approached him and said, "I just asked Russell if Silky had any cigarettes on him. He said he did, and guess what brand, cuz?"

"Newports, but all the brothers getting locked up are smoking either them or Kools."

"Yeah, I know," said Reeny. "But hear me out. I call my man Brienzo, down in the D.A's office, and get him workin on a court order to swab Silky for DNA. Then we check to see if the smokes at the homicide crime scene were tested yet. Hopefully, we get a match. We then wait for his B.C.I. photo and try to locate the witness to show him an array. We ain't got nothing else, unless he gives it up in the box. The court order should be no problem, we got a reliable informant, and this was a big media case man, innocent pregnant girl and all, and we got a possible witness."

"Yeah, true-dat," O'Laughlin said. "I just hope they don't want a positive I.D from the witness before the judge will issue the court order. Tell Brienzo we need the court order because this assault is a weak case and Silky will probably get bailed. The D.A's office won't want a stone-cold killer walking around the streets. It should work. A'ight, you make the call and I'll give our boy a go."

While Reeny got busy on the phone, O'Laughlin walked back to the interview room. Before going in, he looked through the one-way mirror into the room, only to see Silky with his head lying on his folded arms on top of the desk. While studying Silky, the detective thought it best, before talking about the homicide, to tighten up the current assault case against Silky. This would provide more support to keep the original Assault 2nd degree charge. Silky might then get a higher bail, and, give them more time to get the court order for the DNA. O'Laughlin walked into the room, and slammed the door behind him.

"What's the matter, Gary? You tired?" asked O'Laughlin.

"Yeah, man, I'm tired." Silky said. "Tired of all this bullshit, when am I getting outta here?"

"Well, you got a problem, my brother," said O'Laughlin. "I just spoke to Kings County Hospital and it seems your boy is in a coma. That was a major-beat down you threw him. You want to tell me your side of the story?"

"I tol you, man," said Silky. "I was defendin myself. Muthafucka attacked me for no reason!"

"I hear that. We been kinda hearing the same thing," O'Laughlin said. "I need you to tell me exactly what happened, and we'll give your version to the D.A. and get this all straightened out. But before you tell me, we just got to get something out of the way. I know you might have been the victim here, but I still have to read you this. It's just a formality." O'Laughlin then removed a Miranda Warning sheet from his folder and laid it on the desk. "Okay, first you have the right to remain silent. Anything you--"

"A'ight, Mr.Detective," said Silky. "You can save your breath." Silky leaned back in the chair and dusted off some imaginary lint off his $155.00 Alex Mill cotton-flannel, navy-blue shirt. He then said, "I think I want to emphasize my congregational rights and remain silent. Also, I want to take the one that talks about getting a lawyer. If you look in my wallet, I got his card right in there, so the only person I want to be talking to is my Jew friend. You feelin me?"

*This is one cool, devious muthafucka,* thought O'Laughlin. *He played dumb, but he is a smart as a fox.* O'Laughlin knew better than to mention the double homicide. *With a perp like this, the less he thinks you know, the better off you are,* he thought. O'Laughlin looked at Silky, who was staring back at him with cold, dark eyes. The detective thought there was no doubt that the man sitting across from him could have shot and killed the drug dealer, along with his pregnant girlfriend.

Although Silky was taller than O'Laughlin, the detective outweighed the prisoner by about thirty pounds, and it took quite a bit of self-control for him not to leap across the desk and pound the shit out of the preening, pompous killer sitting across from him. Finally, staring back at Silky, O'Laughlin said, "You keep eye-fuckin me, homeboy, you gonna be joinin your victim in Kings County."

Silky shook his head and grinned. Sucking his teeth, he said, "I think we about done here, home-boy."

Suddenly and without warning, O'Laughlin grabbed the edge of the desk in front of him and pushed the desk into the unsuspecting Silky, pinning him in his seat against the back wall of the room. Silky grabbed the edge of his side of the desk, but without any leverage he was unable to push it off his stomach. With the wind knocked out of him, he could only stare at the face of the detective, as O'Laughlin continued to push the large table into Silky's mid-section. O'Laughlin finally said, "Now you listen to me, muthafucka, we be done when I say we're done. Now, do you feel me?"

Silky managed to shake his head, yes. O'Laughlin pulled the desk back, and Silky collapsed off the chair, falling to the ground, desperately trying to catch his breath.

The detective stood up, walked out of the room, and went over to his Reeny's desk, "How'd you make out with Brienzo?"

"He gave me a little bit of a hard time," said his partner. "But he's typing out the application as we speak. We get the night court judge to sign it, we'll swab the scumbag tonight. How 'd you make out in the box with him?"

"That's one slick operator in there, son." O'Laughlin said. "He played me and then lawyered up. I don't think he knows we suspect him for the homicide, but he might after the Q-tip is stuck in his mouth. But we got to do it tonight. He makes bail, we might not find his ass again for a while. Call Russell up to take the piece of shit back downstairs. Let him sit in that funky-smellin cell down there. Hopefully, someone will throw up on those crispy threads he's sportin."

O'Laughlin grabbed the handcuffs out of his back pocket, and walked back into the interview room. He pulled Silky out of his chair, threw him up against the back wall, pulled Silky's arms behind his back, snapped the cuffs on the prisoner's wrists, and made sure the heavy metal dug into Silky's wrist bones. Silky winced, but did not complain.

"I'm sure you're gonna beef to your lawyer that you were physically abused, so I'll save you time and trouble. My name is O'Laughlin. That's O, apostrophe, then L,A,U,G,H,L,I,N."

Silky laughed. "You got me all wrong, D.T. I ain't no punk snitch. That ain't the way I roll. I gots the better of you, now you did what you felt you needed to do, I respect that."

O'Laughlin walked Silky out into the squad office to the waiting Officer Russell. The detective saw his partner was already gone, on his way to Brooklyn Criminal Court to walk the court ordered DNA application through the system. "Hey, Russell, did my partner talk to you before he left about what you need to do?"

Russell nodded knowingly. "Yeah. This arrest paperwork is gonna take some time."

*

Detective Reeny was not only successful in obtaining the court-ordered DNA swab, but he was also able to convince the A.D.A. handling Silky's assault case to maintain the Assault 2nd degree charges, which made Silky's crime a felony. The A.D.A. also kept the charges based upon the information provided by Reeny of Silky's possible involvement in the Church Avenue homicides, not that it mattered much, since at the arraignment the next day the $10,000 bail set by the judge against Silky was quickly posted by Bam-Bam.

This was somewhat disconcerting to the detectives, but they had accomplished what they had set out to do when Silky first walked into the squad room. Before he was released on bail, they got to swab inside his cheek for the DNA sample. O'Laughlin deferred to his partner in obtaining the sample, since his relationship with Silky seemed to have gotten off to a rocky start.

As far as Silky was concerned, it had been a bad day. From hearing the complaints from his fat-assed aunt, to his arrest, nothing had gone well. Silky had watched enough "C.S.I-New York," to know that the taking of the DNA swab meant nothing but trouble.

# CHAPTER 13

As part of a moral-building initiative, the Commanding Officer of the 75th Precinct had decided to reward his active rookie officers with assignments to the detective squad for one week. As a mere formality, he had discussed the idea with the squad boss, Lt Fisher, who readily agreed with the Commanding Officer that it was a brilliant idea. After all, it was the Commanding Officer of the precinct who assigned the precinct parking spaces, and Fisher was no fool. He had a prime spot in the lot, almost adjacent to the walkway to enter the rear of the precinct. God forbid he should have to park in the street and walk along Sutter Avenue, especially in the dark. Just the thought, made Fisher feel for his gun.

Linc's arson/homicide arrest made him a shoe-in as one of the officers to be assigned to the squad, along with Ira Gleason, a very active Operation Impact cop. Unlike his fellow rookies, who were generally twenty-one to twenty-five years of age, Gleason had been almost thirty when he had graduated from the police academy. With his age also came a certain amount of wisdom and guile.

His personal folder listed him as both Jewish (his mother) and Catholic (his father), but you have a better chance of finding a Sunni in a synagogue, or a Catholic Church for that matter, than finding Ira in either house of worship of which he claimed membership. By listing both, however, Gleason was able to claim almost all the religious holidays as his own, thus giving him preference when it came to granting days off.

He had also discovered a second cousin on his mother's side was part Spanish, so he also checked off "Spanish" in the ethnicity box on his police application. At the time he figured he might be able to pick up some points on any future promotional exams. Gleason spent much of his off duty time searching Ancestry.com, in hopes of finding a distant Native American relative, so that he might receive even more points on the Sergeant's test. Gleason was short and stocky, with a simian appearance.

His appetite was legendary, and, upon entering the squad room he had said to Linc, "Hey, I always heard the detectives ate well. You don't think there gonna make us pay for our food, do you?"

At the mention of food, Shawn, who had been emptying a garbage pail, suddenly looked up at the oversized cop and eyed him suspiciously. He also looked at the tall, black kid who was standing next to the fat cop. His brain began trying to process where he had seen the black kid. The portion of the brain that controlled Shawn's hunger impulses suddenly took control, however, and thoughts of the black kid suddenly disappeared.

Shawn, sensing gastronomic competition from the gorilla-looking cop, put the pail down on the floor and ran into the squad's kitchen. He quietly opened the refrigerator door, and studied the interior for any leftovers, knowing the big rookie would soon discover the refrigerator and clean out any hidden goodies. Spotting one lonely Dannon Yogurt, Shawn quickly grabbed it and placed it in the right pocket of his army fatigue jacket.

Linc was preoccupied, thinking of last week's meeting with Silky, and never heard Gleason's question. The meeting had not gone well. Silky had mentioned that an Applicant Investigation detective had visited the address that Linc had listed on his police application as his permanent residence. Silky had tried to convince Linc not to be concerned, that everything was going to be straightened out, but Linc was not so sure.

To make matters worse, when Silky had handed Linc the investigator's card, the name on the card read, "Detective Matthew Boyd." Linc knew that anyone who had worked with Monahan for as long as Boyd had must be a competent detective. It would only be a matter of time before the whole charade was exposed.

Silky had told Linc to call Boyd, but Linc was putting it off as long as possible, hoping Boyd had a shit-load of other cases and would place Linc's on the back burner. Linc tried to explain his concerns to Silky, but was brushed off. In addition, Silky screamed at Linc about the lack of information Linc had provided, or failed to provide, in the recent weeks. Linc allayed Silky's anxieties, explaining that he was being temporarily assigned to the detective squad for one week, and a veritable gold mine of information could be forthcoming.

The pressure was becoming unbearable for Linc. Linc knew that between school, helping his brother, providing Silky with intelligence, and performing his job, his resignation with the N.Y.P.D. might come sooner than later.

"Hey, Linc, you hear a word I said?" asked Gleason.

"No, Ira. I'm sorry, man. Got my mind on a thousand different things."

"Well, nothing to worry bout now, my brother. We're out of uniform, gonna be workin decent hours, and most importantly, we ain't gonna miss a meal!"

*

"This is total bullshit!" said Monahan. Once he had heard that the two rookies were being assigned to the squad for a week, Monahan had stormed into Lt. Fisher's office. When he had first observed Monahan walking towards his office, Fisher had attempted to pick up the phone, as if he had received a call, but he was too late.

"Now calm down, Kevin. It's only for one week," said Fisher.

"I don't care if it's for one day," Monahan said. "Since when did babysitting become part of our job description?"

"It's only an experiment. The C.O. wants to reward his good cops."

"Nothing is an 'experiment' on this job. Once something starts, it never stops. I guarantee, if two more rookies aren't up here next week, they will be here the week after. Hey, why not give them all lollipops when they make a good collar? This coddling bullshit has got to stop. Most of these rookies have been coddled all their lives.

"Even in sports, as they were growing up, they were given "participation" trophies. What kind of shit is that? Oh, Johnny is sad because his team did not come in first place, so he didn't get a trophy. Hey, let's give everyone a trophy, so nobody feels bad. So what's the incentive for coming in first? I would say, 'Johnny, you want a fuckin' trophy? Work harder and practice more, then maybe your team will come in first, and then you get a trophy!'"

Monahan was just getting started. "Another thing, everything with them is 'why?' I'm at a crime scene, I tell them to move the crime scene tape back to extend the scene, and it's 'why?' I tell them to voucher something, it's 'why?' Every fuckin thing is 'why, why, why?' Other than the ones that were in the military, I never hear, 'Yes, sir. You got it, detective!'"

Beads of sweat began forming on Fisher's forehead as Monahan continued, his voice becoming louder by the minute. "And another thing, everybody's always on a fuckin cell phone. At a shooting the other night, I go to speak to the first officer on the scene. As I walk up to him, he's on the phone, so I figure he's speakin to his Sergeant. He puts up one finger, tellin me to wait a minute, when I hear him telling his girlfriend he might be late because, 'some savage just got shot!' I knocked the fuckin thing out of his hand and I thought he was gonna start cryin. They are either on the phone or lookin at the fuckin thing. And now we have to entertain them in the squad office? What the fuck has this job come to?"

"Do you have a problem with either of the two cops out there, Kevin? If you do, I'll ask the C.O. to send up someone else," said Fisher, desperately trying to placate the ranting detective. Fisher had always felt intimidated by Monahan, and he now began to roll his chair as far away from the detective as he possibly could.

"No. If any cops deserve *attaboys,* it's the two cops out there. But why assign them to the squad? All they're gonna do is answer phones and file shit. Those two should have been detailed to either Anti-Crime or S.N.E.U. for the week. This way they could do what they do best, catch crooks."

"The Chief of Detectives is on board with this Kevin, so it's a done deal," said Fisher, instinctively feeling for his gun at the mention of the Chief of Detectives.

"Of course he is, Chief, 'I'm smarter than anyone in the room,' would be on board with such an idiotic idea. Here's a guy that could not find a collar in a shirt factory, dictating policy to the greatest detectives in the world. The grapevine has it that he is going to come out with a checklist we will have to complete before we can close a case. What the fuck are we, airline pilots?

"No wonder they can't find competent squad bosses any more. No one wants the job. Everything you do is second-guessed, and you constantly have to implement these inane ideas. This squad produced some of the best bosses in the whole city. Guys were climbing over each other to be a squad boss here. Look at you. Those guys couldn't wait to get here, and you can't wait to leave."

"That's enough, Monahan. You said your piece. Now it's time for you to leave. I have work to do."

Monahan turned around and began to walk out of the office, "Yeah, I'm sure you do."

*

Fisher had decided to split up the rookies. One was to perform day tours during their week in the squad, the other night tours. Much to Shawn's chagrin, as he was in the office during the day, Gleason chose to work the day shift. Gleason figured that by working during the day he would be able to get two free meals, breakfast and lunch. Shawn was not happy, since he viewed the ape-like cop as culinary competition.

Linc was just as happy working nights, as it allowed him to attend his day classes. In addition, the nights were busier, so for the most part the detectives were out of the office, responding to various jobs. This would allow him to peruse various cases and files for any intelligence he might provide Silky, hopefully keeping the drug dealer off his back.

During the past few weeks, Silky had instructed a seventeen-year-old psychopathic killer, fittingly called "Bedbug," to dispatch as many of the Boulevard Houses gang as possible. Bedbug had been born and raised in the slums of Kingston, Jamaica, and had arrived in Brooklyn when he was eleven-years-old. By the time he was sixteen, he had been arrested three times, once for gun possession and twice for assault. Since he was a juvenile when he had been arrested, his records were sealed, and Nigel, recognizing the crazed teenager's talents, began using him strictly as an enforcer.

Bedbug's mission against the Boulevard gang had begun as a result of a conversation between Nigel and Silky. Both had decided that a message should be sent to Boulevard that there would soon be a new sheriff in town. Fortunately for the Boulevard gang, Bedbug had failed to spend much time at a shooting range, so the four victims he did manage to hit had all survived, although one, a sixteen-year-old, would remain in a wheel chair for life. Silky pressed Linc to find out if the 7-5 Squad had any leads on the erratic shooter.

As luck would have it for Linc, however, Monahan was also scheduled to work night tours for the week. The detective made Linc nervous, and his uneasiness was only exacerbated during his first night tour with the inquisitive detective.

Monahan approached Linc, puttting his big right hand out in greeting. "Welcome, Linc. I haven't seen you in a while. I am not a big fan of this program, but if any of the rookies deserve to be up here, it's you." Monahan slid his chair out from underneath his desk, "Have a seat, Linc." The detective then sat on the corner of the gunmetal gray desk, his legs dangling over the side. He was now staring down at Linc, who began to feel very warm. Linc unconsciously loosened his poorly-knotted tie, one he was required to wear as long as he was assigned to the detective squad.

Monahan continued to look at Linc for a few seconds, although it seemed more like a few minutes to Linc. Finally, Monahan spoke. "Basically, Sergeant Dover wants you to stay in the office for the majority of the tour. You can file our Want Cards, and answer the phones when no one is around, or if everyone is busy. I know our cold case homicide folders need cleaning up. Guys pull them out and never put them back in order. I think Fisher gave that job to Gleason, but it's a lot of work, so if you have free time you could help out in there also. Take your time and go year-to-year, making sure the case numbers are in numerical order. Start with last year first."

"You got it, detective. Anything I can do to help."

"Help, yeah. Hey Linc, that reminds me. Remember I asked if you knew anyone in the Linden projects? I needed help finding a witness to the Williams homicide, the kid they called Tarface?"

Without even realizing it, Linc began to slowly push his chair away from the desk, away from Monahan's steady gaze. "Um, yeah. Vaguely I remember something about that."

"I'm sure you do. I remember you telling me you had no dealings with those particular projects, and I said that was a shame because I had a C.I. that identified the shooter as a thug from Boulevard named Glee, but I needed a witness."

"Oh, yeah. Now I'm starting to remember. You said you couldn't use your C.I. to testify. How'd you make out? Did you ever find a witness?"

Monahan's stared at Linc, "Well, now I need another witness, Linc. Seems our boy, Glee, what are the words to that song from *The Ramblin Man*? The song was before your time, but one of the lines in the lyrics is, "He wound up on the wrong end of a gun". Yeah. Person, or, we think, persons unknown lit homeboy up over on Flatlands Avenue a little while back. Right down from the Boulevard Houses. Hey Linc, you said you didn't have dealings with Linden. How about Boulevard? Ever down there? Know any of the players?"

"No, not really. Again, me and Sgt.Kolitoski are usually in the northern sectors of the precinct. We almost never patrol down south, either in Linden or Boulevard."

"Yeah. I remember seeing Kolitoski that night that Glee got smoked. You weren't with him, though. The big cop, Williams, was driving him. Were you off that night?"

Linc began to feel the back of his neck and his hands becoming very damp, "I'm not really sure, Detective. I would have to look it up in my date book. Any particular reason why you're asking?"

"No. Don't bother looking it up. Just curious. Okay, kid, why don't you set up at Boyd's old desk. If you have any questions, or need anything, just let me know."

Linc, unnerved by the conversation with Monahan, sat at Boyd's desk all night, straightening out the Want Card File and filing old cases. Searching for information for Silky was the last thing on his mind that evening.

The next evening, however, the whole squad emptied out of the office to investigate a double homicide up on Jamaica Avenue, in "La Compania" territory. Linc was left alone in the office, directed to man the phones in case the detectives at the scene required any information.

Comfortable that no one would return for quite a while, Linc knew that there was one order of business he needed to take care of before even thinking about gathering information for Silky.

He got up from his chair and he walked over to the storage room behind the squad room. He opened the door, turned on the light switch, and the soft fluorescent lights began blinking in the ceiling. He stepped into the musty room, and he walked over to the gray metal filing cabinets that lined the walls of the room.

His eyes scanned the index cards that had been placed in the metal slots at the front of each file drawer, stopping at the card labeled "1996." Taking a deep breath, he pulled open the file drawer and began thumbing through all of the brown tri-fold case folders until he came to the one marked "Homicide# 22, Victim-Watson, Delbert, 7/12/96."

Holding the folder under his arm, Linc opened up a folding chair that had been placed against the filing cabinets on the opposite side of the room. He knew he would be safe reading the folder inside the room rather than at Boyd's desk, since one of the rookie's assignments was to ensure that all the old homicide case folders were in chronological order. Although the assignment had been delegated to Gleason, Linc figured he could just say he was helping Gleason out, as Monahan had asked him to. Hopefully it would never come to that.

Linc sat down on the metal chair and slid the brown elastic band off the trifolder. He pulled out of it the beige manila folder that contained the D.D.5's, the forms that documented the investigation into his father's death. As he pulled it out, a clear plastic envelope dropped to the floor-- the crime scene photos. Linc looked at the first photo, and his hands began to shake. The color photo showed his father lying on his back, blood soaking the front of one of his favorite shirts, a light blue T-shirt that had, "New Lots Yards" on its back. It was his father's softball T-shirt.

Tears of sorrow and anger began rolling down his cheeks, as Linc thought of his brother inside that store, looking at the same scene. Only then it had been real. Not some photo. Unable to look at another photo, Linc began reading the D.D.5's that revealed the steps of the investigation. Linc discovered the lead investigator's name was Charlie Rowe. He had been the kind, big, black detective who had provided much comfort to the Watson family. Rowe must have either retired or been transferred, as Linc knew there was no one by that name currently assigned to the 7-5 Squad.

He quickly read through the D.D.5's, and realized that Rowe had done a thorough job. He and his partner, a detective named Sapricone, had canvassed the area for almost two straight weeks, looking for any witnesses. They had recorded the plate numbers of all the cars parked in the vicinity of the bodega, tracked down all the owners, and questioned them. Unfortunately, in-store security cameras were rarely used back then, so there was no video footage recording the incident. All they had were two young, male blacks, one tall and heavy, the other slightly shorter and thin. The perps were wearing pulled-down ski masks, so the bodega owner could not provide a good sketch.

The one so-called witness they had located could only tell the two detectives that she had seen the males running towards the Linden Projects. As far as evidence was concerned, all that was vouchered, besides his father's clothes, were two .32 caliber slugs recovered from inside his father's body, and a grape Nehi bottle that the bodega owner claimed the shooter had been drinking from. *I guess they weren't able to lift any prints from the bottle,* thought Linc. He was dismayed to read the last D.D.5 in the folder, especially the typed line that stated "Case Open."

Linc carefully placed the D.D.5 folder, along with the Crime Scene photos, back into the larger accordion folder. He wrapped the elastic band back around the folder, and squeezed it back into the file drawer, right behind Homicide # 21. He placed the folded metal chair back in its original spot, shut off the light switch, and exited the room.

A distraught Linc knew he still had to find some information for Silky, and he knew he might not have much time to do it. The detectives would be arriving back soon. He began to look at some of the case folders on the detective's desks, and he hit pay dirt at McQuirke's desk, finding a folder labeled, Boulevard Houses Shootings. Reading through the D.D.5's, Linc discovered that the detective had unearthed Bedbug's street name.

It seemed that during each of the shooting events the mentally deficient psychopath would yell, "Bedbug be in the house, mon!" before emptying the clip from his Tec-9. Two witnesses, whose names and addresses were both listed on the DD-5's, had conveyed to McQuirke what they had heard.

McQuirke, however had had no luck discovering Bedbug's real identity. The nickname file revealed three Bedbugs. One had been in jail during the time of the shootings, and the other two were much older than the young teen described as having committed the shootings. Bedbug's juvenile arrest file had been sealed, and McQuirke was going to have some difficulty determining the shooter's true identity.

Looking around the squad office, satisfied that he was alone, Linc pulled out his burner cell phone and dialed Silky's number.

After the second ring, Bam-Bam picked up, "Who?"

"It's me, he there?" asked Linc.

"Hol' up."

Linc could hear Bam-Bam walking along the linoleum-covered floor, the rubber soles of his sneakers squeaking with each step. Bam-Bam then must have placed his hand over the mouthpiece of the phone, and Linc could only hear garbled voices at the other end.

Linc turned suddenly as he thought he heard the entrance gate slam. It was the cleaner, not Shawn, shutting the cleaning supply closet. The cleaner waved at Linc, who returned the wave, and the cleaner walked back towards the stairs leading down to the front desk. *Shit, Shit,* thought Linc. *Hurry the fuck up Silky.* Finally, Linc heard, "Wha's up, cuz?"

"Got something for you."

"Bout fuckin time," said Silky. "Every time I pass that bench in front of the building, I think about your lean ass sittin on it, doin some work. What you got?"

"They know he be called Bedbug." There was silence on the other end. "Silk, you there?"

"Yeah, man. I'm here, just thinkin. How they know?"

"Stupid muthafucka yelled out his name before he start blastin. What wrong with that nigga?" Linc could hear chuckling on the other end.

"Yeah, that him. He stone cold crazy B. He don't give a fuck bout nothin. Who told the D.T'S they heard his name?"

Linc would never dream of providing Silky with the witness names or addresses. Both witnesses were in their mid-thirties, working people, civilians. No need for them to, how did Monahan put it? "Wind up on the wrong end of a gun." In this case it would

178

be Bedbug's gun, and from what Linc read in McQuirke's note, if Bedbug started spraying, people had better start praying.

"All the D.T.'s notes say is that he got it from a confidential informant. No name, no nothing. Silky, you better get that crazy muthafucka back to East Flatbush."

"Yeah, yeah, I hear that. Just wished he coulda got a few more them, Nigel ain't gonna be happy."

"Listen, I got to go," Linc said. "I ain't done up here, man. I still have some time to get you more shit, bro."

"A'ight. Try get me that C.I.'s name, or at least some righteous names and apartments for some Boulevard homeys. You feel me?"

"I hear that. K, Silky, chill, talk at you soon."

*

Wednesday evening was fairly quiet, as was most of Thursday, until Linc received the call that turned his world upside down. Halfway through his tour on Thursday, Linc had completed all his filing, and was actually looking forward to returning to patrol. Secretarial duties were just not for him. The detectives, specifically Monahan, had not left the office on Wednesday, and it appeared it would be the same for Thursday, so Linc was unable to gather any more viable intelligence for Silky.

With his filing completed, Linc pulled out a number of books from his backpack and placed them on top of Boyd's old desk. He grabbed one of his speech therapy exercise books, and began to study. Monahan, whose desk was located right across from Boyd's old desk, slammed down his phone.

"This is the bullshit I can't stand. I just received a short notification for court tomorrow, so now I have to do a day tour. Now I'm going to have to take some lost time so that I can get some sleep."

"If it makes you feel any better, detective, I've got court tomorrow also," Linc said. "Grand Jury appearance for a gun collar I made a few weeks back. That's why I'm only working until ten tonight."

Monahan nodded. "Don't get me wrong. I don't mind going to court as long as I get called to appear. This is a homicide case, and it's my third notification for a Mapp Hearing. The other two times, I just sat down in the A.D.A"'s office all day, with the A.D.A. telling me it "should go on any minute." Waste of my fuckin time." Monahan then asked, "What are you reading, Linc?"

"Just some material for school. I'm trying to get my degree in Speech Pathology at L.I.U. Eventually, I'd like to teach."

Monahan leaned back in his chair and locked his hands behind his head, "Good for you, kid. This is a tough place to make a career. I don't envy cops coming on today. Everyone and anyone has a camera. One mistake, and the incident can be seen by anyone with a computer. Then there goes your pension. Besides that, even with the short time you have on this job, you have probably noticed the job taking a toll on you, both mentally and physically. Am I right?"

Not waiting for an answer, Monahan continued. "You see things no one should see, and you can't talk about it to anyone, except another cop. So you lose a lot of your old friends, you become very cynical about everything, and you don't trust anybody. It's no way to live. You'll be much better off, physically and mentally, if you teach."

Monahan was quiet for a little while, and Linc noticed the detective's eyes had a faraway look. Breaking out of his reverie, Monahan slowly shook his head, and asked, "Why Speech Pathology?"

Linc knew better than to provide the probing detective with any personal information so he said, "I did a little research and found that there are not enough qualified speech pathologists to teach." *And that wasn't a lie,* thought Linc.

Monahan then stood up and came around to Linc's desk, his eyes focused on one of the books. He picked up a brown paperback, and chuckled, "*Dante's Inferno*? The nine circles of hell. I hope you realize that by working here, you yourself have begun the tortuous trek with Virgil, whether you are aware of it or not."

Taken aback by the detective's knowledge of the classic, Linc asked, "You've read this?"

"Oh, yeah. When I was stationed in the Middle East with the Marines, I was in kind of a bad place, mentally. There was not much to do, other than work out, train, and read. I found a great deal of comfort from the philosophers: Voltaire, Camus, Goethe."

*This son of a bitch continues to amaze me,* thought Linc. Looking at his books, Linc replied, "I finished *The Plague* not that long ago. It's funny, when I started on this job, I found a lot of what Camus said was right on point. You know that we, as human beings, really have no control over shit, man, that people really don't give a shit bout one another, and that the world has no rational meaning or order. As a cop, now, I can see that. People just don't give a fuck about one another, and there just seems to be so much bad shit out on the streets."

Monahan laughed. "You see, this job is beginning to eat away at you, kiddo. You better get that teaching job, and quick. I'd hate to see how you feel in five years." Silent for a moment, Monahan then quietly said, "Linc, Camus also said that there is an innate capacity for good within every person. So, even if you are on this job a short while longer, don't give up. There are a lot of good people living in those projects, and our "thin blue line" is the only thing keeping them safe."

The detective once again became silent, seemingly floating off to a distant place. Linc began to feel uncomfortable, and was about to speak, when Monahan continued, in a voice that seemed strangely detached, "You have to judge each person as an individual, but sometimes you make mistakes. A person you thought to be good, could, in reality, be evil, and vice versa. There are consequences for all your actions. The consequences might be here, or wherever we go after we've left here.

"Okay, enough with the philosophy dissertation. Tell me about your family. Your mom and dad, what do they do for a living?"

Linc hesitated, "My moms works for the T.A. My pops passed away when I was eleven. He had a heart attack. I have one brother younger than me. He's still in high school."

Monahan looked at Linc and shook his head, "Eleven years old. Shit, I'm sorry, Linc. I lost my mom when I first came on the job and my father soon after, but eleven years old, that had to be tough on you and your family. Hopefully you're still living with and taking care of your mom and brother. You are, aren't you?"

Linc was now beyond uncomfortable, but thankfully the conversation was suddenly interrupted. A desperate voice came through the radio that had been placed on McQuirke's desk. "Central, I need a 10-85, forthwith! I have a male shot, likely, corner of Sutter and Georgia. Have the sergeant and the squad respond!"

The squad room was eerily quiet as all the detectives stared at the radio, waiting for additional information. The "likely" in the officer's request meant the victim was likely to die, so the detectives knew their response to the scene was imminent. Each detective's mind was racing, as they tried to process the information already received. They tried to picture the location, Sutter and Georgia, as well as trying to connect the voice coming through the radio with a face.

Central said. "Identify yourself, unit."

A breathless voice came back over the radio. "Central, this is 7-5 Boy. I have a description, male, black, early 20's, wearing either a dark blue or black sweatshirt." The cop, obviously running, stopped talking momentarily in order to catch his breath, "Suspect also wearing a dark blue cap, possibly Yankee hat. Male was last seen running north on Georgia towards Belmont, armed with black handgun."

Wordlessly, the detectives began putting on their sport coats or suit jackets. Some grabbed radios, the others car keys. Within seconds Linc was once again alone in the office, hearing the screeching tires and blasting sirens outside the window on Sutter Avenue, as all the units sped towards one of their brothers calling for help.

Linc looked at the large clock on the wall and realized he only had two more hours left in his shift. Monitoring the radio, he heard that the detectives had arrived at the scene and were requesting the Crime Scene Unit to respond to the location, which usually meant that the victim had not survived the gunshot wounds.

Putting his feet up on Boyd's desk, Linc leaned back in his chair and resumed reading his textbook. After three pages of the extremely dry material, Linc felt his eyes beginning to close, and he jumped when the loud ring from Monahan's desk phone pierced the silence of the squad room. *Monahan is probably calling, searching for information concerning the shooting victim*, thought Linc, as he stepped over to Monahan's desk. Almost all the shooting victims in the 7-5 had some sort of criminal record, and one of the first things the detectives did at a crime scene was to attempt to get a victim profile.

Linc picked up the ringing phone. "7-5 Squad, Police Officer Watson, can I help you?"

"Yeah. Hey, buddy, this is Nuciforo, DNA Liaison from the Medical Examiner's office. Is Monahan there?"

"No, sorry. He's out in the field on a shooting. Can I take a message?"

"Did you say you were a P.O.? Are you a white shield assigned to the squad?"

"Yeah, just temporary. Last day is tomorrow." There was silence at the other end of the phone, as it was obvious Nuciforo was deciding whether to trust Linc with whatever information he had.

"Well, okay. I got to get out of here soon, so I can't wait for a callback. You have a pen?" After Linc answered in the affirmative, the detective said, "We had a DNA submission from the 6-7 Squad on one of their double homicides. We got a hit on their homicide, but we also had a hit on one of the 7-5 Squad's old cases. The submitting detective was Charlie Rowe, but I know he retired after 9/11. Since it's a cold case I'm figuring Monahan would probably be working it."

*Rowe, that was the detective that had worked his father's case,* thought Linc. *He probably worked hundreds of cases. What were the chances,* he wondered, as he felt his stomach muscles begin to tighten.

"Yeah. Monahan and McQuirke usually work the old cases," Linc said, his voice becoming more and more excited. "What is the message? I'll make sure he gets it."

"Okay. It was from a homicide of one Delbert Watson. Date of occurrence was 07/12 of 1996. Rowe had submitted a grape Nehi bottle for testing."

Linc quickly cut the detective off, "I thought they were not able to get prints from the bottle?"

An annoyed Nuciforo said, "Who said anything about prints, partner? We got a DNA hit off the bottle. How do you know about the case? Hey, wait a minute. I'm lookin at the last name I wrote on my pad, your last name. It's the same as the victim's in this case. Please tell me there is no relation."

Linc, felt his insides churning. He realized he should have said nothing and just copied down whatever information Nuciforo gave him. "Uh, well I have been making sure all the old homicides are in order while I've been assigned here. I read through a few, you know, just to pass time, and that was one I remembered reading. You know, because we had the same last name. Relax. There is no relation."

Nuciforo digested the information and decided to change the subject a bit, "So, you've been basically filing all week, heh? I bet you can't wait to get the fuck out of there. Well anyway, a hit came back for a recent collar made by the 6-7, guy by the name of Gary "Silky" Pitt. Pitt's NYSID number is 48543557Y. His DNA swab taken from that collar matched DNA from the "Nehi" bottle. Tell Monahan to give me a call when he can at --."

Linc never even heard the phone number. He had written Silky's name on a yellow legal pad, and now he was staring at it. The next thing he heard was Nuciforo's voice. "Hey kid, you still there?"

"Yeah, yeah. I'm sorry. Um, you sure it was a match to this guy Pitt? And what kind of DNA came off the Nehi bottle?"

Nuciforo laughed, "What are you, a fuckin defense attorney now? I'm sure you've watched C.S.I., kid. You know the probabilities of a DNA hit. After all, every fuckin perp that has a T.V. knows the percentages. We got the hit off saliva from the top of the bottle, same as with the cigarettes he smoked at the double homicide. This boy is fucked.

"Listen, I'd love to stay and chat with you all night about DNA helixes, chromosomes, and shit like that, but I gotta go, they ain't payin me no overtime here. Just make sure he gets the message. Tell him I banged in tomorrow and I'm off on weekends, only good thing about this gig, so he can call me Monday. Do me a favor and make sure you put the message into the Telephone Message Log. Got it, kid?"

Linc managed to mumble an acknowledgement before hanging up the phone. Linc ripped off the top sheet of the legal pad that contained Silky's name, shredded the sheet, and placed it in the garbage pail. He assumed that a more formal notification containing the DNA hit would be sent to Monahan in the future, and he had no intention of writing Nuciforo's information in the Telephone Message Log. By the time Monahan received a formal notification, Linc would have taken care of business with Silky, and his resignation would come shortly thereafter. Linc would be very careful, and if Monahan ever put two and two together, Linc would hopefully be a civilian by that time.

Linc stood up on shaky legs and walked over to the storage room. He turned on the light, and went straight to the file cabinet that read "1996." He opened the drawer, and pulled out Homicide

#22, his father's case. Linc placed the thick folder under his arm and hurried out of the squad room and down the stairs, intent on reaching the parking lot. He opened the heavy metal door that led to the parking lot, and stepped out onto the ramp, only to meet Sgt.Kolitoski, who had been walking up the ramp to enter the precinct.

Kolitoski said, "Linc! Your vacation up in the squad almost over? You ready to come back onto the streets to do some real crime fighting?"

Linc was startled and remained speechless for a couple of seconds, but quickly recovered, "Shit, yeah, Sarge, I can't wait to get back in the car with you. I'm sick of all the bullshit secretarial work they got me doing up there."

Kolitoski's eyes drifted down towards the homicide folder that Linc had in his right hand, "Are you sure? That looks like a case folder you have in your hands. You bringing work home to study?"

Linc looked down at the case folder and laughed nervously, "Nah, Sarge. I just borrowed a folder to keep some of my schoolwork papers in order. You can file a lot of shit in these folders."

"Okay, pal, I won't tell anyone that you're "borrowing" department property." Kolitoski stepped aside to let Linc pass, "Let me get inside, rookie. We're talking on my meal hour, and you know how valuable they are. I'll see you Monday." The sergeant finished his walk up the ramp, opened the door, and entered the precinct.

Linc stood still for a moment, and took a couple of deep breaths in order to slow down his rapid beating heart. He then looked over the entire parking lot in order to avoid any further suprises. Seeing none, Linc walked over to his car, opened the passenger side door, and placed the folder under the passenger seat. He then jogged back into the building, ran up the stairs, and re-entered the squad room.

He picked up a phone and he called the front desk. He spoke to Keavney, and asked that a cop be sent up to the squad to monitor the phones. He explained to Keavney that he was not feeling well, and needed to take an hour of lost time.

Within five minutes, Linc's relief, a cop named Lichte, entered the squad room. Linc explained that the detectives should be back shortly. All Lichte needed to do was answer the phones and take any messages for the detectives. Leaving his Request for Lost Time form on Sergeant Dover's desk, a still stunned Linc walked out of the 7-5 Precinct, perhaps for one of the last times.

*

While driving home Linc pulled up alongside the Gershwin ball fields, and parked in just about the same spot as the detectives had the day his father had been murdered. It was a cool, almost cold, March evening, as winter seemed reluctant to release its grip on Brooklyn. A light rain had developed, which suited Linc just fine. The isolation he now felt would hopefully enhance his powers of concentration. As he sat in the darkness of his car, he thought back to that hot July afternoon in 1996. He closed his eyes and leaned his head back, trying to recall all the details of that day.

He remembered his father and Harris had missed seeing his first at bat, and it wasn't until he had taken the field that he saw the two of them standing outside the chain link fence, right behind Linc's team bench. In his mind he pictured a smiling Harris, his small hands gripping the fence, staring proudly at his older brother. His father was standing besides Harris, one hand on the young boy's shoulder, the other also gripping the fence. Linc shut his eyes tight and began to concentrate hard. He knew he was missing something.

The mind's subconscious is comparable to a large filing cabinet. Everything a person observes is stored and filed away. The inconsequential and insignificant is stored in the back, perhaps not to be referred to again as long as a person lives, but significant, notable events, such as the death of a loved one, are stored in the front, easily accessed at any time. The events of that memorable day occupied a special place in Linc's subconscious.

His intense concentration now began to bring those same events flashing through his mind. It was almost as though he was viewing the scene from an old eight-millimeter camera. Colors were faded and movements were choppy, but there they were, part of the background on that hot July afternoon. Linc saw Silky and Bam-Bam walking past his father and Harris. Both were laughing, Linc remembered Silky playfully pushing Bam-Bam into a group of girls who were walking by the two. They both stopped and said something to the girls, then they turned around and continued walking east on Stanley Avenue towards the bodega.

It made sense. The physical descriptions provided by the bodega owner matched both Silky and Bam-Bam, and the witness had remembered watching the two bodega suspects running towards the Linden projects. They were running back home! Linc quickly started his car, and continued the short drive to his apartment. He parked, and rushed into his building, and through the lobby. Unwilling to wait for the elevator, he flew up the stairs, taking them two at a time. Breathless, he finally arrived at his apartment door. He keyed his way into the apartment, gently shut the door, and looked down the hallway towards his mother's room. Satisfied her door was shut, he removed his shoes and silently padded along the hallway to his bedroom. He entered the bedroom and stood still for a minute, allowing his eyes to adjust to the darkness.

Linc slowly made his way towards Harris's bed. He squatted, and watched his brother's chest move slowly up and down. A slight snore came from the young man's nostrils. Looking at Harris in such a peaceful repose, Linc realized how much he had come to love his younger brother. He thought to himself how that muthafucka Silky had caused this gentle boy such problems, both mental and physical. He gently shook his brother's shoulder, "Harris. Harris. Wake up, little man."

188

Harris slowly opened his eyes, "Wha,-whats the ma,-matter, Linc?"

"Nothin, little man. You gots to keep your voice down. Don't want you waking up Moms. Listen to me, Harris, I know this is gonna be hard, but I want you to think back to when Pops got hurt, you know, inside the store."

Harris closed his eyes and turned away from Linc, "I do,-don't wan,-want to th,- think b,-bout that."

"This is important, Harris. You remember back then, once in a while, I would hang with a dude named Silky. You used to see me and him at the basketball courts. You remember him?"

"Ye,-ye,-yeah, so?"

"In the store, could the guy that hurt Pops be that Silky? Think hard. I know those boys were wearing masks, but did you hear any of them talking?"

Harris, thinking back to that fateful day, remained silent for a while. Then he spoke. "I hear,-heard one of th,-them b,-b,-boys ta,-ta,-talking at the A,-Arab man. Ye,-yeah Linc, it d,-did s,-s,-sound like your f,-f,-friend. Di,-di,-did he-hur,-hurt Pops?"

"I don't know yet, little man, but I'll find out. You go back to sleep."

Harris turned over quickly and looked at Linc, "Na,-na,-now your po,-po,-police Linc. Ya,-ya,-you can ar,-ar,-arrest him."

"Yeah, you're right, Harris, I can," said Linc as he stood up. *But I'm going to do one better that that,* he thought to himself.

*

The next day, his last day assigned to the detective squad, Linc was exhausted. He had had a sleepless night, thinking of the various ways he could deal with Silky. Adding to his exhaustion was the fact that he had gotten up early in order to attend court. After testifying in front of the Grand Jury about his gun case, he had punched out of court and headed back to the precinct in order to sign out. He also wanted to make sure Monahan had not heard from Nuciforo concerning the DNA hit on Silky.

Linc pushed open the gate to the squad room, and his heart began to race as he saw Monahan on the phone. *Shit,* Linc thought. *What if that's Nuciforo?* He remembered that Nuciforo had told him he was taking the day off, but what if he had changed his mind? Linc pulled out the chair to Boyd's desk and slowly sat down, looking at Monahan.

Monahan hung up the phone, "Well, I hope you had better luck in court than I did." he said. "That was the A.D.A.. I went to court this morning, sat there until lunch, then the douchebag tells me I can return to the precinct but I'm on phone alert. That was just him. The case has been postponed once again."

"Yeah," said Linc, "I got to testify. Grand Jury indicted the guy. Just came back to sign out and say thanks for all your help during my week here."

Monahan stood up, "No problem, kiddo. My pleasure. Hey, I saw you banged out for an hour last night. Everything okay?"

Linc began rubbing his stomach, "Yeah. Just a little stomach problem. Might have been from that Chinese food we had for dinner."

At the mention of Chinese food, Shawn strolled out of the squad kitchen. He looked at the young cop who had mentioned Chinese food, and suddenly he matched the face, "Hey, what were you doin by my building that night?"

Linc stared at Shawn, trying to make sense of the question, "What the fuck you talking about, your building? Where you live at?"

"Boulevard!" yelled Shawn, as he stuck his thumb in his mouth and began walking back to the kitchen, deciding that the kid was lying about any available Chinese food.

Linc felt Monahan staring at him. Not wanting to look Monahan in the face, Linc shook his head and said, as if to himself, but more for Monahan's benefit, "That boy be crazy!"

Linc heard Monahan slowly say, "Yeah, he must be. I remember you saying you were never in the Boulevard projects."

Monahan paused before continuing. "You did say that, didn't you?"

Still not daring to look at Monahan, Linc said, "That's right. I don't know what that green-jacket-wearin, crazy muthafucka is talking about." Linc began nervously searching for a black pen in all his pockets, "I got to sign out. You need anything before I leave, detective?"

Monahan stood up and walked over to Linc. Holding up a black pen, he said, "Here you go, kiddo. No, I don't need anything from you, for now."

Linc hurriedly signed out in the Detective Command Log. He handed the pen back to Monahan, finally looking the detective in the eye, "Well, if you need me, you know where to find me. Thanks for the pen."

Linc slowly walked down the stairs to the front desk area. *Shit,* he thought, *I should never have come back from court to sign out. I should have just called, had someone sign me out, and taken some lost time. I had to run into that dim-witted fuckin Shawn.*

As he walked out the front door towards the parking lot, he thought back to the night he and Shortfinger had met up with Glee. It didn't take him long to remember the bum wearing the green fatigue jacket, with that stupid looking black watch cap, walking along Ashford Street. He remembered the uneasy feeling that had coursed through his body when he looked across the street at the bum. It was Shawn! Linc felt the walls closing in on him.

*

Monahan watched Linc walk down the hall towards the exit stairway. He then walked over to the window that faced the front of the precinct, onto Sutter Avenue. He watched as Linc exited the front of the precinct and made a left towards the parking area. Monahan turned around and strolled over to his desk. He unlocked his bottom drawer and pulled a Devil Dog out of an opened eight-pack box. He walked into the squad kitchen, and saw Shawn sitting in a black office chair, leaning back, staring at Fox News Channel. His thumb was in his mouth.

"Hey, Shawn, let me ask you a question."

"I didn't throw it out. Boyd did it!" said Shawn, still staring at the television.

Monahan laughed. "No, nothing like that, Shawn. You're not in any kind of trouble. Matter of fact, look what I brought you. You can have it, if you promise to help me." Monahan stuck out his hand that contained the Devil Dog. Without taking his eyes off the television or pulling his right thumb out of his mouth, Shawn's quickly snatched the Devil Dog from Monahan's grasp. He stuck it into his jacket pocket and grunted.

"Where exactly do you live, Shawn?"

"I jus tol you. Boulevard!"

*This is going to be like pulling teeth,* thought Monahan, "Yeah, I know, but where in Boulevard?"

"Stanley Avenue. I don't know the number, I know the building."

Monahan thought to himself, *Glee was seen in the lobby of 920 Stanley on the night he was killed.* The detective got up and quickly walked back to his desk to get the case folder. He pulled out the folder from the drawer, and walked back into the kitchen. Sitting down in a chair next to Shawn, Monahan pulled out a B.C.I., or mug shot, photo of Damon "Glee" Miller. He then extended his hand containing the photo, "Shawn, did you ever see this boy before?"

Shawn snatched the photo almost as fast as he had snatched the Devil Dog. He put it in front of his face and stared at it. Monahan watched as Shawn closed his eyes, as if in deep concentration, opening them only to once again stare at the photo. This ritual continued on for almost three minutes. Shawn finally said, "Seen him in my lobby. My Moms said don't talk to him."

Monahan smiled and said soothingly, "Your Moms is a smart woman, Shawn. You should never talk to any of those boys that hang out in your lobby." Monahan took the photo back from

Shawn and said, "Now, Shawn, the young cop that was sitting out in the office before. You said you seen him by your building?"

"The kid that ate all the Chinese food?"

Monahan laughed. "Yeah, that kid. I promise that before I leave I will order you some Chinese food, because you're helping me out. Okay?" Monahan watched as Shawn smiled and nodded his head up and down. "Shawn, you've got to think hard. When did you see that kid Linc by your building?"

"At night."

"But what night, Shawn? Was it last night, last week, last month?"

"Yeah, it was then."

Monahan realized that Shawn had no conception of time. Frustrated, he opened the case folder to put Glee's photo back, when he suddenly had an idea. He pulled out the Crime Scene photos and looked at them for a few seconds. He noticed that in the background of some of the photos there was a thin layer of snow covering the grassy strips that separated the sidewalks from the street. "Shawn, the night you saw that boy, was it snowing?"

Shawn nodded. "It stopped, though. That's when I came back from the stores, when it stopped."

Monahan thought about stores in the area. Shawn's mother was very careful with her disabled son. She would not let him up go to the stores on Stanley Avenue, especially at night, so Monahan asked, "The stores on Pennsylvania Avenue?"

Shawn nodded, as Monahan began to draw a rough sketch of the streets, beginning from the stores on Pennsylvania, and ending at the Boulevard project building at 920 Stanley Avenue. The detective then showed Shawn the sketch. Giving Shawn a pencil, he asked him to trace the streets he traveled when he went home each night. Once satisfied that Shawn knew the streets he walked, Monahan had Shawn mark where his building was located on the sketch. It was the 920 building.

He then asked, "If this is your building here, Shawn, where did you see that kid on the night it was snowing?"

Shawn placed a dot on the drawing. The dot was right on Ashford Street. If someone wanted to watch someone in the lobby of Shawn's building, that dot was the place to be.

# CHAPTER 14

While Shawn was busy drawing on Monahan's map, Matty Boyd had also come to a realization. The job was fucking him once again. The promise of easy work and plenty of overtime, working in Applicant Investigation, had slowly turned to shit. All the details in the N.Y.P.D. start off as sweet gigs. Then some Chief realizes that the cops in a particular unit are actually enjoying their work, and that sweet gig suddenly blows up. It is one reason why cops seem to act miserable all the time, even though they actually relish their assignment. They know that if they express happiness, someone upstairs will do their best to fuck it up.

Boyd had been doing plenty of overtime. He was making local background visits to Brooklyn and Queens and never missed a meal. He was a happy detective. Soon enough, however, his caseload began increasing, and he and his partner, Angelo, were being sent on address checks all over the state, and sometimes out of state. Within the last two weeks, they had traveled four times to New Jersey, and twice to Pennsylvania.

It seemed that some of the recruits who had signed the affidavit promising to move into the five boroughs or contiguous counties once they had graduated from the academy felt the N.Y.P.D. could wipe their ass with that affidavit. The detectives had discovered that one rookie lived as far north as Albany and another as far west as Port Jervis. These rookies would sleep in the precincts, or bunk with another cop during the days they worked, and return home on their days off.

Boyd, at every opportunity, complained to his supervisors about the trips, and at one point even began contemplating filling out magazine subscription cards for a couple of those supervisors. His relentless bitching finally broke the supervisors down, and he was back to working his cases once again.

The Applicant Processing Division office in Queens was located on the Horace Harding Expressway, which allowed the investigators easy access to either the Long Island Expressway or the Grand Central Parkway, two of the main thoroughfares that traversed Queens. The antiseptic offices there were quite different from those found in precinct squad rooms. They were clean, well stocked with office supplies, and only a few of the desk chairs were broken.

Boyd had settled into one of those desk chairs that Friday morning, and he glanced over at his partner, Joe Angelo. Angelo was finally happy. He was actually smiling as he was cutting coupons out of newspapers he had *borrowed* from other investigators' desks. The last two weeks had been a living hell for Boyd, as he traveled with Angelo all over the state.

From the moment he got into the car, Angelo would never stop complaining about their assignment. At one point, Boyd actually thought about driving the Crown Victoria off the Tappan Zee Bridge, just to put himself out of his misery. The difference between Boyd's complaining and Angelo's whining, was that Boyd had the balls to complain to the bosses. Angelo would never do that, lest he might be sent to a detective squad in a precinct by some pissed-off Applicant supervisor.

Boyd thought about putting his feet up on his desk and reading the newspaper. After all, he had been on the road for almost two weeks, and it was Friday, his last tour for the week. Then he saw the Watson folder. He opened up Linc's folder in order to see what he had done on the background check. Boyd read over his notes on the visit to the Ozone Park address, the address where Linc supposedly lived. Remembering that he had asked the aunt, or godmother, or whatever the fuck she was, to have Linc call him, Boyd checked for any messages that the kid had called. There were none. *There is definitely something not right here,* Boyd thought.

Boyd then continued reading through Linc's file. The kid had graduated from the academy at the top of his class, and was still attending college, working towards a four- year degree. He was receiving good grades as well. His evaluations at the 7-5 Precinct were exceptional, and he had even been put in for a number of commendations.

Boyd was about to put the folder down, when he noticed that the original investigator on Linc's case had paper-clipped a copy of a Criminal Court summons to Linc's application. Boyd was surprised that he had missed it. The summons was for Trespass, and the location was 190 Wortman Avenue. Boyd was familiar with the building. It was in the Linden projects, the 7-5 Precinct. A Housing cop by the name of Malone had issued the summons. Boyd turned the summons over, and read the narrative written by Malone when he had issued the summons to Linc:

"At T/P/O respondent was observed loitering in the lobby at above location. Lobby of the above address is also a known drug location. Respondent could not produce any documentation to indicate that either he or a relative resided at location which is N.Y.C.H.A. property."

Boyd continued to examine the summons. Linc had received it in the summer of 2003, when he was eighteen years old. A disposition sheet attached to the summons by Linc's original investigator indicated that Linc had pled guilty, and had paid a twenty-five dollar fine. Boyd just shook his head, remembering the days when a criminal court summons for trespass, especially at a known drug location, would have meant an automatic rejection for any applicant.

The detective examined the face of the summons and came to the line that was particularly revealing, the address of the respondent. Boyd read the address, and it was not in Ozone Park. The summons stated that Linc resided at 180 Wortman Avenue, Apartment 8B. Boyd knew that building to be the one right across from where Linc had received the summons. The only question Boyd had was whether Linc had produced identification to Malone, or had the Housing cop just written down what Linc had told him.

"Hey, Angelo," he said, "I'm going over this Watson kid's folder, and in it there was a C summons. The original investigator was a guy by the name of Paul Turano. Do you think he would have reached out to the cop that wrote the summons to get some background on the ticket?"

Angelo never looked up from his newspaper, "Who? Peepin Paul or otherwise known as 'Paul the "Perv'?" Affecting a British accent, Angelo said, "Not bloody likely, mate!" He put down his paper and looked at Boyd. "Paul was a legend amongst us in the office. He wore these thick glasses, although we all knew he could see perfectly well. He felt the glasses made him looked distinguished, and although he had been born in Bensonhurst, Paul would speak with a British accent because he read somewhere that women dug men with British accents.

"What got Paul in trouble, however, was that whenever any of the females would go into the 'loo,' as he would call it, he would wait a minute or two, place his glasses on his desk, and walk into the ladie's bathroom. You see, many of the stall locks were damaged, we figured by Paul, and the woman would have to hold the door shut while they squatted."

Angelo then paused for dramatic effect. "Well, Paul would walk in, push on the stall door, and pull down his pants as if was going to take a shit. For some reason he thought this move would turn some of the woman on, and they would invite him for some 'stall sex.' Needless to say, it never worked, and when the woman complained to the Captain, Paul would say he couldn't see the sign on the door because he had left his glasses on the desk. Paul lasted here about two months. They sent him to Psych Services, and now I think he's logging in cars at the pound. So, to answer your question, I doubt very much if Paul would have called the cop."

*This is just great,* thought Boyd, *I'm following up on a case that had been handled by a sexually perverted Anglophile.* Boyd picked up the phone and called over to P.S.A. #2, the Housing Police Service Area that covered the Linden projects. He was informed by the desk sergeant that Malone had been transferred to Narcotics. Boyd knew that trying to find someone who had been

198

assigned to Narcotics was like attempting to find a particular individual named Singh in India. It was virtually impossible.

Boyd turned on his computer, and accessed the CARS system. He scrolled through the screens until he came to the address menu. He punched in 180 Wortman Avenue, Apartment 8b, and he sat and waited. The screen blinked, and suddenly the address appeared in front of the waiting detective. Boyd discovered that one Gary Pitt had given that address on a recent arrest. He clicked on the arrest number associated with Pitt's arrest, and saw that Pitt had been collared recently in the 6-7 Precinct, for Assault 2 degree.

*Well,* thought Boyd, *at least it was not a narcotics arrest. But why was this guy in the 6-7, a precinct known for it's proliferation of Jamaican drug gangs? It could be nothing, but I have to speak to Mr.Pitt.* Hopefully, he was a relative to Linc, and that would be a partial answer to the address mystery.

Boyd pulled out Linc's photo from the case folder, and said, "Come on, Joe, we're going to beautiful Brooklyn."

"Oh, come on, Boyd. You're fuckin kiddin me, right? My ass can't take being in a car seat any more, and, besides, I'm only halfway through the weekend coupons!"

"Let's go, you cheap fuck. You know you're gonna be trying to switch prices on half the shit you buy, anyway."

Slowly getting up from his chair, Angelo remarked, "Fuckin store scanners have been the death of me."

*

Traffic was fairly light for a Friday, and since Boyd knew all the back-street shortcuts in his old precinct, the partners were parked in front of 180 Wortman within thirty minutes. Boyd had noticed that as soon as they began driving south on Pennsylvania Avenue, Angelo had suddenly become quiet. His complaining had stopped.

Looking around at all the black faces, Angelo whispered, "Where the fuck are we, Boyd?"

Boyd laughed. "I'm home, Joe. I'm home."

The partners rode the elevator up to the eighth floor, Angelo never taking his hand off the off-duty .38 caliber revolver strapped to his waist. Angelo almost shit his pants when Boyd began jumping up and down in the elevator, causing it to shake, finally getting retribution for all the complaining during the road trips upstate. The eighth floor was the top floor of the building, and as Boyd got off the elevator he made a left down the hallway, knowing 8B would be the corner apartment, looking out towards Pennsylvania Avenue.

Angelo, still shaken up from the elevator ride, began running down the hall after his partner, saying, "Wait up, Boyd, wait up!"

Standing to the side of the door, Boyd rang the bell to the apartment. Receiving no answer, he continued to press on the bell, the annoying noise reverberating through the apartment.

"A'ight muntafucka, stop with the fuckin bell! Who dat?"

Boyd stuck his detective shield in front of the peephole. "Po-lice. Open up."

Some whispered conversation was going on inside the apartment. Finally, the voice on the other side of the door asked, "What you want? Who you lookin for?"

Boyd had gone through this same scenario many times. "Ain't nobody in trouble. Just lookin to talk at Gary Pitt."

"Ain't no Gary Pitt here."

Boyd sighed. "Listen up, muthafucka. Don't make me go down to the tenant office and find that there is a Gary Pitt on the lease, cause if there is, I'm comin back here with Emergency Service, and I'm gonna knock this fuckin door down. And if I find someone else's name is on the lease, then I'm gonna come up here with Emergency Service, knock the door down, and throw Pitt's ass out into the street. You feelin me, cuz?"

There was more whispered conversation, then, "A'ight. Hol' up."

Boyd turned around, almost knocking Angelo to the ground. His partner was standing as close as possible to Boyd. The partners heard a number of chains and locks being unclasped and unlocked.

Finally, the door was partially opened, and Bam-Bam's enormous body covered the entrance to the apartment, "What up?"

"You Pitt?" asked Boyd. At that moment the door opened wider, and Silky gently pushed Bam-Bam back into the apartment. "I'm Pitt."

"Mind if we come in?"

Silky studied both detectives. He finally said, "No, I don't mind, as long as you show me a warrant."

Boyd knew at that moment that the smooth-talking son-of-a-bitch standing in front of him was not about assaults. Boyd knew a drug dealer when he spotted one. He had to play this right. Pulling out Linc's photo, he displayed it to Silky. "You know this guy?"

Silky took a quick glance at the photo, "Nah, man. Am I supposed to?"

Continuing to hold out the photo, Boyd said, "I hope so. He said he lived here."

"Well I guess that brother be trippin, cause I ain't never seen his ass before."

Boyd placed the photo in his pocket, "Why would he say he lives here, then? Why did he pick out your apartment?"

"Don't know. You the detective. Some of these boys be buggin, give any address just to get the po-po off their back."

Boyd knew Silky was hiding something. He stared at Silky. "Or maybe the boys give the po-po your address cause you like having boys up in your apartment. Maybe you got a young boy in there now. Is that the way you roll, Gary?"

Silky began to feel his heart racing as he unconsciously clenched his fists, "Man, you better get the fuck outta here before I---" Silky stopped, knowing the cop was intentionally trying to piss him off.

Boyd stepped up right in front of Silky, and while speaking in a low calm voice he poked Silky in the chest with his index finger, "Before you what? Listen, you lying muthafucka. I made my bones chasing down and catching shitheads like you in these projects. So this ain't my first rodeo douchebag."

Bam-Bam tried to get around Silky to get at Boyd, but Silky held him back.

Boyd said, "I know you're hiding something and I'm gonna make it my mission to find out what you're all about. Bet on it."

The two adversaries stared at one another, until Silky finally stepped backward and slowly closed the door in Boyd's face.

*

As soon as the detectives got back to their office, Angelo ran to his desk, opened the top drawer, and pulled out a roll of toilet paper. He then sprinted into the men's room. While Angelo was afraid he had soiled his pants doing some real police work, Boyd picked up the phone and dialed the number of the 6-7 Detective Squad.

After three rings the phone was picked up. "6-7 Squad, O'Laughlin."

"Yeah, hey, bud. I'm Matty Boyd from Applicant Investigations."

Before Boyd could say another word, O'Laughlin cut him off, "Now hol' up, brother. I made it off probation about fifteen years ago. Ain't there some type of statute of limitations for the shit I did before I got on the job? Wasn't my fault you muthafuckas didn't catch it."

Boyd laughed. "Naw, man. This ain't about that. One of your uniforms collared up a smooth-talking scumbag by the name of Gary Pitt. I was wondering if you debriefed him or could give me any information on what he's about."

"You mean Silky? I'll tell you what he's about. He's hopefully about to be collared for a double homicide. Me and my partner are putting together a case against that nasty muthafucka. Gonna be bringing it down to the D.A. soon. Looking to get the okay to arrest his ass for murders. We got a call last night on a DNA hit for Silky, heard he also had a hit on a 7-5 case too."

Boyd was scribbling down the information on his yellow legal pad, "In the 7-5 heh? That double homicide in your precinct, was it drug related?"

O'Laughlin laughed. "My brother, everything in the 6-7 is drug related. That double might turn out to be a triple. The dealer and his girlfriend bought it, and she was about six weeks pregnant. That's gonna be up to the A.D.A., though. We think Silky did it on the say-so of a major dealin Jamaican by the name of Nigel."

"Okay. Just one more thing, O'Laughlin. Did you get Silky's cell phone number when he was collared?"

"Shit, Boyd, of course. What you think, we work for Sheriff Andy Griffin over here in East Flatbush? What does Applicant have to do with this nasty muthafucka, anyway?"

"It's a long story. This works out, I'll tell you all about it over a beer. Got the cell number?" Boyd wrote down the number given to him by O' Laughlin, thanked the detective, and hung up the phone. *Drugs,* thought Boyd, *I knew it.* But he still hadn't tied Linc to Silky, not yet, at least.

Boyd called a retired detective he had once worked with who now worked at Verizon. Boyd promised to fax over a subpoena, but in the meantime he asked his friend to do an expedited run on Silky's cell phone for all incoming calls for the last four months. He then called the Brooklyn A.D.A's office and spoke to one of his A.D.A. friends. The A.D.A faxed the subpoena over to Verizon, and now Boyd had to wait.

Boyd spent the next hour listening to Angelo tell everyone in the office how he and Boyd almost beat the shit out of two gangsters in a Brooklyn housing project. Of course, with each story both Silky and Bam-Bam got bigger and bigger, and by the time the last story rolled off Angelo's tongue, the two detectives had almost got into a shootout with the two "stone cold killers." Boyd was extremely pleased to hear the chirp of the fax machine.

The detective pulled the four-page Verizon report off the fax, and walked back to his desk. He began examining the numbers that had been called into Silky's cell phone, but none matched the phone number Linc had recorded as his cell number. Boyd was about to give up, when he noticed one number on the sheet that looked familiar. It was the number Linc had listed as his home number, his "home" in Ozone Park. Boyd then checked the date the call was made to Silky's cell. It was the same date, and about the same time, that he and Angelo had ended their visit with Linc's "Godmother," Dorita.

# CHAPTER 15

It was Saturday the day after Boyd had called O'Laughlin at the 6-7 Squad office. Not far away from the 6-7 Precinct, Monahan was sitting in the rectory office of St. Jeromes in East Flatbush, waiting for his brother, Timothy, to finish morning Mass.

The office was fairly large, by rectory standards, and could be described as warm and comfortable. It had retained the original oak flooring, with bookcases lining one wall, while a leather couch occupied the other. A large mahogany desk took up most of the space in the rear of the room, and it faced the entrance to the office.

St. Jeromes, like most of the churches erected in Brooklyn during the 1900's, was built to last. No expense had been spared to accommodate the priests who presided over the parishes at that time. Today the parish would barely be able to afford the mahogany desk.

Monahan was seated on the leather couch, and above him was a framed photo of the current Pope, Benedict XVI, as well as the obligatory picture of the only Catholic President, John F. Kennedy.

Monahan had been keeping himself busy by reading Friday's edition of the *New York Post*, when his brother entered the room. "You've chosen to read the New York Post over the Bible that's lying on the table in front of you Kevin? And it's yesterday's paper at that!"

"I'm a murder cop, Timothy, and I think I can read about more murders in the Post than I can even in the Bible."

Monahan's cell phone suddenly rang. It was Boyd.

"An Applicant Investigation detective working on a Saturday? What the hell? Oh, sorry, Tim, what the heck is this job coming to?" asked Monahan. "How's my one-time favorite partner?"

"Who are you with," Boyd asked. "Your brother? What have you got to confess? You overtip, you say 'thank you' to the squeegee guys, and the only time I hear a foul word out of you're mouth is when Lt. Fisher pisses you off. Ain't you working today?"

"Yeah. I'm going in for a night tour later," the detective said. "What's up, pal?"

"Kev, I'm working on an applicant case that's been bothering me. Doreen and the girls are going to her folks for the night, and I thought I might hook up with you later to talk about it."

"Sure, bud, anything for you, you know that. I have to drop my car off when I get back to Rockaway. My mechanic is going to do an inspection and oil change, Devaney is giving me a ride into work. Why don't you come by the precinct about ten? I'll take some lost time, and you can drive me back to Rockaway. We'll have some beers at McKeeferys. What is the case about?"

"I don't want to bother you with it now," Boyd said. "You're with your brother. I'll tell you all about it later. Just a quick question. Did you get a recent DNA hit on an old homicide? The perp is a mutt named Gary Pitt? Street name is Silky."

"Not that I am aware of. I'll check the Telephone Message Log when I get in. I'll also see if any new case file DD-5s came in."

"Okay, thanks buddy. I'll see you around ten. Tell your brother to say a prayer for me. God knows I need it."

Monahan hung up the phone and looked at his brother, now seated behind the desk. A cop ages in a busy precinct, and Monahan could see the same thing happening to his brother, aging quickly in a tough parish. Timothy's once thick dark brown hair was thinning, and flecks of gray had began appearing. Deep set lines had formed on his forehead, bags were under his light blue eyes, and prominent crow's feet were spreading from the corners of those eyes.

"You okay, Tim? You look tired."

Timmy shook his head, "I don't have to tell you, Kevin, Friday nights in this neighborhood keep me busy. I got a call from one of my parishioners about 1 a.m. Her son had gotten shot in the Vanderveer Houses. I met her at Kings County Hospital, where they had rushed her son, a sixteen-year-old boy running with the wrong crowd. He didn't make it. I didn't make it back here until almost 5 a.m."

Both brothers were silent for a moment, and Kevin was first to speak, "If you think about it, Tim, our work is very similar. We try and provide comfort to people in the very worst of situations. There is nothing on this earth that causes more anguish to a human being than the loss of a son or a daughter.

"At least you can provide some comfort with prayer, and convincing them that their loved one is in a better place. All I can do is promise them I will do my best to find the killer. Unfortunately, it is often times an empty promise. There is nothing worse for a family than knowing that the person that took their loved one is still roaming the street, breathing fresh air."

Kevin put his head down. "And that's why I'm here, Tim. For forty years I have been mailing the Mickens family a check each month. After all those years, I've finally come to the realization that I only do it to make myself feel better. They're no different than the families that I deal with now. They have a right to know that the killers of their son are no longer walking this earth, and hopefully it will bring them some comfort. I want to visit them to tell them everything, and I would like you to come with me, if you could."

Father Tim stared at his younger brother. "So instead of confessing to me like you do each time you've taken a drink or two, you would like to confess to them? I'm very proud of you, Kevin, although I have to say this should have been done a while ago. You understand what the ramifications might be with your job, don't you? If the Mickens family decides to report the incident you could be in a bit of trouble."

Kevin lifted his head, "Yeah, I know. But, Tim, I just can't take the nightmares any longer, and I truly believe it's the right thing to do. Hopefully, when I tell them that the two animals that killed their son are dead, it will help to ease their pain. Whatever happens, and you should know this better than anyone, it's in God's hands. We all have to pay for our sins sometime."

"Okay, Kevin. You know I'll be with you. When were you hoping to leave?"

Kevin leaned back into the leather couch. "I am off tomorrow and Monday. Tomorrow being Sunday, I know you couldn't go, but how about Monday? I have plenty of vacation time on the books, and I know Fisher wouldn't give me a problem taking off."

"Monday it is, then," said Father Tim. "I'll call you tomorrow afternoon. I overheard you telling Matty that you had brought your car in for service. I'm figuring you knew the car would be taking a long trip. Either way, if I had said yes or no, you planned on taking this trip. Am I right?"

Kevin stood up and laughed, "You should have been the detective, my brother." He walked over and hugged Father Tim, "I'll talk to you tomorrow."

*

The first thing Kevin did when he walked into the 7-5 Squad office was to fill out a "28" for vacation time for the following week. A 28 was the N.Y.P.D. form designation for a Request for Lost Time. He then brought the form over to Sgt.Dover, explaining that he needed the next week off to take care of some personal business. Dover readily signed the form as the authorizing supervisor, approving Monahan's request. Monahan then took the form and placed it on the Administrative Aide's desk, so that when she came in on Monday she could make the necessary adjustments to the roll call sheets.

After placing the sheet on the desk, Monahan walked over to the Telephone Message Log. Many of the notifications in the log were from Assistant District Attorneys, requesting various detectives to appear at court on a particular date. Other messages often received were notifications from Internal Affairs, the Medical Division, and the Detective Borough Command.

Monahan went through the past week's messages twice but there were no notifications about a DNA hit from the Liaison Office. He picked up the nearest phone and dialed the number for the Liaison Office, hoping somebody might be there on Saturday. He had no luck, however, as a message informed all callers that the office was closed for the weekends, and the caller should call back on Monday at 8 a.m.

The detective then walked over, sat down at his desk, and turned on his computer. He scrolled to the screen showing "Case Files" and hit *enter*. Once the screen appeared, a message alert flashed at the bottom of the screen. He clicked on the alert, and waited a few seconds before the message appeared. It was from the lab, informing him that, indeed, there was a DNA hit regarding a Gary Pitt. The 6-7 Squad had submitted evidence for DNA testing concerning a double homicide. The submitting detective, O'Laughlin, had apparently gotten a court order to swab Pitt. The message further stated that in addition to the hit on the 6-7 case, there was also a hit on a submission made by Detective Charlie Rowe of the 7-5 Squad, back in July of 1996.

Monahan knew Rowe as a sharp detective, and it did not surprise him that Rowe would have submitted a soda bottle for DNA testing. Back in 1996, DNA testing in law enforcement was in its infancy. There were too few labs, and the ones that were available were very expensive. But Rowe must have known, back in 1996, that in the near future DNA testing would become an invaluable tool for law enforcement. He more than likely also figured, quite correctly, that testing would become a standard step in a detective's case management. Monahan read on. The case Rowe had been investigating happened on July 12, 1996, Homicide #22, and the victim's last name was Watson.

*Watson?* thought Monahan. *What were the chances?* Monahan stood up and walked into the room containing the cold cases. He found the file cabinet that read "1996," pulled open the drawer, and searched for the folder labeled Homicide #22. It was missing. Figuring it was just filed incorrectly, Monahan went through each folder in the drawer. No # 22. He closed the the file cabinet drawer, exited the room, and walked into the supervisor's office. Stopping in front of Sgt. Dover's desk, he asked, "Hey, Sarge, did you also get the notification on the DNA hit submitted by Rowe on that cold case?"

Dover closed the case folder he had been reading and said, "Yeah. I was about to ask if you had a chance to look over the case?"

"Well, I would have loved to look over the case, but it's not in the file cabinet. I went through every folder for 1996, figuring it was just misplaced, but it's not in the drawer at all."

"Check with the cop Gleason, I had him go through all the cold-case homicides to make sure all the folders were in order. Maybe he pulled that case out for some reason."

"I think both he and Linc are off for the weekend. Let me check the electronic case file. If I'm lucky the case might have been entered in there."

At that moment Detective McQuirke entered the supervisor's office, and said, "Hey, Kevin, can you give me a hand running a lineup? I got the Chinese delivery guy here that had been shot in the leg during the robbery in one of the Cypress Project buildings. The lineup fillers are all here, they're in the lineup room right now. Sarge, I'll give you a yell when we're all ready."

"Any lawyer involved?" asked Dover.

"No. Miraculously, the Chinese guy picked out the suspect from our robbery photo book, and the suspect has no open cases."

Sgt.Dover breathed a sigh of relief. If the suspect had a case pending in court, or had been picked up on an arrest warrant, the right to an attorney would have immediately attached. That would have meant that when the victim viewed the lineup, the suspect's attorney would have to be present. Generally, this caused logistic problems as often the attorney made some kind of excuse not to appear at the precinct at a particular time, and the lineup would have to be re-scheduled.

The re-scheduling often caused problems for the victim, especially for those employed by Chinese restaurants, as they sometimes worked six-days-a-week, eighteen-hours a day. More often than not, the restaurant owners would dismiss the robberies as the price of doing business, and refuse to allow their employees any time off.

Dover then said, "Joe, refresh my memory on the case."

"Happened about two months ago. Male caller calls in an order for ribs, and a quart of chicken lo-mein and shrimp chow-mein. The delivery guy, our victim, goes into the lobby with the food. Three savages pop out of the stairwell, one with a gun, and they tell the vic to give up food and money. Unfortunately, the vic tries to make a run for it out of the building. Suspect with gun fires one shot, hitting vic in leg. Vic falls to floor, whereupon said savages take the food, rifle his pockets, and get thirty-two dollars. They also take his cell-phone. They then run out of the lobby to parts unknown. No witnesses, of course."

"What's our suspect look like?" asked Dover.

"Good chance it's him," said Joe. "Twenty-six-year-old shithead named Horace "Sneaky" Fletcher. Lives in one of the Cypress buildings, been taking collars since he was fifteen, mostly strong-arm robberies. He's out on parole right now. C'mon, let's get this going, Kevin, our victim is getting antsy. Says he's got to get back to work."

Kevin walked out of the office and over to the cell area. He opened the cell and had Fletcher walk backwards to the cell door. At that point Kevin snapped handcuffs over Fletcher's thick wrists. Fletcher was short and beefy, solid throughout from the generous amount of time he had spent working out in prison. Kevin grabbed one of Fletcher's muscular arms and led him into the line-up viewing room.

Inside the viewing room were seated five males, all in their mid-twenties and all of a similar build to Fletcher, or as close as possible. The fillers had come from a men's shelter, and it was obvious none had eaten quite as well as Fletcher in the recent months. They were happy to be used as fillers, as they received twenty dollars each just for sitting in a chair for about five minutes. Kevin spotted one problem however. All the fillers had hair, and Fletcher was bald. If the victim viewed the lineup as it was, the identification would be prejudiced, and when the case went to court, the identification would be thrown out at a Wade Hearing.

The detectives were prepared for such situations, and Kevin went over to a box in the corner of the room, opened the box, pulled out six plain white baseball caps, and handed them out to the six males in the room. Monahan then pulled out six pre-printed eight-by-twelve-inch cards from the same box. Each card had a large number on it, the numbers running from one to six.

"What seat do you want, Fletcher?"

"I want the seat in my muthafuckin livin room! Ain't nobody tol me why I'm in here, man! Ain't this some bullshit!" He was looking towards the five fillers for sympathy, but he found none, as they figured any agreement with the bald-headed bruiser could put their twenty dollars in jeopardy, so all remained silent.

An irritated Monahan said, "Listen, you want to know what this is all about? Pick a seat and you will find out soon enough! The longer you take to decide, the longer we're all gonna be standing here."

"A'ight, the faster I get out of this funky-smellin room the better I be. Man, did one of you muthafuckas shit yourself?"

Monahan had to admit that the smell in the room was becoming unbearable. Apparently none of the five fillers had availed themselves of the shower facilities at the shelter. The aroma that filled the room was similar to that of a locker filled with week-old sweat socks. Once the fillers had vacated the room, Shawn would be called in to mop the floors down with straight ammonia, and an industrial sized fan would attempt to clear out the stench.

Fletcher had finally decided. "Yo, give me seat number five. That's how many kids I got, I think."

Monahan handed Fletcher card number five, and the suspect sat in the fifth seat from the left. The fillers grabbed the remaining cards and filled in the empty seats. Monahan then placed the white caps on all six individual's heads.

"Okay. Everyone sit straight up, keep the cards in front of your chest, and look straight ahead." Monahan then walked over to the one-way mirror and placed his hand between the shade covering the mirror and the mirror itself. He then gently rapped his knuckles on the mirror, indicating to McQuirke and Dover that the lineup was ready to be viewed. He then heard McQuirke's voice, "Okay, Kevin. Pull it up."

Monahan lifted the shade and stepped to the side of the one-way mirror. Standing on the other side of the mirror were McQuirke, Dover, and the victim, Eddie Shen. Shen was a twenty-two-year-old South Korean who had arrived in America when he was fifteen years old. Standing only five-foot-six inches tall, the delivery man weighed maybe 120 pounds soaking wet.

His lack of weight was largely caused by the twelve-hours-a-day he rode a bicycle around East New York delivering food. A young Oriental male riding around the streets of East New York on a bike, carrying Chinese food and money, was like an American soldier driving around Fallujah in a convertible Mustang. He was playing Russian roulette. Shen's hours had been recently cut down to ten, as his boss felt sorry for Shen because of his newly acquired gunshot wound. Thankfully, the bullet had been a through-and-through to Shen's left calf. If the bullet had been two inches to the left and had hit Shen's tibia bone, the bone would have shattered like a vase dropped off a ten-story project roof, as Shen's bones weren't much larger than those of a Thanksgiving turkey.

McQuirke asked Shen to step up to the mirror and look at the six individuals seated inside the room. Shen at first refused, fearing that he could be spotted by the seated men. It took McQuirke and Dover a few minutes to convince the slight South Korean that only he could see inside. The men could not see him. All the while, Monahan was on the other side of the mirror, kicking himself in the ass for not remembering to bring the jar of Vicks Vapor rub that he kept in his desk drawer. Finally, the delivery man stepped up to the window.

McQuirke then spoke to Shen, "Mr.Shen, I want you to take your time. Look at the men seated in front of you and tell me if you recognize any of them. If you do, tell me how and why you recognize that person."

Shen nervously stepped closer to the mirror and looked back and forth at the seated men for several minutes. The prolonged viewing by Shen began to make McQuirke and Dover a bit concerned, but in a way they expected it. Asian victims had a very difficult time identifying their American assailants. Most detectives figured that all non-Asians looked alike to them.

Finally, McQuirke said, "Mr.Shen, do you recognize anyone seated in front of you."

Much to the detective's relief, Shen said, "Yes I do."

"Which one, Mr.Shen, and how do you recognize that person?" asked McQuirke.

"I recognize aw of them! They aw rob me in robby."

McQuirke looked at Dover and shook his head, "Okay, Mr.Shen. Thank you for your time. We will be in touch with you." The case was now basically closed, as Shen's failure to identify his assailant, and more importantly, the fact that he identified five innocent men from a shelter, indicated that the victim could not I.D. Unless Fletcher or one of his accomplices confessed to the robbery/shooting, the case would be closed.

McQuirke then banged on the glass, letting Monahan know that the lineup had concluded. Monahan quickly shut the shade as Sgt. Dover entered the lineup room. No people were happier to see Dover than the five shelter inhabitants, as he peeled off twenty-dollar bills, and handed one each to each of the lineup volunteers.

"The first thing I'm doin is getting me some goot Chi-nie food!" said one, unaware that the restaurant he might dine in was one that a certain delivery man had just accused him of robbery.

While Dover was handing out the money, Monahan's first move was to turn the industrial-sized fan on high. He then motioned for Fletcher to stand up, whereupon Monahan reared-cuffed the prisoner and led him back to his cell.

"Will somebody tell me what the fuck is goin on?" asked Fletcher. After uncuffing Fletcher and placing him back in the cell, Monahan turned around and walked away. As he walked back to his desk, he saw McQuirke come into the squad office.

McQuirke had just escorted Mr. Shen out of the precinct and was in a foul mood. He shook his head at Monahan, "I know that scumbag did it, but, not surprisingly, our victim could not identify. No. I'm sorry. He could identify. He identified Fletcher and all the skells sitting in the room as the perps." Monahan could not help but laugh.

"It's not funny, Kev. I know he ain't gonna talk cause he already mentioned a lawyer, so now I have to release this shithead and void the arrest," said the distraught detective. The N.Y.P.D. frowned upon releasing prisoners, and in order to get the point across they did not make it easy for the arresting officer to void collars. With a voided arrest there was always the specter of a lawsuit for false arrest. In Fletcher's case, McQuirke had had the right to make the collar, since Shen had picked Fletcher out of a photo array and had signed paperwork attesting to that fact, but the threat of a lawsuit, and all the bullshit that came with it, was always in the back of a cop's mind after a voided arrest.

McQuirke would have to release Fletcher immediately and return any property that had been taken from him. He would then have to escort Fletcher down to the front desk and explain to the desk officer why he was releasing his one-time prisoner, whereupon that supervisor would have to make a blotter entry in the command log indicating the time Fletcher was released and why. McQuirke would then have to call down to Brooklyn Central

Booking and ask a supervisor to prepare an On Line Booking Sheet, and an arrest number would be assigned. The supervisor would have to mark the arrest as "voided," and McQuirke, as well as every other cop, knew that once you asked a supervisor to do any paperwork he was not normally required to do, it became a problem.

McQuirke walked over to the cell and opened it up, "Cmon, Sneaky, you're outta here."

"You gonna explain to me what that was all about, or is my lawyer gonna have to ask you?"

McQuirke knew this was the worst part of releasing a prisoner-- the shit you had to swallow. "You were picked out of a photo array and you needed to sit in a lineup. You got lucky. The vic could not I.D."

"Course he couldn't I.D. I didn't do shit. I gonna get paid for reparations like them stinky muthafuckas that were sittin in the room with me?"

A pissed-off McQuirke said, "You ain't getting shit. Just be thankful you're walkin out of here. Now let's get this done." McQuirke returned his prisoner's property and brought him down to the front desk. The detective explained to the desk officer the circumstances of the release and told Fletcher to get the fuck out of the precinct.

Fletcher just sucked his teeth and looked at McQuirke, "Tell that Chinnie muthafucka that shrimp lo-mein sucked anyway." The bald-headed bruiser then hitched up his pants and strode out of the precinct's front door.

Up in the squad room Monahan glanced at the clock hanging on the wall and was disconcerted to see that it was almost seven o'clock. He was planning on meeting Boyd at ten, and he had yet to try to find the old homicide case in the computer. In addition, he was taking the whole next week off to visit the Mickens family, and there were still some loose ends he wanted to tie up on a few of his current cases.

He had just sat down at his computer, hoping that the Watson homicide had been entered into the Case Management System, when the radio emitted an unnerving three beeps. The beeps were generated by the Communications dispatcher and indicated to all cops listening that a heavy job was about to be transmitted over the radio. Sgt. Dover heard the beeps and he walked out of his office to join his detectives. They stared at the radio. "Units, be advised we are getting multiple calls of a male shot in front of 1260 Loring Avenue. Any units to respond?"

The detectives heard yelling in the background as a cop was apparently about to transmit a message. "Central, this is the Pink Houses post. We are 10-84 at the location. We do have a confirmed male shot numerous times. Have EMS respond. We're also gonna need a supervisor here, and you might as well notify the 7-5 Squad."

Monahan looked at Dover and the sergeant said, "Sorry, Kev, but I'm gonna need you and Archer to respond there. I want McQuirke to finish up the paperwork on Fletcher, and Kalergios and Courtney are gonna be transporting Courtney's prisoner down to Central Booking."

Monahan shut down his computer, and he and the big, black detective Benny Archer grabbed their jackets. Archer grabbed a set of car keys from the hook hanging outside the supervisor room door and made an entry in the log that he and Monahan were responding to 1260 Loring Avenue in RMP 824. Monahan grabbed their two radios.

*

The two detectives arrived at the scene within ten minutes of leaving the precinct. The scene was chaotic, as it often is during daytime and early evening shootings, especially on a Saturday. For the detectives, the scenario had good and bad points. More people at the scene meant the potential of more witnesses, but, on the other hand, the crime scene itself was difficult to hold together, as the numerous bystanders tried to get as close as possible to the victim. Their physical closeness to the victim afforded them the

217

opportunity to regale their friends and neighbors with the story of how they were there, when-so-and-so got lit up, and they could accurately describe his wounds and how much blood he lost. All the while they were inadvertently kicking shell casings and stepping in blood.

Monahan noticed that this scene was not as chaotic as others, and he quickly ascertained the reason why. Shock and Awe were securing the crime scene.

"If you don't move, I'm gonna split your skulls like fuckin coconuts!" yelled the huge, black cop, Fulfree, at a couple of young thugs who were refusing to back away from the crime scene tape. After doing the requisite teeth-sucking, the two teens slowly sauntered away, displaying for the gaggle of giggling young girls just how tough they were. Both knew, however, that they were more than likely going to receive slaps to the back of the head by the two crazy giant cops at a later date.

Monahan walked over to the cop. "Evening, John, you got anything on this for me?"

Fulfree turned to face the detective, "Hey, Monahan. Yeah, the vic is a local. Lives in this building, at 1260, in Apartment 3-D. His name is Tyrell Simpson. When we got on the scene I had one of my snitches come up to me and tell me some shithead named Bedbug did the deed. This Bedbug is supposed to be this crazy little fucker that's an assassin for a drug gang out of East Flatbush."

"So the victim was selling?"

"Naw, man, that's just it. Truth, that's his street name, used to dabble a little, but since his granmoms died he's been pretty straight. Word is she left him and his brother, Thomas, some money. The granmom's death hit Truth hard, and since her death I heard he got on with a construction crew and has pretty much straightened himself out."

"Who's the next of kin, his brother? Where is he at?"

"Thomas is a sergeant in the army, 82$^{nd}$ Airborne. I spoke to him when his grandmom's died. I notified the Army about her death and told them I had to get a hold of him. After about an hour he called me from somewhere in the Mid-East, couldn't tell me where he was, some secret squirrel shit. That's one tough muthafucka, Monahan. He's been deployed in Afganistan, on and off, since 2003. Joined up right after 9/11. Think he's stateside now. Plans on getting out, he said. I think I got a number for him, I'll get it to you guys."

"Appreciate it, John. Now, what about your snitch?"

"As soon as we get some relief here, which should be soon, I'm gonna meet him in the parking lot of the diner on Pennsylvania Avenue and Linden. I get any info, I'll come up to the squad with it."

Monahan nodded and lifted up the yellow crime scene tape. He made his way under the tape and walked over to the lifeless body of Tyrell Simpson. The sky was quickly becoming dark, and the amber lights from the front of the project building cast an eerie glow over the scene. Detective Archer had grabbed a sleeve of small, white plastic drinking cups from the trunk of the detective's RMP and was placing those cups over the shell casings lying on the walkway. The cups would protect those casings until the Crime Scene Unit arrived and placed their own numbered plastic protectors over the casings.

The bright white plastic cups were in sharp contrast to the deep black walkway. Tyrell was lying on his back, his arms outstretched, almost as if he had been crucified. The black walkway upon which he lie was absorbing the blood seeping out of the bullet holes in his back. It seemed to be sucking the precious crimson liquid from the young man's body into the earth.

Monahan walked over to Archer. "I got an I.D on the victim. Lived in this building. Might even have a street name for the shooter. Gonna firm that up later. Wanna start canvassing for witnesses? Maybe someone else knows the shooter, and hopefully we can get a good I.D."

The taciturn Archer simply nodded and pulled out his Reporter's Notebook. He then made his way into the crowd.

Unbeknownst to the detectives, if they wanted a good I.D, all they had to do was look across the courtyard and up to the third floor terrace.

*

It had been early afternoon when Bedbug had sat down on the bench in front of 1260 Loring Avenue. After having waited two hours on the bench, Bedbug's target had finally exited the building. Bedbug might have been a psychopath, but he was a patient psychopath. He knew any sudden moves would spook the dude named Tyrell, so when Tyrell had nodded at Bedbug, the killer simply nodded back. The sun had not completely set, and there were still quite a few children running and playing in the courtyard, but Bedbug couldn't give a shit less. A job was a job.

Bedbug waited for Tyrell to pass him on the bench, and then he stood up and called Tyrell by his street name, but first he pulled out the 9mm Glock he had secured in his waistband.

Then Tyrell Simpson heard the last words he would ever hear again on earth, "Yo, Truth, what up?

Tyrell turned around and stared at the thin, light-skinned black youngin who had been sitting on the bench. The gun the young boy had been holding then began barking, and four 9mm bullets exploded inside of Tyrell's chest cavity. Bedbug had been so close that the bullets slamming into Tyrell's chest actually knocked Tyrell off his feet.

Bedbug did not bother to pick up the ejected shell casings. He just calmly turned around and walked inside the project building where Tyrell Simpson had resided all his life. The screams from the children in the courtyard made Bedbug smile, as he walked through the lobby and exited the building through the back door. From the back of the building he made a left and walked onto Loring Avenue. He crossed the street at Loring and walked east to Autumn Avenue. Passing the killing site, Bedbug saw the first police units arrive.

Once he hit Autumn Avenue, he made a left, and strolled a short while, until he came to the back of building number 1258, the sister building to 1260. Once again, he entered the back door and took the stairs up to the third floor. His feet had begun to swell inside the tight, tan Timberland boots he was wearing, and he knew he needed to sit down. Exiting into the third floor hallway, Bedbug walked over to the door leading to the terrace. He looked through the door's small window, out onto the terrace, and he was pleased with what he saw.

Not only did the terrace provide an excellent view of the crime scene, but an older woman was sitting in what appeared to be a comfortable beach chair on the terrace. The woman looked to be in her mid-seventies, and she was wearing a flowered housedress partly covered by a blue New York Mets windbreaker. Despite the chilly March air, she was wearing white, open-toed sandals. In her hand was a cup of tea, and the woman seemed to be thoroughly enjoying the entertainment of the frenetic crime scene taking place in the courtyard below her.

Bedbug opened the door, stepped onto the terrace and walked over to the woman, "Yo, ol lady. Ya gots to give up that chair. My dogs be hurtin."

The old woman looked at Bedbug, shook her head and continued to watch the entertainment unfolding before her in the courtyard. Bedbug felt like pulling out his gat and capping the old bitch in the head, the way she was disrespecting him, but instead he pulled a cigarette from his pack of Newports and fired it up. Standing next to the woman he began blowing smoke rings in her face.

The woman finally spoke, "What if I yell down to the police that you're bothering me with that smoke? How would you like that?"

Bedbug calmly said, "Ya worried bout smoke, ol' lady? Well, ya yell to the Babylon and I gonna find out where ya apartment is and put the muthafucka on fire. Ten ya can worry about da smoke. Now get ya wrinkly ass up and give me dat chair. I ain't gonna be more den a half-hour. Ya go watch some shit on T.V. fo a lil' while and come back in half hour. Ya chair be here."

The woman stared into Bedbug's crazed eyes and stood up, thinking that perhaps she might be better off watching Wheel of Fortune, than dealing with the young lunatic in front of her.

As soon as the woman left, Bedbug settled into the beach chair, took off his Timberlands, patted down the tight cornrows atop his head, and fired up a spliff. He watched the scene below, paying particular attention to anyone who spoke to the police at the scene. He wasn't happy about having to do a job for that sneaky muthfucka, Silky, but he enjoyed his work all the same. Nigel told him that the dude Truth had been a player a few years back, but somehow he ran afoul of Silky.

From what Bedbug had heard at a recent meeting amongst Nigel's lieutenants, one of them had reminded Silky about the time Truth told Silky to get off Pink Houses property or suffer an ass-whipping. All the lieutenants at the meeting had begun laughing, and Silky flew into a rage, wanting to kill Truth right then and there. Nigel had calmed Silky down, and promised Silky he would take care of it. He had reminded Silky that the East New York drug dealer didn't need another run-in with the law. Nigel called Bedbug the next day, and Tyrell Simpson's fate was sealed.

*

Matty Boyd left his house in Bayside a little early. Knowing he wasn't meeting Monahan until ten, he figured he might just make a quick stop at 180 Wortman Avenue. It was only ten to fifteen minutes driving time from 180 Wortman to the 7-5 and Matty didn't plan on staying long. He just wanted to knock on a few doors to see if anyone on the 8th floor recognized Linc.

Boyd also did not plan on staying out very late, as he was to meet his dad, a retired N.Y.P.D. cop, out on Long Island the next morning. His father lived out in East Islip and was a member of the Ancient Order of Hibernians. Each year, members from the local chapter of the Irish organization marched in the St. Patrick's Day parade along Montauk Highway. It had become a family tradition that Matty would march in the parade with his dad.

Matty was especially excited because this year his nineteen-year-old-son, Michael had agreed to join his pop and grandfather in the march. When he was younger, Michael had thought it not-cool to march with a bunch of old men down the streets of East Islip, but he had suddenly developed some pride in his Irish heritage.

Boyd drove down the Cross Island Parkway and took the westbound split for the Belt Parkway. Even the notoriously slow moving Belt had little traffic, and within fifteen minutes of getting on the Belt, he was exiting off onto Pennsylvania Avenue. He drove north on Pennsylvania and made the right turn onto Flatlands Avenue. From there he made the left on Vermont, and quickly found a parking spot in front of the public school across from 180 Wortman. He locked his car and began walking across the street to enter the building.

Standing on the side of the building, watching the white guy get out of the silver Camry, was Maurice Allen, known as "Pumpkin" on the street. Pumpkin was one of two enforcers employed by Silky to watch visitors coming into 180 Wortman, and both enforcers were instructed to be on high alert after being told of the shooting of Tyrell Simpson. Silky was taking precautions in case of any possible retaliation. Pumpkin pulled out his cell phone and immediately called Bam-Bam, advising him that a lone 5-0 was coming into the building. Pumpkin was directed to follow the cop.

Boyd entered the lobby of the building and walked over to the elevator. Before pressing the button, Boyd began to get an uneasy feeling. Maybe he should call the 7-5 Precinct and have a sector car meet him. If any trouble started, Boyd didn't even have a radio. Then he thought that, as it was a Saturday night, all the sector cars would probably be busy, and for him to call for back-up before there was even any trouble would make he seem like his scared-ass partner, Joe Angelo. *After all,* he thought to himself, *I've worked this precinct for years. These are my projects.* He pushed the elevator button.

The elevator arrived, and the doors groaned open. Boyd was glad there was no one else on it. He pressed the button for the top floor, the eighth, and stepped back. Someone must have used the elevator car for a toilet, because the enclosed space smelled like piss. The doors once again began groaning to close, but just before they shut, a hand came between the two doors. The doors opened. Boyd instinctively placed his hand on his off-duty, Smith-and-Wesson thirty-eight caliber revolver. The gun was strapped to Boyd's belt, underneath his navy blue windbreaker.

Boyd eyed the young male entering the elevator. The male looked at the eight buttons on the floor panel for just a little bit longer than Boyd felt necessary. Boyd's button, number eight, was lit, and the male pressed seven. Boyd was glad he had his back to the wall, and he kept an eye on the male's hands, which at that moment were hanging down by his sides. The elevator door closed once again, and the elevator lurched upward. Boyd noticed the male was wearing a black-and-silver FUBU sweatshirt. A Yankee cap sat perched atop his head, and designer jeans were tucked into a spotless pair of white Air Jordans. The male's cologne helped mask the urine stench.

The elevator finally shuddered to a stop on the seventh floor, and the male exited. Boyd saw him turn and walk to the right. Boyd stepped over to the control panel, not taking his hand off his revolver, and pushed the *door close* button. He then moved into the front corner of the elevator, opposite the control panel, feeling safer at that location. The doors finally closed, and the car began its upward journey, one more stop.

*

Linc had just finished cleaning up the table after dinner. His mother was settled in the living room watching a reality show, and Harris was in the bedroom, catching up on school work. Linc had finalized his plan on how he was going to repay Silky for his father's murder. He had rehearsed the plan again and again in his head, and he had found no flaws.

He was in no rush, as he knew Silky would be home, even though it was a Saturday night. Ever since Silky had gotten locked up for the assault in East Flatbush, he had been lying low. Silky had been released on bail, and didn't want to fuck anything up before his next court hearing, so Linc was sure Silky would not set foot out of 180 Wortman. The first step in Linc's plan was a phone call.

Linc walked into the bedroom and asked Harris if he wouldn't mind studying out in the kitchen. He explained to his brother that he was tired, and just wanted to lie down for a spell. Harris picked up his books and walked out of the bedroom towards the kitchen. Linc took out his cell phone and hit the speed dial for his best friend.

"Yo, Shortfinger, what you doin, cuz?"

"Nothin much, B. Probably goin over to a party at Moniques. You know that girl lives over in the 240 building?"

"Yeah, I know her. You ain't workin for Silk tonight?"

"Naw, man. It quiet. I don't know what happened, but he don't want nobody slingin in front of the building tonight. Only guys workin are Pumpkin and some other dude. All they doin is watchin the building, though. Some shit musta gone down."

"I hear that. Listen, man, you got to do me a big favor, and you can't ask me about it right now. Me and you tight right. Been that way since we pups."

"Yo, cuz. You know it. What you need, you know I be there."

Linc explained to his best friend what he wanted him to do, and although Shortfinger was somewhat confused, he agreed. Linc's repayment plan for Silky was in motion.

*

After exiting the elevator on the seventh floor, Pumpkin walked over to the stairwell, opened the door, and ran up one flight of stairs to the eighth floor. He opened the eighth floor stairwell door a crack, and heard the doors to the elevator open. Peeking out,

Pumpkin saw the cop emerge from the elevator and look down the hallway towards Silky's apartment.

*

Boyd stepped off the elevator and saw the hallway was empty. He looked down the hall towards Silky's apartment, and decided there was no way he could knock on the door right across from 8B, Silky's apartment number. That left only two other apartments on that side of the hallway he could canvas. If he struck out there, he would have to knock on the four apartment doors to the right of the elevator.

He walked quietly down the hallway and stopped in front of Apartment 8C. Taking his shield out of his pocket he began to knock on the heavy green door. He knocked quite a few times, and, hearing no response, he put his ear to the door. He heard nothing, not even the sound of a television or stereo. He turned around and stopped in front of Apartment 8D. Once again, holding his shield in his left hand, he knocked on the thick apartment door. He heard footsteps inside the apartment approach the door.

"Who's there?" asked a deep male voice.

Boyd did not want to yell "police" in the quiet hallway, so he just put his shield up to the peephole.

"One second," said the male.

Boyd heard an unending number of chains and locks being opened. Finally, the door was opened by a clean-shaven male in his mid-fifties. Once the male got a good look at Boyd he opened the door a little wider. Boyd could see that the male was a postal worker, as he was wearing gray slacks with thin blue piping down the sides, black, thick-soled shoes meant for walking, and a white T-shirt.

Speaking in a voice barely above a whisper, Boyd said, "Sorry to bother you, sir. Would you mind if I came in?"

"I would rather you didn't. Me and my family are just ready to sit down for dinner. Can I help you with something?"

Boyd quickly glanced down the hall towards Silky's apartment. All seemed quiet. In a low voice Boyd asked, "I was just wondering if you could look at a photo and tell me if you have ever seen the male in the photo up on this floor?"

Boyd took the picture of Linc out of his windbreaker pocket. He handed the photo to the male, who turned on the hallway light inside his apartment.

The male studied the photo for a short time, and nodded. He stepped outside his apartment door and glanced down the hallway towards the elevator. Seeing no one was in the hallway, he pointed towards Silky's apartment and nodded. He handed the photo back to Boyd, stepped back into his apartment, and quickly shut the door.

Standing in the middle of the hallway with Linc's photo in his hand, Boyd thought to himself, *Son of a bitch, the kid is working for a murdering drug dealer.* Boyd turned around and walked over to the elevator.

*

Pumpkin had watched the events in the hallway unfold through the small opening in the stairwell door. Unsure what to do, he decided to continue watching the cop. He closed the stairwell door, turned around and sprinted down the flights of stairs. Within a minute, he had reached the bottom floor, and was about to open the door into the lobby when he heard someone in the lobby call out "5-0". He caught a quick glimpse of the cop walking by the stairwell's small window. Pumpkin waited a few seconds, and then stepped into the lobby. He pulled out his cell phone and dialed Silky's number.

Silky answered on the second ring, "What up?"

"Yo, Silk," said a breathless Pumpkin. "The cop be talking to one of yo neighbors. Showed the dude some type of picture, and the dude nodded at yo door to the muthafucka. I'm in the lobby. The cop just left the building. What you want me to do?"

Silky knew the picture Boyd had shown the neighbor. It had to be the same one he had shown Silky, a picture of Linc. "You know where he parked his car? This is what yo gonna do."

*

Boyd had an uneventful ride on the elevator until he reached the lobby. As soon as he stepped off the elevator, two young knuckleheads getting on, yelled out, "5-0". It didn't take Sherlock Holmes to realize that any white guy in the building on a Saturday night had to be either nuts or a cop. Boyd was going to start fucking with the two, but decided there was no time. He had to get hold of Monahan. He exited the rear of the building, stopped on the walkway and pulled out his cell phone. He dialed Monahan's cell number, but it went right to voicemail.

Boyd spoke into the phone, "Hey, Kev, it's me. Listen, I was at 180 Wortman, eighth floor, and it's hard for me to process what I just found out. I think one of your cops is a fuckin mole, just like some spy shit, brother. I thought if you were in this area you could stop by. You're probably out on a job. You don't have to call me back, I'm gonna head over to the squad now anyway. I'll tell you all about it over some beers. It's some fucked-up shit man."

Boyd hung up and looked up at the windows of the eighth-floor corner apartment. Lights were on. "I told you I'd get you, you slick son of a bitch," he said out loud.

As he crossed Vermont Street, Boyd pulled out his car keys and hit the remote, opening the locks on his Camry. He glanced around to make sure no one had followed him, opened the door of the car, and slid into the driver's seat. He looked at his watch and saw it was only 9:15. He wasn't supposed to meet Kevin until ten. He pulled out Linc's photo once again, looked at it, shook his head, and slid the photo into the zippered pocket on the inside of his windbreaker. Then he heard a banging on his window.

Boyd looked through the glass, and although it was dark he recognized the male standing outside the window, it was the kid from the elevator. The detective's survival instincts immediately took over. Boyd reached for the gun on his waistband, while trying to climb over the stick shift to get to the passenger side of the vehicle. The driver's side window suddenly shattered from the impact of the 9 milli-meter bullet fired from the kid's gun. Boyd was now on his back, trying desperately to get his gun out of his holster, but there was no time. He was lying on his back on the passenger seat, his feet in the air. He began kicking his feet, as if they would somehow deflect the bullets that were now raining into the car.

The fourth bullet fired from Pumpkin's gun entered the soft tissue underneath Boyd's jaw, and that bullet sped through the detective's pallet and nasal cavity before entering the base of the brain. The 9 milli-meter, 124 grain bullet was traveling at about 1300 feet per second when it left the barrel of the gun. The soft tissue of the brain was no match for the incredible speed of the lead slug, and the bullet sped through Boyd's brain, destroying any tissue it came in contact with. It exited the top of Boyd's skull leaving a larger hole than the one underneath his jaw. Matty Boyd's body shut down.

Now, instead of marching along the streets of East Islip with his dad and grandpops, listening to the bagpipes play the light, airy tune of, "When Irish Eyes Are Smiling", Matty's son, Michael Boyd, would be listening to those same bagpipes airing the mournful dirge of "Danny Boy" at his father's funeral.

Pumpkin jumped into the driver's seat of the Camry, started up the car, and pulled away from the curb. Behind him was Bam-Bam, in a 2007 black Jeep Cherokee. Pumpkin made a right turn onto Wortman Avenue, drove east to Schenck Avenue, made another right, and followed Schenck south to a desolate area by the sewage treatment plant. He pulled to the side of the road, popped the gas latch, and exited the vehicle. Bam-Bam ran over to the Camry and stuffed an old t-shirt into the mouth of the Camry's gas tank, lit the shirt, and ran back to the Jeep. Both he and Pumpkin then drove off, back to 180 Wortman.

*

Two partners in an E.M.S. bus were enjoying a quiet meal, parked on Seaview Avenue, just west of Schenck. They had ten minutes left in their meal hour when they noticed flames flickering off the blacktop, not far in front of them, on the corner of Schenck and Seaview. The driver threw what remained of his coffee out of the window, started the bus, and roared up the block to Schenck. Making the left onto the block, he pulled the bus across the street from a car fire, which had almost fully engulfed a Camry.

Both men jumped out of the truck and ran over to the car. The taller of the E.M.S. techs looked into the driver's side window, hoping the vehicle was empty of passengers. There was no one in the driver's seat, but the tech thought he saw a pair of legs and feet lying across the passenger seat. The tech put heavy canvas gloves on his hands as he ran to the other side of the vehicle. He knew he had to act quickly, as the vehicle's gas tank was likely to explode at any moment.

The intense heat coming from the vehicle nearly pushed the tech back, but he heroically grabbed the hot door handle on the passenger side door and yanked it open. A white male was lying on the floor in the well underneath the glove box dashboard. The tech grabbed the victim underneath his armpits and dragged him onto the street. His partner, who had radioed for the fire department, shoved the radio back into his jacket pocket and ran over to assist him.

While the taller tech had his hands underneath the victim's armpits, the shorter one grabbed the victim's legs, and they ran, carrying the victim across the street to their truck. Once across the street, they heard the gas tank explode and saw a large orange flame burst through the roof of the vehicle. Black, acrid smoke poured out from the interior of the car, as the cloth seats began burning. One look at the numerous bullet holes in the victim caused the shorter tech to get back on his radio, and request police response to the scene for an apparent homicide.

*

Monahan and Archer had finished the homicide scene at the Pink Houses and were loading up the equipment into the trunk of their car. Looking at the clock on his cell phone, Monahan saw it was almost 9:50, and he noticed that he had a voicemail waiting. He accessed his voicemail and heard Boyd's message. He wondered what the hell Matty was doing at 180 Wortman, and who the mole was he was talking about. He hoped his ex-partner hadn't decided to start drinking early and was playing a prank on him. He wouldn't put it past the Merry Prankster. It was almost ten, and Matty should be at the precinct, thought Monahan.

Although Archer had caught the murder case of Tyrell Simpson, Monahan knew he would have to spend at least an hour typing out the DD-5s on his interviews from the scene. Boyd would not be happy about losing an hour of drinking time.

Monahan slipped into the passenger seat of the unmarked car, and as Archer began to pull away from the curb, Monahan's cell phone rang. "Kev, it's Dover. I guess you didn't hear the radio, but they got a body down by the sewage plant on Schenck, a little north of Seaview. Victim shot multiple times. E.M.S pulled the vic out of a burning car. I'll meet you down there."

"Oh, shit, Sarge. I'm supposed to meet Matty in the office at ten. We were gonna go out for some St. Paddy Day beers. Don't you have anyone else to go? A murder case with a burning crime scene will be a bag of shit, anyway. It has to be a dump job."

"McQuirke is done with his Chinese robbery case, so he will take the murder. I just need you and Benny to go down and give him a hand. You probably won't be long, because you're right. More than likely it's gonna be a dump job."

"10-4. See you in a little while."

# CHAPTER 16

It was a little after ten o'clock when Linc noticed his mother had fallen asleep in her favorite chair while watching T.V. He shut the T.V. off, placed a blanket over her legs, gave her a kiss on the forehead, and walked into the kitchen.

"Hey, little man, you can go back into the bedroom now," he told his brother. Harris had just about fallen asleep while studying at the kitchen table. In a sleepy daze Harris stood up and walked into the hallway. As he walked into the hallway, Harris noticed the baseball bat placed against the wall near the front door.

"He-he-hey Linc, a-a-ain't th-th-that your T-T-Tony Gwynn bat?"

Linc had hoped his brother wouldn't spot the bat. "Yeah. Jus gonna show it to Shortfinger."

His brother nodded, rubbed his eyes, and began walking down the hallway to the bedroom.

"Harris, hol' up." Linc walked down the hallway and hugged his brother to his chest. "Sleep well, little man. You know I love you, right?"

Harris nodded his head into Linc's chest, then stepped away, turned around and continued walking to the bedroom. Linc's watched his brother go into the bedroom. He then walked to the door, grabbed the bat, and exited the apartment.

*

Monahan and Archer pulled up in front of the crime scene tape that had been strung across Schenck Avenue. As soon as Monahan exited the car and went underneath the crime scene tape, he saw Sgt. Dover. Dover was talking to McQuirke, but as soon as he saw Monahan, he stepped away from McQuike and began walking over towards him. Dover looked upset.

"What's up, Sarge? Don't tell me it was a kid."

Dover could not look at Monahan. "No Kev. I don't know how to tell you this. Its Matty Boyd."

Monahan felt the air being knocked out of him. He rushed past Dover and ran over to to the back of the E.M.S. truck, where the body of Matty lay, covered by a light blue canvas blanket. Monahan lifted the blanket and gazed at the face of his old partner. The gunshot wound to the underside of Boyd's jaw, had shattered the jaw, causing Boyd's mouth to hang open. His blondish hair was tinged with red, and it was matted down, wet from the blood that had seeped out the exit hole in the top of his skull

"Why the fuck is he still in the street?" yelled Monahan.

"Take it easy, Kevin," said Dover. "We put a rush on the M.E.'s van. They should be here any minute."

"He was working on something, Sarge, over at the Linden Projects. Was he searched?"

Dover shook his head. "We didn't know he was working on anything. We thought he was driving through the area to meet you at the precinct. We figured it might have been a carjack-- they found he was a cop, panicked, and shot him. Me and McQuirke will search the car, or what's left of it." Dover called for McQuirke, and the two of them began walking over to the burned Camry.

Monahan then removed the blanket covering Boyd. He put on the pair of latex gloves he had in his suitjacket pocket, and he began going through his ex-partner's pockets. He unzipped the right front pocket of the windbreaker and pulled out Boyd's shield case. It still contained his shield. Monahan thought to himself, *if it was a carjack, the mutts would have taken this and gotten rid of it quick.*

Continuing his search, he found Boyd's wallet in the left front pocket of the green Dockers pants Boyd was wearing. He opened the wallet, and counted out seventy-six dollars in cash. He knew Boyd's murder was no robbery. Finding no other items, Monahan removed a plastic zip-lock bag from his suitjacket and deposited both wallet and shieldcase in the bag. He then zipped up Boyd's windbreaker, and as he did, he felt something soft inside.

233

He opened the jacket, saw a pocket, unzipped the pocket, and pulled out a photo, a department photo of Linc Watson.

*

Linc crossed Wortman Avenue and followed the walkway to the front of 180 Wortman. He slowed down, expecting to see Silky's enforcer, Pumpkin, standing in front of the lobby, but he wasn't there. Another homeboy was standing on the walkway, and the way the male continually pulled at the waistband of his jeans indicated to Linc that the male, more than likely, had a gun tucked inside that waistband. This could be the dude that Shortfinger had spoken about, a newcomer from East Flatbush now working for Silky. Linc wasn't worried, as the punk was in an animated conversation with two girls, and had no clue as to what was happening around him. *Amateur*, thought Linc.

Keeping the bat pinned against the right side of his leg, Linc quickly walked into the lobby. Not wanting to take the chance of being seen by the new enforcer in the well-lit lobby, Linc opted to take the stairs up to the eighth floor. He took them two steps at a time to reach the top floor. He continued up the final set of stairs to the door onto the roof of the building. He pushed open the heavy steel door and he stepped out onto the gravel of the roof. With the blue and gray gravel crunching underneath his feet, Linc walked over to one of the large gray exhaust units that dotted the rooftop.

Taking a deep breath of the cool March air, Linc looked up to the bright, almost full, moon. It was a night or two shy of reaching its full brilliance, but still bright enough to showcase the hundreds of stars surrounding it. He watched as thin, wispy cirrus clouds, pushed by a brisk northwind, passed quickly in front of the moon. The light from the moon illuminated the clouds with a reddish hue. To Linc, it seemed as if every one of the feathery clouds was paying its respects to the brilliance and beauty of the moon, which on that evening, ruled the night sky.

He had always made a point of going up to his project rooftop whenever he knew he could get a clear view of a full moon. His project was fourteen floors high, so he felt closer to the glowing orb there then he did on this night. He would sit on the edge of the roof, fifteen stories above the ground, and stare up up at a night sky, so bright it gave him his only chance to spot an elusive shooting star. His grandmother had once said that a shooting star was actually the soul of a loved one, traveling across the heavens. It was a sign, indicating to the watcher that the departed were always there for them, but Linc, who had desperately wanted to see a sign from his father, had never been lucky enough to spot one of space's beautiful phenomena.

He comforted himself with the thought that he would finally bring closure to the painful death his father had suffered, as well as all the mental and physical suffering Silky had brought upon Harris. The bat that he held in his hand would serve two purposes. One, he knew he could never bring his gun into Silky's apartment, because he was sure to get searched by Bam-Bam, and he did not want to take the chance of leaving the gun up on the roof, unattended, even for a short while. The other reason for using the bat was that, when Silky had shot his father to death in the bodega, Linc was standing not far away, holding that very bat, waiting for his brother and father to return to watch him play.

Satisfied there was no one on the rooftop, Linc walked back to the steel door. He stood the bat up, barrel side down, against the edge of the doorsill. He took one more look around, opened the door and descended the one flight of stairs to the eighth floor. He walked down the hallway to Silky's corner apartment, pulled out his cell phone, and texted Shortfinger, typing in the word, NOW! Linc waited outside the apartment door until he heard the shrill ring of Silky's cellphone inside the apartment. He then knocked on the door.

Linc heard footsteps approach the door and then the familier booming voice of Bam-Bam, "Who?"

"Yo, it's me, Bam. Open up." Linc heard Bam-Bam's voice lower, as he apparently began to talk to Silky. Linc could not hear any of the words exchanged between the two, but, after a few seconds, he heard the sounds of chains and locks opening up on the other side of the door. Bam-Bam opened the door and nodded for Linc to enter the apartment. As he stepped into the small foyer area he was gently pushed up against the wall by Bam-Bam.

"You know the drill, cuz," said Bam, as he began frisking Linc. He patted Linc down, from his shoulders down to his calves. Satisfied Linc wasn't carrying, Bam finally said, "A'ight, step on inside."

Linc walked down the small hallway and spotted Silky standing in the living room. On one couch was a duffel bag stuffed with clothes. "Yo Silk. What's up? You goin somewhere?"

"Naw, man. My boy Bam need to see some relatives out of town for a while."

"Everything a'ight?"

"Yeah, everything cool. What brings you up in here?"

Linc took a few steps inside the living room so he could keep an eye on Bam-Bam. "Just wanted to update you, Silk. Haven't hollered at you in a while. Jus letting you know the D.T's still ain't got nothin on yo' boy Bedbug."

"Yeah, well, that good, cause he did nother' piece of work for me tonight. Yo B, speakin a' D.T.'s, you ever get hol of that D.T., that nosy, cowboy-boot wearin muthafucka, that be investigatin yo' for the po-lice job?"

"Naw, man. Been real busy. Maybe Monday," said Linc. He then watched as Silky looked past him and smiled at Bam-Bam. The smile made Linc feel uneasy.

"Hey, listen up, yo," said Silky. "Jus got a call from yo boy Shorty. He tell me he got the one of Boulevard boys that set up our boy Tarface. Muthafucka was stupid enuf to be layin up with some honey right here in this building. Shorty say he grabbed him when the dude was comin out her apartment. They up on the roof right now. You lookin to take a walk wif me?"

Bam-Bam quickly said, "Let Shorty do it, Silk. Yo got enuf problems right now. Or let me take care of it."

"Naw, man, you got to finish packin yo' shit up an jet the fuck out a here. Tarface was my boy yo, he worked fo' me. How it

236

gonna look if I don't take care of the homeys workin for me, gonna make me look weak. I gots to do this, cuz." Silky then walked into the kitchen and opened a drawer. He pulled out a silver Smith and Wesson, .380 caliber, semi-automatic handgun. He looked at Linc. "Let's do this son."

Linc followed Silky down the hallway to the front door. Silky then turned around and said to Bam-Bam, "Yo, finish packin you shit. We ain't gonna be long."

Silky opened the door and stepped out into the project hallway, with Linc right behind him. The two men walked quietly down the hall to the stairwell door. Silky looked up and down the hallway. Seeing it was all clear, he opened the door and he and Linc stepped into the stairwell. They then began to walk up the short flight of stairs to the roof.

*

At the moment when Linc was entering Silky's aparment, Monahan was checking his voicemail once more to be sure of the address. Listening to the message, he confirmed that Boyd had said 180 Wortman Avenue, eighth floor. Holding Linc's photo, Monahan ran over to Dover, "Sarge, I'm taking a car. Matty had left me a message that he was lookin into something at 180 Wortman, on the eighth floor. This was no carjacking, Sarge."

"All right. Have Benny go with you."

"No, Sarge, there's not enough guys to work this scene as it is. I'll have uniforms meet me at the location. You're gonna have Chiefs crawling all over this place soon enough. You've got to make sure you work this scene right."

Dover nodded his head, "I trust you, Kevin, to call for backup once you're over there. It looks like we're dealing with some stone-cold killers here. You need anything, call me. Got it?"

Monahan nodded, and ran to the car. He jumped in, started the car, and sped away from the scene. As he made a left onto Flatlands Avenue, he called Central on his portable radio and requested that a patrol car meet him at 180 Wortman Avenue.

Shock and Awe had just got done meeting with their Tyrell Simpson snitch. They pulled out of the parking lot of the Galaxy Diner and made a left onto Pennsylvania Avenue. As soon as they pulled out onto Pennsylvania, they heard Monahan's request for back-up come over the radio. Officer Hannigan, A.K.A. Awe, informed Central that he and his partner would respond, since they were only minutes out from the location.

The two partners pulled up to the rear of 180 Wortman just as Monahan was exiting his car. Monahan was glad to see the two huge cops were his backup, not only because of their size, but more so because of their experience.

Fulfree was the first to speak. "What do you need, Detective?"

Monahan walked over to the two partners. "My old partner, Matty Boyd, was shot and killed tonight." Both cops appeared stunned. "He left me a voicemail saying he was investigating something, but I don't know what, at this location, on the eighth floor. I honestly don't know what we're looking for, but we have to start banging on doors on that floor to find out if anyone knows anything. Be real careful. We're dealing with cop-killer or killers here. One other thing," Monahan pulled Linc's photo out of his jacket pocket. "Matty had this cop's photo in his pocket when he died. I don't know if the cop has anything to do with this, but if you see him, stop him. C'mon. We're wasting valuable time."

The two partners followed Monahan up the walkway to the rear door of the building. As they walked into the lobby, Monahan said, "You guys got all your gear on. It will be easier if I take the stairs, you guys take the elevator. This way we'll have the exits covered. When you get to the eighth floor, just start banging on doors. Ask anyone if they saw a white cop up on that floor tonight. I'll meet you up there."

"But we really don't know what we're lookin for, Monahan," Fulfree said.

"You two guys have worked these projects long enough to know what doesn't seem right, something that's out of the ordinary. Trust your gut, and guys, please be careful."

Fulfree and Hannigan walked over to the elevator and pressed the down button, while Monahan began going up the stairs, taking them two at a time.

*

While Monahan was trying his best to make it up eight flights of stairs as quickly as possible, Silky pushed open the door and stepped onto the roof. The moon acted like a bright streetlamp, illuminating the rooftop so much that he could see from one end of the roof to the other. Holding the .380 in his right hand, Silky yelled out, "Yo, Shorty, where you at?" Looking across the landscape of the gravel covered rooftop, an annoyed Silky again yelled, "Cmon, man, where the fuck you at?"

At that point, as he began to turn around to speak to Linc, he was suddenly falling. Linc had swung his bat, hitting the gangster square across the back. The gun flew out of Silky's hand and bounced across the gravel. Silky's face landed flush on the hard, sharp edged rocks that covered the roof. Turning onto his back he saw Linc standing over him, a baseball bat gripped in his two hands. "What the fuck, nigga?" yelled Silky.

Linc stood over the prone drug dealer and quietly said, "Its' payback time, bitch. You see this bat? You know who gave me this bat, muthafucka? My pops, that's who. You knew my pops, Silk. Matter of fact you were the last one to see him alive. Weren't you, you punk bitch!" Linc brought the bat down, slamming it into Silky's right kneecap, instantly shattering the bone. Silky screamed at the excruciating pain he felt, a searing pain that traveled from his foot to his hip. As he tried to get up, Linc brought the bat down once more, hitting Silky in the right side of his ribcage, breaking two of his ribs and knocking the wind out of the drug boss.

"Naw, man. It wasn't like that," whispered Silky. "Yo, it was Bam-Bam, cuz. He did the deed. You know I would never do harm to yo' pops."

"You lying, coward, little bitch! Be a man fo' once in yo' life, an admit what you done."

Sensing the futility in protesting his innocence, Silky propped himself up on his elbows and stared at Linc. "Why, you buggin punk? Cause after I lit up yo' old man, yo brother become a stuttering fool?"

An enraged Linc brought the bat down once again, this time shattering Silky's right collarbone. Silky managed to scream before he collapsed onto the gravel.

*

Monahan had just reached the eighth floor, and had stepped out into the hallway, when he heard the scream from the rooftop. Fulfree and Hannigan had reached the floor before Monahan, and were walking down the hallway in the direction of Silky's apartment, about to start knocking on doors. Monahan turned around, opened the stairwell door and raced up to the rooftop. Gun in hand, he slammed into the rooftop door and almost fell onto the roof. Regaining his balance he looked up and saw Linc, bat held over his head, standing over a male who was lying at Linc's feet.

Training his Glock 9 millimeter on Linc's chest, Monahan yelled out, "No, Linc. Put down the bat. Let me take care of this. Whoever this guy is, or what ever he did, let me take care of it!"

"Help me, po-lice man," Silky screamed. "Pleez get this crazy muthafucka away from me!"

Linc, bat still over his head, looked at the detective. "Whoever this guy is? This guy, Monahan, is pure fuckin evil. You remember Dante's Inferno? The gates of hell? Well, this piece of shit is gonna be the toll collector. As a po-lice I seen what justice is, there ain't none. The only true justice is out on these streets, I see that now. And now I'm gonna give this muthafucka his sentence." Linc began to bring the bat down onto Silky's skull, when Monahan, remembering what a bat had done to a young man on a desolate road in South Carolina, fired one round from his service weapon. The blast lit up the night sky as the 9 millimeter bullet exited the barrel, traveling faster than the speed of sound, straight into Linc's chest.

The bat flew out of Linc's hand, as he fell backwards onto the project rooftop. The March night air seemed suddenly colder to Linc. Although he couldn't move, a peaceful calm spread through his body. He had to get his eyes open just one more time, he thought to himself, and as his life seeped out of him, Lincoln Watson did manage to open his eyes one last time. He was able to stare up at the bright night sky, and he noticed that just passing below the moon was a bright shooting star.

# CHAPTER 17

Monahan exited Our Lady of the Blessed Sacrament Roman Catholic Church with the Boyd family. He looked out over 203 Street in Bayside, Queens, and as far as his eyes could see, there was an ocean of blue uniforms. The lieutenant from the Ceremonial Detail had just given the command, "Detail, Attention!" over the loudspeaker and it was followed shortly by the command, "Present Arms!" At that moment thousands of white-gloved hands snapped to salute, as the casket of a fallen comrade descended the steps from the church to the street, and into a waiting limosine.

The haunting, mournful dirge of the bagpipes filled the otherwise silent air. The tradition of the bagpipes dated back hundreds of years, when Scottish warriors about to enter the field of battle, would blow the pipes to intimidate their enemy. Today they were used to accompany a modern-day warrior to his final resting place.

Monahan stood on the steps watching, as the Boyd family entered their limosine. He was waiting for his brother to meet him in front of the church. Father Timothy had assisted the parish monsignor to conduct the funeral mass, and now he was changing out of his vestments for the drive down to South Carolina.

The detective had planned to leave with his brother on Monday, but the Saturday night events had blown up that plan. For four straight days after Linc's shooting, Monahan had been inundated with paperwork and interviews. He had also made an appearance before a Brooklyn Grand Jury and provided them with his version of the events that had occurred on the rooftop that evening. After the D.A.'s investigators had interviewed Silky, and a doctor had evaluated his extensive injuries, the D.A. determined that Silky had been one baseball bat swing away from being killed, and that Monahan had been justified in firing his weapon to save Silky's life.

After discovering the extent of Silky's sordid criminal history, and especially after determining the role the drug dealer had played in Boyd's death, Monahan was devastated. Deep inside he realized that if he had had all the information he know knew, he would have never have stopped Linc from administering the street justice that Silky truly deserved. It tortured him that in South Carolina he had not stopped the murder of an innocent man, but on a Brooklyn project rooftop, he had stopped the killing of a guilty one.

Linc had been right. Silky was evil personified. His brother Timothy tried to assuage Kevin's feelings. He attempted to convince him that no human being had the right to be judge, jury, and executioner. It hadn't helped. The night demons that he hoped would vanish on his visit to South Carolina were sure to re-appear when he thought of Linc. As it was, he had had difficulty in falling asleep the past few nights, and he knew there was no way he could take a drink, as the alcohol was sure to transport him to the rooftop of 180 Wortman Avenue.

He remembered kneeling next to Linc, his knees digging into the gravel that covered the roof. Holding Linc's hand, he pleaded with the young man not to give up. He watched as Linc's eyes opened wide, and at that moment he could feel a sense of peace and contentment come over the young cop. Then Linc's eyes had closed, forever.

Monahan's thoughts were suddenly interrupted by a gentle tap on the shoulder. It was Sergeant Kolitoski.

"That was some crazy shit the other night, Kevin. How you doing?"

"Not too good, Sarge. Not too good."

"Hey, we all would have done the same thing. You had no choice. The kid was gonna split that shithead's head wide open. I had always told the kid that we were no better than street thugs if we did shit like that. I didn't realize at the time I was talking to a street thug. He was using us, Kevin."

"It's not as simple as that, Sarge. Linc's life was a complicated fuckin mess. His father was murdered when he was eleven, and his young brother witnessed the murder. His brother became traumatized, and wound up with a speech disability. He had to become the man in the house and look after the brother and mother at too young an age. He tried to do the right thing and go to college, but he knew his mother couldn't afford it. Then he sees all his homeboys making all kinds of money. What would any of us do in that situation?

Monahan paused and then said quietly, "He tried to leave the projects, never realizing the projects would never leave him."

Kolitoski was silent for a few moments. "Yeah. I see your point, but I will never get over the fact that he used us, all of us, for that scumbag, Silky. Speaking of which, what's gonna happen to the piece of shit?"

Monahan went on to explain that after he had fired the shot on the rooftop that night, Bam-Bam had come running out of the apartment, gun in hand. Shock and Awe were also headed to the roof, when they heard the door slam behind them and saw Bam-Bam running towards them. The two cops were about to light Bam-Bam up, when he dropped his gun. Tests run on the gun showed it was the same one used to kill Matty Boyd.

Faced with life without parole, Bam-Bam broke like a Canal Street umbrella. He named Pumpkin as the shooter of Matty, and gave up Silky as ordering the hit. He also accused Silky of ordering the hit on Tyrell Simpson.

Bam-Bam refused, however, to give up the name of the actual shooter of Simpson. Apparently he was deathly afraid of the shooter and the people the shooter worked for. All he would say was that the killer was a member of a Jamaican posse, and that no matter what type of prison protective custody he was placed in, the Jamaicans would find Bam-Bam and kill him.

In addition to the murder of Linc's father, Silky was also indicted for the murders of the couple in East Flatbush, along with the unborn child, so there was an excellent chance that Silky would never draw a free breath again.

As Monahan finished speaking to Kolitoski, Father Timothy came up and placed an arm around his brother's shoulder, "Ready to go, Kevin?"

"You guys going on a family vacation?" asked Kolitoski.

"Yeah. I guess you can say that. Have to take care of some personal business," said Kevin.

Kolitoski shook both of the brother's hands and began to walk away.

"Hey Sarge," called Kevin. "Do you think you can do me a favor?"

Kolitoski stopped and turned around, "Sure. Whatever you need."

Monahan pulled an envelope from his inside jacket pocket. Inside the envelope was a money order for three-hundred-dollars. The envelope was addressed to Mrs. Kitty Watson, at 220 Wortman Avenue, Apartment 3B, Brooklyn, New York. The envelope contained no return address.

"Can you stop on your way back to the precinct and throw this in a mailbox for me?" He handed the envelope to Kolitoski.

"You write the kid's mother a condolence letter?"

Monahan looked at his brother Timothy, who just slowly shook his head. "Yeah, I guess you could say it's a condolence letter," said Monahan, as he and Timothy walked to the car.

# EPILOGUE

As the Monahans were driving westbound on the Belt parkway towards the Verazzano Bridge, for the beginning of a long journey to South Carolina, a green Jeep Cherokee with North Carolina plates was passing them, travelling eastbound. The Cherokee was headed to an area all too familiar to Kevin Monahan -- East New York, specifically, the Pink House Projects.

The Jeep took the Pennsylvania Avenue exit off the Belt Parkway, drove past the Linden Projects and headed north to Linden Boulevard. The driver made a right on Linden and drove eastbound, passing the Boulevard Houses and Gershwin Junior High. The Jeep continued on Linden until it reached Fountain Avenue, where the driver made a right turn and then a quick left onto Loring Avenue.

As the Jeep approached Crescent Street, the eight-story Pink Houses projects came into sight, and Thomas Simpson slowed down. He had only returned to the projects one other time since his first deployment to Afganistan in 2003. He remembered it as if it was yesterday-- October of 2006, his grandmoms' 70th birthday. Although Thomas and his brother had tried to make a big fuss over her birthday, she would have none of it. All she talked about and wanted to celebrate was Thomas's birthday, which had been three days earlier.

It was now a bright summer afternoon in early June, and the trees on the Pink Houses property were in full bloom, trees that now seemed so much bigger than he remembered. At Crescent Street he saw the sign, pink of course, with black buildings painted under the lettering that read "Louis Heaton Pink" across the top. The painted black buildings looked more like the New York City Skyline than a housing project. Thomas laughed, as he always did, at the words written across the bottom of the sign: "A Wonderful Community".

246

Finding a spot on Loring Avenue, he pulled his Jeep almost directly across the street from 1260 Loring Avenue, the building where he and his brother had been raised by his grandmother. Shutting the Jeep off, he sat for a moment and looked at the buildings surrounding him, each one with its own memories. The building he was parked in front of, 1259, was where he and his brother Tyrell had caught two boys from the Cypress projects, wanna-be A-Team punks, tagging the front door of the building. Needless to say, those Cypress faggots were administered a severe beat down.

He looked down the block on Loring, and stared up at the roof of the 1306 building, where, as a fifteen-year-old tough guy, he had been introduced to the oral pleasures only an experienced woman could provide. That experienced "woman" had been seventeen-year-old Vanessa Miller.

His life, he figured, had been divided into two sets of memories, and in a certain respect they were not much different from each other. The first were of him growing up on the often violent streets and sidewalks of East New York, and the second of him growing up once again -- in the often violent mountains and valleys of Afganistan.

Thomas got out of the Jeep and opened up the back liftgate. He pulled out a green duffel bag and slung the strap over his shoulder. He reached into the back, slid a tough-box out, and placed the box onto the street at his feet. He closed the liftgate, paused, and looked around hard at his surroundings. His years on these streets, as well as the years in Afganistan, had taught him to be constantly on point. It had now become second nature for him to eye rooftops, person or persons sitting in parked cars, basically anything that seemed out of the ordinary.

Satisfied that no one was clocking him, Thomas picked up his box and crossed the street. The box probably weighed upwards of fifty pounds, but at 6'2 and packing 225 pounds of solid muscle, Thomas had no problem handling it. He passed through the black, wrought iron fencing and strolled up the walkway to the 1260 building, stopping to look at the basketball courts to his left.

The courts had been a haven for him and his brother as they grew up. He remembered his grandmoms yelling out their apartment window, begging the boys to come up for dinner. Thomas was glad to see the courts were crowded with young boys, many lined up along the fence waiting to play winners.

Entering the lobby, Thomas stopped and inhaled deeply. It had a smell endemic to all Brooklyn project buildings. Housing Authority paint, fried food, cigarette smoke, and a whiff of urine, all contributed to the unique odor that brought back a flood of memories. It was as if he was hearing some old song come on the radio, and he was suddenly transported back to a time where everything was right with the world.

As Thomas was about to push the button for the elevator, the door opened, and a young mother and her daughter stepped out into the lobby. The attractive young woman smiled at the handsome soldier, as the daughter began skipping through the lobby, headed for the front door. Thomas nodded and smiled back at the woman, and as he was about to step onto the elevator he heard her yell in a Jamaican accent, "Tanisha, you no be goin out dat door wit' out me girl!"

Mothers in the projects had learned the hard way not to let their children run out of a lobby without the mother first examining the surroundings. Mothers knew that, all too often, gunfights erupted without a moment's notice, and a bullet had no conscience.

Thomas entered the elevator and was glad to see the young girl had heeded her mother's advice. Before the elevator doors closed, the mother, holding her daughter's hand, looked back at Thomas. She smiled once again, and with her free hand she gave him a sleight wave. The door shut, and the elevator rumbled up to the third floor.

Thomas exited the elevator, made a left turn and walked down the small hallway until he reached apartment 3D. He placed his box on the floor and pulled a set of keys from his pants pocket.

Opening the door of the apartment and stepping inside made Thomas feel as though he had just stepped into a time capsule and had been transported back to the year 2001. Everything was the same, the only exception being the big-screen television that his brother had always raved about in his letters to Thomas. Other than that, all the furniture was arranged just as Thomas had remembered it, almost seven years ago. The apartment smelled a bit musty, though not as bad as he had anticipated, so he opened up two of the windows. He did a quick tour of the apartment, and came back to his tough-box.

He opened the box, pulled out a smaller wooden box, and placed it on the kitchen table. He opened the wooden box, which contained all his ribbons and medals, including one Silver Star, two bronze stars, and his most prized honor, his C.I.B., his Combat Infantry Badge. A glass frame was the next item to come out of the box. Inside the frame was the patch of the 82nd Airborne. The unique A.A. (All-American) symbol, the white double A's within a blue circle against a red background, had been worn proudly by American soldiers since World War I. The division was considered among the elite of the American fighting forces.

Thomas turned back to continue emptying the tough-box, when he suddenly heard a loud banging on the apartment door.

"Who is it?" he asked.

"Open up, soldier, before we re-introduce you to a good Pink House ass-whupping!"

Thomas quickly shut and locked the tough-box before walking over to the door. He glanced out the peephole and smiled. Opening the door, he was glad to see the two Housing cops, Shock and Awe. Their huge frames covered the entire doorway, almost preventing any light from entering the apartment from the hallway. They both rushed inside and began to hug Thomas. It took all his strength to keep them from knocking him to the ground.

The big, black cop, Fulfree, yelled, "Now why the fuck wouldn't you call us to let us know you were back? I gave you both our cell numbers when I spoke to you, right after your brother

--" Fulfree stopped in mid-sentence. "We're both so sorry, Thomas."

"I know, guys, I appreciate it, and I can't thank you enough for taking care of all the arrangements. Where I was, I couldn't get away. How did you guys know I was here, anyway?"

The white cop, Hannigan spoke, "We were running plates on Loring, hoping to come up with a fresh steal. We came up on a green Jeep with N.C. plates and we both got a hard on, figuring it was def a steal. When we run the plate it came back to this knucklehead we knew, Thomas "T-Bone" Simpson."

Thomas laughed, as he hadn't heard his street name, T-Bone, used in seven years. He had never told the guys in his unit the name, or how he got it. They would have ragged his ass without mercy. The name was given to Thomas when he was about fourteen by his homeboys. They gave him the name, as the word on the street was that he was tougher than an overcooked T-Bone steak. He received the moniker right after he had fought off three punks from the Boulevard Houses. The three had jumped him while he was walking along Stanley Avenue.

Fulfree looked over at the box containing Thomas's medals. "Jesus, Thomas, you got more medals than a Russian general! One day, over a couple of beers, you're gonna have to tell us about them."

Thomas just nodded, knowing he could never disclose to the two cops many of the operations that had led to the awarding of the medals. Most were classified. In addition, many of the things Thomas had done were better left within the dark recesses of his mind.

Hannigan then asked, "Thomas, you sure you're done with the army?"

"Well, I got some time if I want to re-up, but I think five years over there was enough. I knew if I re-upped I would probably wind up being a lifer. From what I got from my Grandmoms and Tyrell I'm pretty well set financially, so I'll just relax for a while and take care of some things that need to be

250

done." Thomas paused a minute and asked, "Any more information as to what happened to my brother?"

Fulfree answered, "The lead detective on the case now is this guy Monahan. He is real sharp, Thomas, a tough ex-Marine. One of our snitches gave us information that this psycho killer named Bedbug was the shooter. Supposedly, he's like an assassin for a drug crew out of East Flatbush, run by this Jamaican dude named Nigel. Get ahold of Monahan at the 7-5, and he will be glad to help you out."

"C'mon John, let's let T-Bone finish unpacking," said Hannigan. "I'm sure he has a lot to do, and jobs are probably backing up out there on the street."

Both cops gave Thomas a hug and walked to the front door.

Before stepping out into the hallway, Hannigan turned to Thomas and said, "Remember, you need anything, you call us, and please be careful. It's not as bad as it was in the late 80's, when you were growing up around here, but there are still some nasty muthafuckas out there. Realize that you don't have the firepower you had over in A'stan."

Thomas just smiled and nodded. After shutting the door, Thomas locked it and unlocked his tough-box. He thought, I might not have as much firepower, but what I do have will do just fine. He then pulled out a Heckler-Koch 417 Assaulter rifle with a collapsible stock. Placing it on the kitchen table, he returned to the box and retrieved a much smaller gun, a 9 mm. Beretta, PX-4 sub-compact.

When he had known he was leaving Fort Bragg, Thomas had made a stop on Bragg Blvd. in Fayetteville, a week before he was to be discharged. Knowing he would never be able to purchase a handgun or assault rifle in New York, he had availed himself to the lax gun laws in North Carolina. He stopped at one of the many gun stores along the boulevard, and purchased the two guns using his North Carolina driver's license. He cleared the record check and stopped by the store to pick up the two weapons. The two guns set him back almost fifteen-hundred dollars, but he knew he could never put a price on avenging his brother's murder.

## BE ON THE LOOKOUT FOR THE NEXT IN THE SERIES: *THE CONCRETE G.I.*

21041166R00148

Made in the USA
Middletown, DE
17 June 2015